THE ORIGINAL JAMAICAN

Patois; Words, Phrases
and Short Stories

LAXLEYVAL SAGASTA

Lime Press

The Original Jamaican Patois;
Words, Phrases and Short Stories
by Laxleyval Sagasta

This is not fiction. Apart from the Patwa words and translation, the rest of this work represents folklores, and anecdotes that is rooted in the Jamaican culture. Some of the events have been slightly dramatized and are not intended to refer to particular persons. The opinions expressed in this manuscript are solely the opinions of the author and do not represent the opinions or thoughts of the publisher. The author has represented and warranted full ownership and/or legal right to publish all the materials in this book.

First Published, 2013

Printed in the United States of America.

ISBN: 978-1-954304-31-4 (Paperback)
ISBN: 978-1-954304-30-7 (E-book)

Published by Lime Press LLC
425 West Washington Street Suite 4
Suffolk, VA 23434 US
https://www.lime-press.com/

TABLE OF CONTENTS

Preface

Patois, patwah, patwa or whichever other way it is spelt, is a dialect, a mixture of at least four different languages, mainly English, French, Spanish and Dutch. It is the (*de facto*) national language of Jamaica, sometimes referred to as Jamaican English. Most of the words are not pure from any of these languages, but they are easily understood particularly by people and/ or their descendants of Caribbean islands.

Patwa originated in the early days of slavery in the region and served as the principal way of communication between the slaves. This communication was very essential as the islands had many small plantations, and the slaves were from different parts of Africa with multiple tribal languages. However, even before the Africans were brought to the islands, there were English, Irish, Spanish and Dutch slaves who became slave-drivers of the Africans and taught them enough of their respective languages to enable some form of communication.

The tropical weather allowed year-round agriculture. It was common to move slaves from plantation to plantation to facilitate crop stages. The different slave-drivers taught the slaves only enough of their own languages to enable the necessary communication.

Over a period of years those slaves knew enough of the various languages used by the slave-drivers that they were able to alter most of the words to form a dialect that only they understood. That is the origin of patwa. This was very beneficial to them when factions from several plantations revolted and took refuge in the mountains. Those refugees bonded and successfully defended themselves against the authorities. Those revolting slaves were called the Maroons, and that name stayed with their descendants.

Words are tools by which, outside of sign languages, we communicate. Like most other tools, some words are more versatile than others. A particular word may be used many times for different purposes; sometimes as a preposition and sometimes as an adverb, albeit in different sentences.

Today there exist many types of patwa dialects. This book is concentrated on what is widely believed to be the original patwa, which means that all the words are the same as those used by the slaves. Patwah, spelt with an '**h**' is an evolving dialect. It is mostly a Jamaican Rasta version that involves the original patwa and newly formed words like *Irie* = cool, or agree, and *doney* = money. It also uses established English words to carry additional meanings, e.g. *Seen* = understand, and *water* = sky-juice. Patois, patwa, patwah or patwahz should not be mistaken for slang words. Slang words can be found in almost every language. They are usually mispronounced words of a language. It might be interesting to know that the early generations who spoke the dialect spelt it the way it is pronounced, Patwa.

One salesman joked that he went to Boston and lost the `r' in car but he found it in the *warsh* in Texas. Those are slangs.

One of the main characteristics of patois of any version is that the pronunciations are exactly the way the words are spelt. Another specificity of the dialect is that it ignores gender, plurality and tense. For example, him or her, he or she is spoken as *im*. I drove is I *drive*.

No thought should be entertained that all the people of the Caribbean speak patwa fluently. The dialect is normally spoken with an accent which is different even within a particular country.

Conversing in patwa is a fun exercise. English is the official and only language of most Caribbean countries and is sometimes spoken with a slight accent. This accent sometimes allows less sound emphasis on some syllables of multi-syllabic words ---- photographer is photo-gra-pher instead of pho-tog-rapher.

Most patwa words are really broken English. That is because most of the slave-drivers were British and Irish, and they themselves did not speak proper English. History shows that the majority of them were either indentured slaves, and or prisoners, who on a whole were the uneducated, undesirables of their societies.

In parts two and three of this book, entire sentences or paragraphs of patwa will be written in ***bold italics*** followed by the same sentence or paragraph written in regular English script.

Over the last half a century, occupation and leisure travels enabled this author to meet people, especially seniors from all over the island. Through interviews and casual conversations, he collected the major parts of this work the way it was handed down from generation to generation. He had collected and recorded hundreds each of original words, phrases and short stories. Some of them are vulgar and is outside the scope of this book. One thing that stood out, was that every Jamaican speaks some Patwa, and even though most of them at times speak perfect English, invariably a word or two of Patwa can be found in any conversation they conduct.

The narrative is slightly dramatized, and profanities and vulgarities are removed, but the essences remained, and even the dialogues are close to verbatim. This book will be enjoyed for its' values of history, humor, education, entertainment and as a conversational subject. This book should be an hierloom to every Jamaican, and also to friends of Jamaica and Jamaicans.

PART ONE

***

Commonly used words in English and patwa

A, *prep. A, I, ah, at,* e.g. *a* as in a *fe mi,* meaning: It is mine. I as in: *a see it now,* meaning, I see it now. Ah, same as *a.* I was in at the market, or *a de maakit.*

The alphabet letter *a* is used in patwa both as a letter and as a word. It is also sometimes used to replace other letters such as **o** and **h,** e.g. orange = *aringe,* October = *Acktoeba,* etc.

After, <u>prep.</u> = *Atta.*

Agree, <u>v.</u> = *Gree.*

Air, <u>n</u> = *Eire.*

Already, <u>adv.</u> = *Aredy.*

Alright, <u>adj.</u> = *Ahright,* meaning okay.

Although, <u>conj.</u> = *Aldoah.*

An, <u>prep.</u> Used as *a* also as and, e.g. *a aringe,* (an orange) and *you an mi. (You and me.)*

Another, <u>adj.</u> = ***Anadah.***

Ask, <u>v.</u> = Axe.

At, <u>v.</u> = *Hot,* or *hat.*

Avoid, <u>v.</u> = *Avide.*

Awkward, <u>adj.</u> = *Ackwud*.

Baby, <u>n.</u> = *Be-aiby*.

Bait, <u>n.</u> = *Be-aite*.

Bake, <u>v.</u> = *Be-aike*.

Battle, <u>n.</u> = *Backle*.

Bird, <u>n.</u> = *Bud*.

Boat, <u>n.</u> = *Buout*.

Body, <u>n.</u> = *Bady*.

Boil, <u>v.</u> = *Bwile*.

Boots, <u>n.</u> = *Condum* or *rubbaz*.

Born, <u>v.</u> = *Baan*.

Borrow, <u>v.</u> = *Bawra*.

Both, <u>pron.</u> = *Buout*.

Bother, <u>v.</u> = <u>***Badda***</u>.

Bottle, <u>n.</u> = *Bakle*.

Boy, <u>n.</u> = *Bwoy, bwoy*.

Break or broke, <u>v.</u> = *Bruk*.

Breverage. <u>n.</u> = *Brebidge*

Brother, brothers or brethren, <u>n</u> = *Bredda*.

Burn, <u>v.</u> = *Bun,* to cheat on one's spouse, or to be burned by hot object.

Calf, <u>n.</u> = *ki-af*.

Can, <u>v.</u> = **Caa**.

Cannot, can't. <u>v.</u> = **Caan**.

Captain, <u>n.</u> = *Keyaptin*.

Car. <u>n</u> = *Keyar*.

Careful, <u>adv.</u> = *Kayful.*

Careless, <u>adv.</u> = *Kaylis.*

Carry, <u>v.</u> = *Keyar.*

Catch, <u>v, n.</u> = *Ketch.*

Chew, <u>v.</u> = *Chaw*

Center, <u>n.</u> = *Migle, centa.*

Con-man, <u>n.</u> = *Ginnal,* a trickster.

Cover, <u>v.</u> or <u>n.</u> = *Cova, Keba.* (The cover, n. I will cover, v.)

Craven, <u>adj.</u> = *Greedy, gravalishous.*

Crow, <u>n.</u> = *Jan-cro, john crow.*

Curse, <u>v.</u> = *Cuss.*

Cushion, <u>n.</u> = *Cotta*

Dad, daddy, <u>n.</u> = *Dadda.*

Darling, <u>n.</u> = *Dawling.*

Daughter, <u>n.</u> = *Dawta.*

Day, <u>n</u> = *Deay, dey*

Dirt, <u>n.</u> = *Dut, dutty.*

Dollar, <u>n.</u> = *Dalla.*

Done, finish, complete, stop, <u>v.</u> = *Dun.*

Down, <u>n.</u> = *Dung.*

Drizzle, <u>n.</u> = *Jizzle,* a light rain.

Each, <u>pron.</u> = *All-a-ounu.*

Ears, <u>n.</u> = *Aise.*

Eat, <u>v.</u> = *Heet, nyam.*

Egg, <u>n.</u> = *Heg.*

Everyone, <u>pron.</u> = *All-a-ounu.*

Eye, <u>n.</u> = *Yeye.*

Face, <u>n</u> = *Fe-ace.*

Facety, <u>adj.</u> = *Bay-fe-aced.*

Family, <u>n.</u> = *Faambly.*

Farmer, <u>n.</u> = *fawma.*

Fast, <u>adj.</u> = *Faas, fass*

Father, <u>n</u> = *Puppa.*

Fat person, = <u>n. phr.</u> *Tuco Tuca.*

Favor, <u>n.</u> = *Fava,* a kind gesture.

Fire, <u>n.</u> = *fyah.*

Food, <u>n.</u> = *bickle.*

Friend, <u>*n.*</u> = *pa-cero, combolo, pawdy.*

Fungus, <u>n.</u> = *Junju.*

Gal, <u>n.</u> = *Gyal.*

Ganja, <u>n.</u> = *Marijuana, Pot, weed.*

Ghost, <u>n.</u> = *duppy.*

Give-me, <u>v. phr.</u> = *Gimme*

Glass, <u>n.</u> = *Glaas.*

Go-away, <u>v. phr.</u> = *Gu-weh.*

Going-to, <u>*v. phr.*</u> = *Gwine.*

Go-on, <u>*v. phr.*</u> = *Ga-lang* or go along. *Gwaan.*

Gossip, <u>*n.*</u> or <u>*v*</u> = *susu susu.*

Greedy, <u>adj.</u> = *Lickie-lickie.*

Grind, <u>v.</u> = *Grine,* a sexual act. <u>N =</u> Processing of dried grains.

Handle, <u>n</u> or <u>v.</u> = *Hangle.* (Hold it by *de hangle*, <u>n.</u>, do *hangle* it *sawfly.* v.)

Handsome, <u>adj.</u> = *Ansome.*

Hang, <u>v.</u> = *Heng*

Hang around, v.ph.= *Heng-ke hengke.*

Hard, adj. = *Ard, haad.*

His, him, her, <u>pron.</u> = *im.*

Holler, <u>v.</u> = *Halla.*

Husband, <u>n.</u> = *Usban.*

Idiot, <u>n.</u> = *Idiat, eediat, fool-fool, kunu-munu, quashie.*

Idle, <u>adj.</u> = *Igle.*

Informer, <u>n.</u> = *Infaama.*

Inside, <u>adj.</u> = *Eena.*

Into, <u>Prep.</u> = *Inna.*

Keep, <u>v.</u> *Kip*

Kind, <u>adj.</u> = *Kine.*

Land, <u>n.</u> = *Lan.*

Leave, <u>n.</u> = *Lef.*

Little, <u>adj.</u> = *Likkle, a Kench,*

Long, <u>adj.</u> = *Lang.*

Look, <u>v.</u> = *Coodeh, Cooyah.*

Lost, <u>v.</u> = *Laas*

Make, <u>v.</u> = *Mek.*

Mulatta, <u>adj.</u> = *Malata*

Mark, <u>n.</u> or <u>v.</u> = *Mawk.*

Master, <u>n.</u> = *Massa.*

Me, <u>pron.</u> = *Mi.*

Meager, <u>adj.</u> = *Mawga.*

Mean, <u>adj.</u> = *Cobitch.*

Mister, <u>n.</u> = *Missa.*

Model, <u>n.</u> or <u>v.</u> = *Magle.* (The model, <u>n.</u>, I will model it. <u>v.</u>)

More, <u>adj.</u> = *Mo.*

Morning, <u>n.</u> = *Mawnin.*

Mother, <u>n.</u> = *Madda, mawma, mumma.*

Mouth, <u>n.</u> = *Mout.*

Mud, <u>n.</u> = *Pout-pout, maikey-maikey.*

Natural, <u>n.</u> = *Natral.*

Nature, <u>n.</u> = *Naycha.*

Neither, <u>adj.</u> = *Needa.*

Never, <u>adv.</u> = *Neva.*

Next, <u>adj.</u> = *Nex, nedda.*

No, <u>adv.</u> = *Naa, noh.*

Noise, <u>n.</u> = *Nize*

Nothing, <u>n.</u> = *Nutten, nuttin.*

Only, <u>adj.</u> = *Ongle.*

Open, <u>n.</u> = *Opin, upm.*

Outcast, <u>n</u> = *riffraff.*

Out-of, <u>adv.</u> = *Outta.*

Over, <u>prep.</u> = *Ova.*

Owl, <u>n.</u> = *patu.*

Parson, <u>n.</u> = *Pawsen.*

Part, n. = *Pawt.*

Penis, n. = *Buddy, pem-pem, teely, wood.*

Play, v. = *Ramp, dily-daly, palauve*

Plenty, adj. = *nuff, whole-heap, hope-a.*

Pound, n. = *Pown.*

Prickle, n = *Macka.*

Pussy, n. = *Puss, pum-pum, puniani, cho-cho, cushu, coddu, saul, sus, saul-ting, te-ale.*

Quarrel, v. n. = *Rowow.* (Don't rowow wid mi. v., *wei ha a big rowow.* n.)

Rake, n. = *Re-aik,* (garden tool), *Joke* or *scam.* (*Mi ketch de rake.*)

Salt, n. = *Saul,*

Saturday, n. = *Satdeh.*

Say, v. = *Seh.*

Shirt, n. = *Shut.*

Short, adj. = *Shawt.*

Shove, v = *Shub.*

Shut, v. = *Shet.*

Single, adj. = *Degeh*

Sit-down, v. = *Sidung.*

Soft, adj. = *Sawf.*

Somebody, n. = *Sumaddy.*

Something, n. = *Sinting, supm.*

Stank, or stink, adv. = *Tink.*

Stay, n. or v. = **an-deh**. *(Put **tan-deh** on im. <u>n.</u>, **mek im tan-deh**. <u>v.</u>)*

Stick, <u>n.</u> <u>adv.</u> = **Tick**. (**Dis a fe mi tick**. <u>n.</u>, **tick it ova deh**. <u>adv.</u>)

Strong, <u>adj.</u> = **Trang, tallawah, trapm.**

Sweetheart, <u>n.</u> = **Putus, bonununus.**

Take, <u>v.</u> = **Tek.**

Talkative, <u>adj. phr.</u> = **Labba-abba, <u>Labrish.</u>**

That, <u>pron.</u> = **Dat, Tera-deh.**

These, those, <u>pron.</u> = **dem** or **dem-deh.**

Thing, <u>n.</u> = **Ting.**

Tiny, <u>adj.</u> = **Winji, likkle-bit.**

Trouble, <u>n.</u> or <u>v.</u> = **Choble**. (*A fey u choble*, <u>n.</u>, **a did not choble yu**. <u>v.</u>)

Truck, <u>n.</u> = **Chuck.**

Turn, <u>v.</u> = **Tun.**

Ugly, <u>adj.</u> = **Cunu-munu.**

Under, <u>prep.</u> = **Unda.**

Vase, <u>n.</u> = **Vaas.**

Verandah, <u>n.</u> = **Varanda.**

Voodo, <u>n</u> = **Obeah, Guzzu**

Water, <u>n.</u> = **Wata.**

What, <u>pron.</u> = **Wah.**

Where, <u>adv.</u> = **Weh.**

With, <u>prep.</u> = **Wid.**

Witchcraft, <u>n.</u> = **Beah, Voodo, Guzzu.**

Woman, n. = *Ooman.*

Word, n. = *Wud.*

Work, n. or v. = *Wuk. (A fe mi wuk,* n., *a wi wuk tedeh.* v.)

Worse, adj. = *Wus.*

Worthless, adj. = *Wutlis.*

Yesterday, n. = *Yessideh.,*

PART TWO
***

Popular Jamaican patwa phrases.

These phrases represent the many moods of the natives at different times, and for various occasions. They can be proverbs, admonitions, observations, warnings, etc. Some phrases remain popular for generations; others fade away just as fast as they appeared. In the following sections we will give examples of phrases and dialogues of patwa written in *bold italics*, whether they are sentences or paragraphs, in part or in whole, and immediately repeated in English. The meaning, where necessary, will follow. For example, (patwa) **Neva se cum se.** (*English*) Never see come see. (meaning.) A person who was always poor is now frightened over new found riches.

A bun yu a get. = You are getting burned. = You are being cheated on.

A noh everything good fe eat good fe talk. = It not everything that is good to eat is good to talk about. = Sometimes you have to see things and keep your mouth shut.

A noh one dey monkey waa wife. = Its not only one day that monkey wants his wife. = Your needs are for more than for one day.

A plasta fe every sore. = A plaster for every sore. = An answer, a cause, or a cure for every situation.

A weh yu a ple-ay? = What are you playing? = What are you pretending?

Ahright, no cup noh bruk, noh caafe noh dash weh. = Alright, no cup broke, and no coffee was spilt. = What is done is done and there is no harm.

As lang as fowl a cratch, luck wi cum. = As long as fowl keep scratching, luck will come. = Keep doing what you are doing. One day you will be lucky.

Be-fo han gaa mill, leggo trash. = Before hands go to the mill, let go of trash. = Stop before the situation get out of control.

Butta knife caa butcha cow. = Butter knife cannot butcher cow. = Use the right tool for the job.

Carry buckit to de well every dey, one dey de battam will drap out. = Carry a bucket to the well every day, one day the bottom will fall out. = Keep on taking chances and one day your luck will run out.

Chickin merry, hawk de near. = Chicken is merry, not knowing that the hawk is near. = Beware when all seem to be alright that trouble may be close.

Choble deh a bush, monkey carry cum a yaad. = Trouble is in the bushes and monkey took it home. = Do not bring contention home.

Choble neva set up like re-ain. = Trouble never sets up like rain. = You can never always see trouble coming.

Cock mout kill cock. = Cock mouth kills cock. = Because the cock crows and is noisy, he will be killed. If you talk too much, you may say something to your detriment.

Dawg wid too many yaad, goh to bed wid out bone. = A dog with too many yards goes to bed without a bone. = When you have too many abodes, nobody expects you, or prepares for you.

Dem a bench an batty. = They are like the bench and the behind. = They are close friends.

Dem a like crab in a baaril. = They are like crabs in a barrel. = Crabs in a barrel will not allow a fellow crab to climb on any other to get out.

Dish towil cum tun te-able claat. = Dish towel is promoted to be table cloth. = Critism of someone's promotion.

Doh-na choble wa noh choble yu. = Do not trouble whatever does not trouble you. = What does not trouble you, you should leave alone.

Doh-na fan fly aafa people cow head while fe yu own a spwile. = Do not fan flies off people's cow head while your own is going spoilt. = Don't mind other people's business while your own needs to be taken care of.

Doh-na heng yu baskit furda dan yu caa reach. = Do not hang your basket further than where you can reach. = Do not commit to spend more than what you can afford.

Doh-na jump outa frying pan eina fire. = Do not jump out of the frying pan into the fire. = Do not leave small trouble to get into big trouble.

Doh-na swap black dawg fe monkey. = Do not swap a black dog for a monkey. = What you have is just as good as the exchange.

Duppy know who fe frighten. = Ghosts know who to frighten. = Certain people are not interfered with.

Ef yu caa ketch Quacu, yu ketch im shut. = If you cannot catch Quacu, you can catch his shirt. = This refers to someone who is fleeing a scene. He barely escaped, but his shirt is left in the hands of the pursuer. Similarly revenge is taken on the kin of a wrong-doer.

Ef yu noh goh a fowl rouse, fowl caa shit pan yu. = If you do not go to fowl's roost, fowl cannot filth on you. = If you stay where you belong, no trouble will catch you.

Ef yu waa good, yu nu-ose ha fe run. = If you want good, then your nose have to run. = If you want to be a success, then you have to put your nose to the grindstone.

Empty bag caa tan up. = An empty bag cannot stand up. = A man with a hungry belly cannot work.

Every dangki tink im pickny is a re-ace hass. = Every donkey thinks his cub is a race horse. = Every parent thinks their child is better than the others.

Every dawg have im dey. = Every dog has his day. = Every person has his time to win or to lose.

Every hoe ha im tick a bush. = Every hoe has a stick somewhere. = Every person has a mate somewhere.

Every mickle mek a muckle. = Every little bit counts.

Everyting goh like butta gence sun. = Everything went like butter against the sun. = Everything was wasted.

Feed mawga dawg an im tun roun an bite yu. = Feed meager dog and he turns around and bites you. = Do good to an ungrateful person and be rewarded with displeasure.

Fisha-man neva seh im fish tink. = Fisher-man will never say that his fish stinks. = Your own goods are always good.

Fyah de a monki te-ale im tink a cool breeze. = Fire is at monkey's tail and he thinks it is cool breeze. = Trouble is behind you and you think it is peace and safety.

Gei yu an inch an yu tek a yaad. = Give you an inch and you take a yard. = I am kind enough to give you a little and you take a lot.

Good fren betta dan packit money. = Good friends are better than pocket money. = Good friends are better than money in your pocket.

Gotty gotty don' want it an wanti-wanti can't get it. = Who has it don't want it and who wants it can't get it.

Haas dead an cow fat. = The horse is dead, but the cow is fat. = An excuse by one who is unable to pay his debt as arranged. The horse typifies how he was expecting to pay his debt. However, the cow will soon have calf, so there is hope for him to have earnings in the future to pay his bills.

Han goh han cum. = Hand go hand come. = Kindness from one is rewarded by another.

Head cook an chief bokkle washa. = Head cook and chief bottle washer. = Someone who is in charge of a fete.

Maasta has, maasta grass. = Master's horse, master's grass. = What belongs to the owner also belongs to his appointee.

Man weh noh dun walk noh dash weh im tick. Man who is still walking does not throw away his walking stick. = Never discard something that you will need later in life.

Mi an yu ha no fish fe fry. = You and I have no fish to fry. = You and I have no quarrel.

Mi an yu noh plant peas a line. = You and I do not plant peas at our boundary. = You and I do not get along.

Neva put san eena sumady shoes or yu may jus fine gravel eena fey yu. = Never put sand into someone else's shoe, or you may just find gravel in yours. = Do unto others as you would have them do unto you.

New broom sweep clean, but ole broom noh carna. = New broom sweeps clean, but old broom knows corners. = The new mate makes extra effort to impress, but the old mate knows the habits.

No sankey noh sing soh. = No Sankey hymn book's song is like this. = What is in the Sankey hymn book is absolutely right, so anything else is absolutely wrong.

No tek mi fey poppy-show. = Never take me for a poppet-show. = Do not make fun at my expense, or think that I am a fool.

Noh tek one man fat fry de adda. = Do not take one man's fat to fry the other. = Do not punish one man for the other man's wrongs.

Ole fyah tick easy fe ketch back. = Old fire wood is easy to re-light. = Old lovers are quick to get back together.

One monkey noh stop no show. = One monkey does not stop the show. = If only one person is missing from group, the play must go on.

Paishen man ride dangki, = A patient man rides donkey. = Do not be in a rush.

Pawsen crissen fey him pickny fuss. = Parson christens his child first. = The leader takes care of his needs first.

Pinetid finga neva seh look ya, it always seh look deh. = A pointed finger never say look here, it always says look there. = The fault finder never point to himself, he always point to someone else.

Ple-ay wid puppy dawg an him tun roun an lick yu mouth. Play with puppy dog and he will turn around and lick your mouth. = Be careful how you associate with someone who is not afraid to show their affections.

Puss an dawg noh have de se-ame luck. = Cats and dogs do not have the same luck. = What is good for you may not be good for someone else.

Puss belly full im seh rat batty tink. = When the cat's belly is full he says the rat's behind is stinks. One gets lazy when he or she is full.

Puss gone, rat tek cha-age. = When the cat is away, the mouse will play. When the boss is away, the servants will take charge.

Re-aine a fall but de dutty tough. = Rain is falling but the dirt is tough. = A line in a popular Bob Marley song, meaning that: although I am earning, times are hard.

Se mi a one ting, cum live wid mi is anada. = To see me is one thing, but to come and live with me is different. = Until you live with me, you don't really know me.

Siddung neva seh git-up. = Sitting down never will say to get up. = It is hard to get out of one's comfort zone.

Sum a dem a jang-cro, sum a dem a dawg. = Some of them are ravens, some of them are dogs. = Lines from a folk song describing bad-minded low-life people.

Teef noh like fe se teef carry bag. = Thief does not like to see another thief carrying a bag. = Thieves do not like competition.

Te-dey fey yu, tomara fe mi. = Today is for you and tomorrow is for me. = Everyone has his time for good or bad.

Tree noh grow inna mi fe-ace. = Tree does not grow in my face. = I am not ugly.

Wa a man doan know olda dan im. = What a man does not know is older than he is. = The older man usually knows more than the younger.

Wa gone bad a mawnin caa cum good a evelin. = What's gone bad in the morning cannot come good in the evening. = What starts bad cannot come good at the finish.

Walk fe nutten betta dan siddung fe nutten. = Walking for nothing is better than sitting down for nothing. = Sitting in one place all the time will do no good.

Wah eye noh se, haut noh leap. = What the eyes does not see does not make the heart leap. = Don' be afraid of what you cannot see.

Wah sweet nanny-goat a goh run im belly. = What is sweet for the goat will soon run his belly. = What is joyful now will soon become sorrow.

Wata more dan flowa. = Water is more than flour. = Times are hard. The expensive commodity is in small quantity.

Weh it mawga it will bruk off. = Where it is meager it will break. = Where supplies run out, the work will stop.

Wen bad dawg a sleep noh wake im. = When bad dog is sleeping, do not awake him. = Do not interfere where there is potential trouble.

Wen bread butta pon two side, yoh noh nooh how fe huole eh. = When bread is buttered on both sides, you do not know how to hold it. = When you have too much luxury, you do not know how to behave.

Wen mi duppy cum mi affi goh. = When my ghost comes I will have to go. = When death comes I will have to go.

Wen plantin waa dead, de fus ting im do is shoot. = When a plantain wants to die, the first thing it does is to shoot. = The known symptom of impending trouble, resulting mostly; to the detriment of the trouble-maker.

Wen yu tek tongue tie knot, not even teet caa pull it. = When you use tongue to tie a knot, not even teeth can pull it. = When you make a verbal agreement. It lives forever.

Yu cum ya fe drink milk, yu noh cum ya fe count cow. = You come here to drink milk and not to count cows. = This remark is usually directed to visitor to one's home who finds fault with the host and or things with the home.

PART THREE

***

Short stories.

It is often said that Jamaican rum, coffee, girls and marijuana are the best in the world. Jamaican stories whether they are true or false follow the same vein. Here are a few that echo those sentiments. Some names and places have been changed for the characters' protection.

Ivan.

Ivan had met a girl whom he liked very much and expressed that to her. She subsequently invited him to her house to meet her parents. There was just one problem. The girl lived at one end of the island and Ivan lived at the other, and he had no transportation.

Ivan asked his friend Dan to take him on his motor-cycle to the girl's house on a Sunday when they both had time. On the day appointed they left their homes early in the morning in order to visit and be back by night-fall, but they were delayed by rain, and did not get to the girl's house until mid-afternoon. Three hours later than what they had planned.

After a very jolly greeting, the girl's mother asked them to stay for dinner, which would be served at five o'clock. They reluctantly agreed, knowing that their return journey would be further delayed. But there was another problem. Ivan knew that his friend was quite a glutton and could embarrass them both around the dinner table, so he took him aside and said.

"A doh-na waa yu mek wei look she-aime roun de people dem te-able. So hea wah yu du. Jus watch mi an anyting mi do, yu do de se-aim. Wen fe mi belly full mi wei touch yu wid mi foot unda de te-able an wei bu-out stop eating."

"I do not want you to make us be ashamed around these people's table. So here is what you must do. Just watch me and whatever I do, you do the same. When my belly is full I will touch you with my foot under the table and we can both stop eating".

At five o'clock sharp, dinner was on the table. The father sat at the head of the table and the mother sat opposite to him. Two pre-teen children, a boy, sat next to his father, and the girl, sat next to her mother. Ivan sat next to his girlfriend and Dan sat opposite to him. A grace was said and the maid piled food on everyone's plate.

Dan was not used to eating with knife-and-fork and within the first minute, he had dropped the utensils on the floor several times. Finally, the father told him to use whatever he was comfortable with. He was more than glad for the advice and wasted no more time trying to be polite. He picked up a spoon and was shoveling food into his mouth with lightning speed when the family's cat walked under the table and touched his feet. Suddenly, he remembered what he had promised Ivan.

Up until that time Ivan had not eaten very much; as in between mouth-full he was talking to his girlfriend and answering questions from her father. But seeing that Dan had stopped eating, he stopped too. Everyone else ate, and the maid cleared the table.

Just as Ivan and Dan were about to bid goodbye the rain came in a torrential down pour. This disappointed them very much as they were both still very hungry, and they both were thinking; albeit unknown to each other, that they would stop at the nearest grocery shop for snacks. The news came over the radio that the roads were washed out, and it was advised that, for safety; no one should attempt to cross certain areas.

"Seems as if you guys are stuck here for tonight", said the father. "We have a spare room, so you both can stay."

They had no choice but to agree. Other than the rain, their overwhelming present situation was that they were hungry. They stood in one corner of the verandah, out of ear-shot of everyone else.

"Man mi hungry still," said Dan. *"A how yu touch mi soh quick?"*

"Man, I am still hungry. Why did you touch me so soon."

"A noh mi touch yu," replied Ivan. *"A mus e de puss."*

"I did not touch you. It must have been the cat."

The rain did not let up, and about nine o'clock everyone retired to bed.

At about mid-night Dan was railing with hunger. Ivan was fast asleep. Dan tiptoed down the hallway into the kitchen. He searched around in the dark to find something to eat; while being very careful to be silent so no one would be awakened. He searched until finally, he found a pot with some liquid that was the left-over from the yams that were boiled as part of the dinner. He was glad to find it and drank a belly-full. Then he poured some in a cup to take to his friend.

As he came from the kitchen he took a wrong turn and went into a room he thought his friend was in. He went to the bedside and started to shake the person covered up on the bed.

"A drink mi belly full an a bring sum fe yu," he said quietly.

"I drank my belly-full and I brought some for you."

Just then the father, who was being shaken out of his sleep, reached to the night-stand and turned on the light. Dan was so startled that he ran out of the house, jumped on his motor-bike and sped down the driveway with the dogs in chase.

Next morning Ivan awoke to find his friend gone. No one told him what had happened the night before. The father took him to the bus-stop, but there were no buses running as the roads were damaged. He knew he would have lost his job back home for not showing up Monday morning, and even if buses were running he wouldn't have gotten home until sometime late Tuesday.

As he stood by the side of the road pondering his fate, a sub-contractor to the Public Works Department offered him a job as a helper to repair the damaged roads. After work that day, he walked into a Bed-and-Breakfast establishment and asked to stay on credit until payday.

Things went very well for Ivan. He was a good worker and the roads were always in need of repairs, assuring him a somewhat permanent source of employment. After pay-day he rented a furnished room in the area and told himself that being close to where the girl lived, transportation would no more be a problem.

After many months Ivan again met the girl who told him that she had been away at college and that she had written many letters to him and got no reply. He shared his story as of his last visit and she again invited him to her house.

The day of the visit was a Sunday, just like it was for the first. Ivan rode his bicycle to the house and got there in time for dinner. This time there were no mishaps or surprises at the table. Everyone ate to their heart's content, but just like the first time, the rain came down and would not let up. At about eight o'clock Ivan and the father were in the living-room talking about this and that.

"Seems like we are gonna have an all-night rain Ivan", said the father. "You'll have to stay for the night."

"Yes Sir", said Ivan as he walked toward the door and looking at the falling rain.

A few minutes later, with the rain still falling, no one had noticed that he had jumped on his bicycle and left.

"What did you say to him Daddy?" asked the girl, after she looked around, and couldn't find Ivan.

"Nothing, I simply told him that he could stay for the night," answered her dad.

They were both perplexed and concerned for his safety. Half an hour went by and the girl suggested that they go and see if he was okay. The father reluctantly agreed. It was still raining, and just as he was getting into his Jeep, Ivan appeared with a plastic bag under his arm. He was soaking wet.

"Where did you go?" screamed the girl.

Very calmly Ivan answered.

"*Oh mi jus goh an get mi pejama.*"

"Oh I just went and got my pajamas."

Note: A fool will make himself known one way or the other.

Doctor Melbourne.

Dr. Melbourne lived in the Mona-Heights area of the city. He had four country-side offices that were within an hour's drive from his residence. On weekdays he would leave home at eight in the morning and be at anyone of his offices by nine o'clock, the latest. He would, on a regular basis, render medical services including giving prescription drugs to the indigents free of charge at the localities where his offices were. His British-born wife was a registered nurse before marriage; worked at the Kingston Public Hospital under her maiden name to conceal her marriage to the doctor, who at the time was head of the staff. Dr. Melbourne himself is an Ethiopian who lived in Jamaica since he was a teenager, and had adopted just about everything Jamaican.

On a typical workday, Dr. Melbourne would be at one of his offices from nine in the morning until one or two o'clock in the afternoon, depending on the number of patients that day; and then he would take an hour lunch break before going to the nearby elementary school to volunteer as Basic Hygiene teacher. By his request, at each of the schools, he was assisted by a sixth-form girl.

During the years of Dr. Melbourne's practice at a particular location, there was a man in his thirties who normally hang out at the local Post Office.

As the story went, when the man was much younger he used to boast to his friends that he was sleeping with Miss Barrett who was a postal clerk that lived on the second floor of the Post-Office building. He would make sure that late at nights someone would see him walking from the back of the building, and assumed that he was coming from Miss Barrett's room. His claim had almost taken root when on a rainy night he fell from an Ackee tree behind the Post Office building where he was sleeping to pass the time. He was taken to the hospital in an unconscious state. When he was revived he demanded to be taken to the Post Office. Ever since then he became mentally unstable, and hung around the post office building day and night.

After the fall; this man could barely speak. His speech sounded like a donkey braying, and whatever he was asked; his answer would be, "Adunnoh". Everyone affectionately called him Adunnoh. He carried a plate into which people from time to time, put food and money. Whenever his clothes looked dirty and scornful someone would always give him some clean ones. The people of the area were always kind to Adunnoh.

One Christmas day he went to a nearby home with his plate. The family was having cow's foot as meat for their dinner. They gave him some, and after he ate the meat from the bones, he put some bones into an open fire. When asked why he did that, he replied with sign language that that was to melt the bones. That provided the family with the laugh of the day, and from then on, Adunnoh with no last name became Adunnoh Meltbone. With the passage of time the `t' was dropped, and Adunnoh Meltbone became Adunnoh Melbone.

Dr. Melbourne's visits to the schools were not purely philanthropic. The sixth-form girls who had passed elementary school age often volunteered their time as teacher's aides. The schools in appreciation for the services of these girls gave them free evening classes to help in preparing them for the Jamaica Local exams which were held once per year.

Dr. Melbourne would choose the prettiest of these girls to assist him with the classes. He then would invite them to his office for free checkups. Any girl who accepted his invitation was made to believe that she was the only one to have such a privilege. In the privacy of his office the girls were sedated and raped, and although he most often used contraceptives, invariably, some girls got pregnant.

One girl who lived with her mother and step-father had no idea how she became pregnant. She thought that her step-father must have violated her while she was asleep. The stepfather flatly denied it, but the girl had told her mother earlier that he had tried to get fresh with her. There was nothing the stepfather could have said or done to convince the mother that he was innocent. The whole district cried shame on him, especially because he was one of the church deacons. People teased him whenever he appeared on the streets. Finally, he could not take it anymore; he killed himself.

Two girls from neighboring districts got pregnant within a month of each other. None of them knew the other. They both gave birth at home and were attended by the same midwife. The mid-wife noticed the resemblances of the two babies even at that early age, especially that none of them looked like the reported fathers.

It was required by law that home-births were to be registered at the local Post Office within thirty days a child's birth. The requirement for registration was a note from the midwife, and if the mother was unmarried, she had to be accompanied by the father. If the father was not alive or refused to show up, then the child would be given the mother's last name. Naming a child after the mother was a stigma, because it was assumed that the mother had slept with so many men that she could not point out the real father.

Both of the girls went at different times to the Post Office to register their child. They each had brought the note from the midwife, but there was no father to accompany them. The first girl was Ned Foster, an eighteen year old who lived with her grandmother and one younger brother. She was of Indian descent, about five-five, slim and very pretty. She took her pre-teen-age brother with her, but the postal clerk refused let him sign as the baby's father.

Being as Adunnoh was always hanging around at the Post Office, the clerk asked Ned if it would be okay to have him put an x on the line for father. The girl anxiously wanted to have her baby registered and knowing that no one in their right mind would ever think that Adunnoh is the father of her child, said yes to the clerk. The clerk then wrote Melbourne instead of Melbone, thinking that Melbone was not a proper name.

Within the same week the second girl, another eighteen year old named Eanti went to have her baby registered. Eanti, was also about five-five of fair complexion and a little bit on the chubby side. She was attended at the Post Office by the same clerk, who having been previously faced with such situation, made the similar request. Eanti, must have felt the same as the first girl did in the predicament, however, she too reluctantly agreed.

Two months later, on Easter Sunday, the two girls went to the parish church to have their babies christened. The entire congregation was amazed at how the two babies looked like twins. By co-incidence one child was named James Robert Melbourne and the other was named Robert James Melbourne. There were whispers that they must be the children of Dr. Melbourne, but it could not be said aloud. Dr. Melbourne was well loved and respected throughout the community, but there was no one else with that name.

The girls were frightened out of their wits. They had never met. They became best friends, and over the ensuing months, they related their life stories to each other, and discovered that there were a few things they had in common, and those things involved Dr. Melbourne. One: They were both teachers' aides and assisted in Dr. Melbourne's classes. Two: They were both invited to Dr. Melbourne's office for check-ups. Three: None of them were sexually active. They figured it out and decided to confront the doctor.

The doctor only visited each office once per week; for four or five hours at a time, so the waiting list was very long. The girls made outrageous promises to the doctor's assistant and succeeded in having their appointments together for two weeks ahead of the normal waiting time.

The day of the appointment came and both girls appeared at the doctor's office dressed alike. The babies were also dressed alike. At nine o'clock when the door opened, they were the first ones to enter. They sat where the sunshine from the curtain-less window shone on them from head to toe, that they could not be overlooked; even by the near blind.

Five minutes after nine the doctor walked in. That day he looked even more spiffed than his usual self, as it was one of his school volunteer days. He was fully dressed in white. Even his hat was white. The only thing seemed out of place was a black doctor's attaché case he carried in his left hand. His attire made him look not a day over twenty-five, although he was well into his forties and must have weighed over two hundred and fifty pounds. He was clean shaven and the smell of his cologne instantly filled the waiting area.

With his right hand he made a half-hearted wave and said good morning to the waiting crowd. He stopped in his tracks as his eyes focused on the girls with the babies for more than a second, then he swiftly walked pass the receptionist, through a doorway behind her.

The girls' names were the first to be called and they went in together. The doctor looked at them, up and down and then up again. He was speechless. The girls enjoyed the suspense for a short while, before one of them spoke.

"Mr. Melbourne, here are your sons Sir".

"What are you talking about?" asked the doctor, in a tone of voice that everyone in the waiting room could hear.

The other girl's voice tone matches the doctor's as he moved swiftly and closed the door.

"Sir, you know very well, and if you deny anything, we are going straight to the police. You know the word rape, and you know the word jail, they sometimes go together, and you know what they do to men like you in jail?"

"Stop, stop", said the doctor. "What do you want from me?"

"*Sopoutance fey u pickni dem.*" said the first girl.

"Support for your children".

"Okay, okay", he said in a much more subdued tone. "I'll give you each ten shillings a week".

"*No sah*", the first girl said. "*Personally mi waa one poun fe de be-aiby an one poun fe mi self fe all de choble yu put mi chue, an den aneda one poun fe noh goh to de police*".

"No sir, personally, I want one-pound for the baby and one-pound for myself for all the trouble that you had put me through, and one-pound for not going to the police".

The doctor was visibly trembling when the other girl spoke and said,

"*An de se-aim ting fe mi to sah*".

"And the same thing goes for me sir".

He took out his bill-fold from an inside jacket pocket and unclipped the notes. Quickly he counted out six, and handed the set to the girls. He showed them a back door from which to leave. They ignored him and left the way they went in.

The following week the girls went to the doctor's office to collect. He refused to see them. One of them waited at the back door to make sure he did not sneak out while the other went in search of a police on the street. She met a cop who was a rookie and was new to the area. He had not heard of Dr. Melbourne and how he was loved and respected in the vicinity, neither did he know why the girl wanted him to follow her to the doctor's office, but she was young and pretty, and he would have gone with her even if she had not promised him ten shillings.

As they stepped into the waiting room, the receptionist ran into the doctor's room and within seconds she returned and courteously said to the girl, "The doctor will see you now".

Without saying a word he handed one of them six one-pound notes. She looked at it and said, *"An ten shilling fe way-tin time"*.

"And ten shillings for waiting time".

The doctor retrieved his bill-fold and opened it. He had no bill of less than one-pound and held it for her to see. As quick as lightning she reached the bill-fold and extracted a one-pound note. She walked backward through the doorway to the waiting area where she handed the one-pound note to the policeman and went outside to the back door to get her friend.

Two weeks had passed and the girls had not showed up to collect. The doctor must have thought his nightmares were over, but on week number five they both returned and promptly ushered themselves into the doctor's office. They were dressed in hot pants, halter tops, knee-high boots and wearing sun shades. They looked like they were beauties on a movie-making set.

No one spoke. The doctor reached into a desk drawer and retrieved some notes and handed the set to one of the girls. She counted it. The lot consisted of one five-pound and seven one-pound notes. The doctor smiled a wry smile. The girls returned the compliments with their own mocking smiles. He expected them to leave, instead they both took seats. One sat in a chair and the other on his desk.

"Get out of my office," he hollered. "You already got what you came for".

"*Not so fass Johnny boy*," teased one girl. Then the other one spoke.

"*De two week yu diden se wei. Wei goh a all de school dem weh yu mess up people pickni life. Tree a dem ha pickni like wei. Now wei waa tree hundred poun fe share up fe all a dem*".

"The two weeks that you did not see us. We went to all the schools where you messed up people's children lives. Three of them have children like we do. Now we want three hundred-pounds to share for all of them".

"This is blackmail," the doctor screamed. "Do you really think you can get away with this?"

"*Well sar*", replied one girl. "*Tree a dem out de, an two a wei ya, das five. Yu eva hear de wud rape, an de wud je-ail, dem two usually goh togeda, an wat dey du to man like yu in je-ail. Yu would neva se dey light as lang as yu live. Yu foot neva touch groung".*

"Well sir, there are three of them out there, and two of us here, that is five. Have you ever heard the word rape, and the word jail, those two words usually go together, and what they do to men like you in jail? You would never see day light as long as you live. Your feet would never touch the ground".

"I do not have that kind of money with me," said the doctor. "I will have to go to the bank".

"We wei we-ate right ya".

"We will wait right here".

The doctor tapped on a small bell and the receptionist swiftly walked in.

"Send the patients home", he said. "I have an emergency. And keep two eyes on these two until I get back".

The doctor slipped through the back door and within seconds the roar of the diesel engine in his Mercedes Benz was loud and clear. One of the girls went to a metal filing cabinet and pulled the top drawer open. The receptionist moved swiftly to close it, but before she could get to it the second girl stepped in front of her and pointed a finger into her face and said.

"Lissen you bitch. You noh why wei deh ya, an ef tings noh goh owa we-ay we wei mek shur dat yu be cha-ahged wid complying wid de commission of crime multiply by five. Yu foot wudn touch groung fe goh a je-ail. An yu wudn se de sun fe de res a yu life".

"Listen you bitch. You know why we are here, and if things do not go our way, we will make sure that you will be charged with being an accessory in the commission of crimes multiplied five times. Your feet would not touch the ground going to jail, and you would not see the sun for the rest of your life".

The receptionist took two or three steps backward and stood in a corner with her arms folded while the other girl flipped through the files in the cabinet. Occasionally she glanced at the receptionist and wryly smiled at her.

The receptionist's name was Nery, and was half-Chinese, but that wasn't very evident as she looked more like her mother who was from Syria. Nary was very pretty and wore a work-casual linen dress that fit her five-foot-nine slim frame like the label on the Red Stripe beer bottle. The doctor was a friend of her mother, and he used the convenience of that friendship to get to her. She was nineteen when she got pregnant with the first child four years earlier. Up until then she had sex with two men, her then steady boyfriend and the gardener. Her boyfriend ditched her knowing that the child could not have been his because, as he said, 'the only time they had done it he wore a condom'. She had no choice but to elope with the gardener. The child was registered in her husband's name, but she knew who the father was.

The doctor had gone a full hour and the girls whispered to one another that maybe they should leave because the doctor might have gone to the police, but then they agreed that if they stop there, that would be the end of them getting money for themselves and their babies, and worst of all, was that the doctor would continue to mess with other students. Apparently, the girls whisper was not soft enough for the receptionist not to hear, and they were very surprised when she stepped toward them and said, "I am with you both. This is a regular practice and many times I had to turn girls away to shield them from the doctor. I was probably the first one that he sedated and raped. He is the father of my two kids. I was forced to marry a man that I do not even like, just to cover my shame. The ten shillings a week extra that he gives me is not worth it for me to keep quiet any more".

It seemed as Nery would never stop talking. The girls hugged her. All three were in an embrace of empathy when they heard the Mercedes pulled up into the carport.

The doctor's eyes bulged as he opened the back door and stepped into his office and saw the two girls and his receptionist holding hands forming a fence blocking him from his desk.

"Nery!" He said loudly. "What the hell is this?"

"Dr. Melbourne", said Nery, softly. "This has been going on long enough, and until now I had no idea it was so widespread. We are putting an end to this, and from now on you will either work for us, or you go to prison. I am ready to testify, particularly on behalf of those girls that you performed abortion on, and remember one thing. I know your wife."

There were tears running down Dr. Melbourne's face. He was allowed to sit in his chair behind his desk. He put his head down and covered his face with his hands. One of the girls put a hand on his shoulder and said.

"Wei hav a baaghin, rememba."

"We have a bargain, remember?"

He reached into his jacket pocket and handed her an over-stuffed envelope, then he looked up at Nery.

"What do you want Nery", he asked.

"The Benz," she said. "Three-pounds a week raise, the supervisor position for all the offices, and to be your assistant at all the schools where you teach, so I can prevent you from destroying young girls' lives".

Note: Your sins will find you out.

Twin Sisters

Two baby girls were born as twins to a well-to-do family in rural part of Jamaica. One was named Mel as part of the father's first name; Melvin. The other baby girl was named Telly as part of the mother's first name; Tellyanna. The twins were the first and only children for their parents. They were also the first and only grandchildren for both sets of grandparents.

Melvin was the only child of a wealthy cattle farmer and Tellyanna was the only child of an equally wealthy sugarcane farmer of the neighboring district. Both sets of grandparents rivaled each other in buying the twin expensive and matching presents.

As the girls grew up, the parents and grandparents made sure that they at all times matched in everything. They had matching clothes, shoes, toys, the same school classes, even the same private tutors.

The girls rewarded their kin folks by excelling in their academics, and were both awarded full four-year scholarships to an ivy-league college in England. They were bright enough that they were able to complete the program in three years and returned to Jamaica. They had just celebrated their twentieth birthday and were glad for the break from a lifetime of studies.

To reward the girls for their achievements one set of grandparents gave them a one-month vacation stay at a four-star resort in Upper Saint Andrew.

The year was 1959 and the Volkswagen beetle was being introduced in Jamaica as the other German-made car. The other set of grandparents, who already owned a top of the line Mercedes Benz, decided that they would not be outdone in awarding presents, so they bought the girls two brand-new Volkswagen beetles.

The salesmen, who delivered the cars to the girls at the Resort, taught them how to drive, and even through their special contacts; helped them to get their drivers' licenses. The girls were very happy. For three weeks they drove around Kingston; to beaches and other fun spots they had barely heard of before. At the end of their stay at the resort, they decided to drive home to the country-side to be with their parents. The weekend before they took the cars to the dealership for servicing.

Bright and early Monday morning they set out to drive from Kingston to their home in Westmoreland. Kingston, where they learnt to drive is all flat roads, so they did not learn how to shift gears when going up or down hills. Both cars had standard stick-shift gear-boxes. On reaching Melrose Hill, the car in the front stalled. The other girl pulled up behind her. Telly released the hood latch of the front compartment and Mel went in front to look in and figure out why the car stalled. She peeped into the empty compartment and hollered to her sister,

"Telly, Telly! ***Dem teif out de ingin outa yu key-ar***".

"Telly, Telly! They have stolen the engine from your car".

Telly was equally startled. She took a few seconds to regain her composure before she said,

"Oh mi neva memba fe tell yu. wen mi goh fe put yu grip dem inna de trunk dis mawnin mi se a spe-aire ingin in deh, so mi put de grip dem pon de back seat".

"Oh I did not remember to tell you that I went to put your suitcases into the trunk this morning and saw a spare engine into it. That is why the suitcases are on the back seat".

Note: You are a fool to what you do not know, and common sense is sometimes better than book sense.

Afraid, times two.

Two brothers who were next-door neighbors and also the fathers of two teenage boys were discussing what to do about their boys staying out late at nights. They, together and separately, had tried many things to discourage the practice but nothing worked. Finally, they decided that they would wrap themselves in white sheets and hide in the bushes where the boys pass by on their way home one of those late nights. There they would jump out of the bushes just as they are passing to make them become scared and believe that ghosts were after them.

The brothers did not know that a juvenile sibling was eavesdropping on their plans. For a hefty reward the junior revealed to one of the teens what the plan was, and for an even bigger reward he revealed to the other teen the date the plan would be put in place.

At the appointed night the teenagers took two white sheets and hid themselves across the path from where they expected their dads to be. It was near midnight. Within fifteen minutes after the boys secured themselves, the fathers arrived and straightaway hid themselves at their designated spot. Each of the boys had with him two short pieces of dried bamboo sticks which when rubbed together make an eerie, ghostly sound.

The first boy rubbed his sticks together and made that eerie, ghostly sound. A few seconds later the second boy who was about ten feet away; rubbed his sticks together and produced that eerie, ghostly sound. Nothing happened. One minute later the boys repeated their antics.

*"**Ben, yu hear dat**?"* asked one father.

"Ben! Did you hear that?"

*"**Yeh mon**",* answered his brother. *"**Nutten to worry bout. A breeze a blow de tree dem**".*

"Yeah man, but there is nothing to worry about. The breeze is blowing the trees".

Another two minutes passed and the boys again repeated their antics.

The first father remarked. *"**But Ben, no breeze nah blow**".*

"But Ben, there is no breeze blowing".

The boys desperately wanted to laugh out loud, and had to put their hands over their mouths to muffle the sounds. Another minute passed and for the third time the boys made the sounds followed by an evil sounding 'meow'.

The two brothers could not take it any longer; they jumped from their hiding places and stood in the path. Just then one of the boys wearing white sheet jumped from the bushes a mere twenty feet away. The two men ran and the two boys wearing white sheets began to chase them. The chase continued for about a hundred feet. The boys stopped and discarded their sheets, afraid that their dads could suffer heart attacks, and they would have regretted their trick. They went back to the streets at a shop where they played dominos until five in the morning. Since then they stayed out as late as they cared to.

Note: There are no flies on the wall. Eavesdroppers come in different sizes and forms.

Dalford Hamm

Dalford Hamm was in his mid-forties, six-foot tall and weighed two hundred and forty pounds. When he talks his voice thunders and at times he seemed to emphasize that, just to intimidate his subordinates. He had been in the Jamaica Police Force for more than twenty two years, and was promoted up the ranks to the post of Senior Inspector. He had been in that position for ten years, and was slated to be promoted to Superintendent within the year, but he really had his eyes on the regional Police Chief's position. He tried to make himself very visible in every situation in order that all the members of the Police Federation would at least know his name, so that when they secretly vote their choice for Police Chief they would be mindful of him.

One night he was leading a squadron of detectives and other police officers on a marijuana field raid. Such a task is quite unusual for an inspector, but this was a big operation and news of it would certainly make headline in the newspaper next morning, and his name would be at the front. During the raid he fell down a precipice and seriously injured himself.

He spent many months in the hospital receiving medical and therapeutic care. He moved around in a wheelchair and had to be assisted as he was crippled from his waist down. Upon his release from the hospital he was placed on light duty, performing office duties while his health was expected to improve. But even light duty was too much for him, and caused him to be excessively absent from work.

Finally, the government placed him on permanent-disability status. With that he was awarded retroactive pay plus a hefty monthly pension. He used his lump sum to purchase a high acreage property in the countryside and had a four bedroom house built. The house was built with special features to facilitate the inspector's physical handicap. All the rooms were accessible to his wheelchair, the ceilings over the carport, his bed and in the bathroom were extra high and fitted with rope blocks and pulleys for him to elevate and lower himself as he needed to. Also, at the back of the house was a large water-catchment tank that supplied water through a hand operated pump to a reservoir on top of the house, which in turn allowed water to flow to the bathrooms and the kitchen. He pumped the water each day, just to exercise his upper body.

When he moved into the area; everything about him was very secretive. He had no visitors. His only acquaintance was an old Englishman named Charlie Hastings who lived in Mandeville, more than thirty miles away. Mr. Hastings owned one of the properties that bordered the inspector's. The inspector's house was more than a quarter of a mile from the public road and had tall fences with bad dogs. For a while, only the people at the Post Office had the least of ideas as to who he was. He had to dismount the mule he rode to go inside the building to sign for the rental of the P.O.

Box. On his subsequent visits he would hand the key to someone standing nearby to retrieve his mails.

Within months after living in the area inspector Ham stocked his property with cattle and adopted two children through the juvenile court system; a fourteen year old boy named Carlton and a thirteen year old girl named Joyce. Carlton was tall for his age, but very slim and Joyce was short and looked three years younger than she actually was. The children did not attend school or church and was only seen on the street near his home once.

No one knew that the children were being abused until some detectives were investigating the theft of animals in the area and the inspector was a suspect of being the recipient of the stolen property.

Unknown to the inspector, surveillance was set up near his house and it was observed that he, on occasion, had tied up both the children to a post on the back porch of his house and had severely beaten them with the whip he used to herd the cows. So as not to blow their cover the detectives did not intervene but reported the matter to their superior. As a matter of showing professional courtesy, inspector Hamm was visited by another inspector and a rookie cop. He denied that the children were being abused but refused to show them. He was outraged that his much guarded privacy was invaded and declared to the officers that,

"My name is Dalford an dis is my prapaty, I call it Hamstead. D fe de devil and D fe Dalford. H fe hell an H fe Hamstead. De devil rule hell, an Dalford rule Hamstead. Nobady tell de devil what to do in hell an nobady will tell Dalford wat to do in Hamstead".

"My name is Dalford and this is my property, I call it Hamstead. D is for Dalford and D is for the devil. H is for hell and H is for Hamstead. The devil rule hell and Dalford rule Hamstead. No one tells the devil what to do in hell, and no one will tell Dalford what to do in Hamstead".

The officers left and no further investigation was made.

Inspector Ham was a self-sufficient man. With the help of the two adopted children he grew everything that he ate. The only things that he bought were rope for his animals, salt, kerosene oil and the daily newspaper.

In a relatively short time, his cattle farm grew so extensive that he had to hire an outside helper, a man known locally as the professor. The man, affectionately called Prof, was a German. He was a six-foot, two hundred pounds, curly hair and courteous person. He and his only brother were sailors who came to Jamaica on a ship that transported bananas from the islands to Britain. On their last shore-leave they both hooked up with some Jamaican women who took them to the inner parts of the island. They spent too many days enjoying the women, the food, marijuana and the rum, their ship left without them. Neither of them had work permits so they were unable to be employed by any establishment.

In search of ways to make a living, the brothers split up. One went to Saint Thomas and the other went to Saint Elizabeth. They kept in touch by letters through the Post Office. The brother that went to Saint Thomas got married, had a family and obtained his Jamaican citizenship. Before the two brothers split up they had joked that the only ship they wanted to see were their citizenship, however, Prof had never pursued his. He was called Prof because he knew a little of everything. He was a carpenter, a mason, a mechanic, a cook, a barber, you name it, and Prof could do it. He even sewed his own clothes and was always ready to give advice on everything from health to religion.

The inspector was glad to have him as his assistant. Carlton and Joyce loved him, particularly because the inspector treated them kindly when Prof was around. Prof's only faults are two words, he smells. He rarely takes a bath, and he wore a pair of knee-high Dunlap-made rubber boots which gives off a scent that was so pungent that when you are near him; your fingers have to take turns making trips to your nose.

Because of Prof's all-round help and his knowledge of animal husbandry, within two years of being with the Inspector, the cattle count doubled. The inspector purchased the neighboring property, from Charlie Hastings, also of high acreage, to accommodate his herds. No longer did he have to spend half an hour getting on his mule. His paralyzed lower limbs did not allow him much agility. Carlton was now almost eighteen. He and Prof, riding mules, herded the cows in a fraction of the time it always took for the inspector to do it.

After herding the cows in the mornings, which was what Prof was hired to do, he would hang around and help Carlton with his chores. He and Carlton developed a very close relationship, and with all the time they spent together, they built pens for goats and pigs and grew an extensive garden. Joyce loved that because it relieved her of working in the garden and gave her more time to do the house chores, which she normally starts at 'sun-up' and finishing one or two o'clock in the mornings. Her chores included washing and ironing clothes, cooking three meals each day and cleaning the entire house, which included all the rooms and porches except a secret room that was always locked.

Things were going so well that the inspector was selling cows by the truck loads. He started to sell milk on a daily basis to the Creamery. He always demanded payment by cash which was sent to him once per month, and which he stored in a room to which only he had the key. He did not keep a bank account for fear the government would know how much he earned and reduce his benefits and also force him to pay income tax.

There was a Land Rover jeep in the carport that was towed there when the inspector moved in. That jeep had not been driven since the inspector had the accident. On rainy days when nothing could be done outdoors, Prof and Carlton worked on the jeep to install hand-operated levers for the brakes, clutch, and accelerator so that the inspector could drive it again. It took Prof, many months of on and off work on that jeep, but he finally got it to where only the brakes were left to be adjusted to the hand lever. He was working on that one Saturday afternoon when a telegram was delivered to him. The telegram read that his brother had passed away, and that the funeral would be the following week Tuesday.

Prof was very distraught. He had not seen his brother for many years and although they kept in touch by letters, the last correspondence was more than a year earlier. He asked the inspector to lend him the jeep, that way he would leave early Monday morning to get to Saint Thomas by night-fall, attend the funeral Tuesday and return by Wednesday night. He explained that if he had to go by bus, he would have to leave Sunday morning to get there Monday night, and then leave Saint Thomas Wednesday morning and wouldn't get back to Saint Elizabeth until Thursday night.

"Take the bus", the inspector said. "Carlton and Joyce can take care of the cows. One week won't kill them".

Prof was upset and disappointed, so he put away his tools and strolled down the long driveway to the public road. The inspector sat in his wheelchair on the verandah and watched him go until he was out of sight before he wheeled himself to the inner part of the house.

The Creamery truck does not pass on Sundays, so the calves did not have to be separated from the cows Saturday night in order to get milk the next morning. Sunday everything went fine. In the late afternoon Carlton secured the calves to prepare the cows to be milked next morning.

Monday morning Carlton and Joyce were awakened by the whip from the inspector for them to get an early start milking the cows. It was still dark and Joyce had never before milked the cows. Carlton tried his best to help her, but they were only able to get half the twenty gallons required before the truck arrived. The inspector was outraged.

That night he attempted to beat Joyce, and Carlton knew that he would be next. They hadn't been beaten for more than two years. Not since Prof came to work there, until that morning. Carlton grabbed the lash of the whip while it was in the air, and just before it was about to violently land on Joyce's backside. No one spoke. The inspector wheeled himself into his bedroom and came out a few seconds later with his rifle. Both Carlton and Joyce ran out of the house. They heard when a shot went off and hoped that he had shot himself. They spent the rest of the night taking turns to watch and sleep in the storage room that was by the detached kitchen.

Tuesday morning found Carlton and Joyce in the attic of the storage room on top of some burlap bags that contained animal feed. There was a slight drizzle, and they felt warm, but not safe. They could not figure out what to expect from the inspector, or what they should do next. "If only Prof was here". Carlton said.

"Yeah, you just love the smell of his boots", Joked Joyce.

Just then they heard the Land Rover's engine started. Carlton jumped down from his perch and peeped through a crevice. He saw the jeep backed out of the carport and headed down the drive-way. As it disappeared he wondered if the inspector was gone to get the police to put them in jail for what happened the night before. He was lost in his thoughts when he heard the crash right where the driveway meets the public road. Without hesitation he ran to see what had happened. The driver of the dump-body truck that hit the jeep was trying to pull the inspector out of the wrecked jeep. A car pulled up and the driver said.

"*Put im inna mi key-ar. Mi wei tek im to de aspital*".

"Put him into my car. I will take him to the hospital".

"What happened?" asked Carlton.

"***Im neva stop***", said the truck driver. "***Im jus cum out soh. Man mi sorry.***"

"He did not stop. He just came out like that. Man, I am sorry".

An hour after the crash the police arrived. The truck driver was still there and he gave them a statement. The jeep was pushed by some on-lookers unto the inspector's property. Then the police asked.

"Where is his son?"

The truck driver pointed to Carlton. He froze, and momentarily his mind went blank. He could not believe that anyone could refer to him as the inspector's son. He knew that the inspector had signed some papers for his release from the court, but had no idea that he was adopted, or what it meant.

"You need to come with me", said the police. "Your dad has been going in and out of consciousness and he had asked to see you. If you are lucky he might hold out until you get there".

Carlton waved to Joyce as he climbed into the police wagon. She did not hear what the police had said to him but she was glad that he was not wearing hand-cuffs. On the way to the hospital Carlton did not speak. He kept looking out the window of the vehicle. He had not been on those roads before, nor had he visited Black River, the capital city. He was very amazed to see so many people all dressed up. This was his first time visiting a place where so many streets and houses were so close to each other, and he wondered if he could ever find his way back home.

At the hospital, Carlton was directed to the inspector's bedside. He could not recognize him. His head was bandaged, so was his chest, his right hand and one of his legs. Carlton put a trembling hand on the inspector's shoulder, but he barely opened his eyes.

"Carry on", he said, very feebly. "I will be back next week".

The inspector closed his eyes again. Carlton stood there not knowing what to do, until a nurse said, "You can leave now. Let him rest".

Carlton stepped out of the hospital building. He was glad to be out in the sun light. He was hungry and the hospital antiseptic smell made him feel faint. The fresh outside air was welcome feeling. He looked around but did not see the police vehicle that brought him there. He wondered what to do, or should he expect the police to take him back home, as he desperately wanted to be home. What if he waited there and the policeman did not come back, and what if he should leave and he came looking for him. He had no money and he knew no one there. Then the thought hit him. Maybe the inspector had money in his pocket when the crash occurred. He rushed to the hospital office and got the clerk's attention.

"Good mawnin mam". He said. *"Me is inspector Hamm son. Im is inna bed upstays. Mi waa tek im clooz home to wash dem"*.

"Good morning mam. I am inspector Hamm's son. He is in a bed upstairs. I want to take his clothes home to wash them".

"Please wait a minute while I call a porter to get them", she told him.

The porter handed Carlton a big brown paper bag. He glanced inside and saw the inspector's blood-stained clothes and his boots. He walked off with the bag. He did not want for anyone to see him going through the pockets. He headed east on High Street and at about three hundred feet away he stopped under a tree and started to go through the pockets. He searched the hip pockets, the back pockets and the shirt pockets and the only thing he found was a small notebook and a house-door key. He secured them into his own pocket. Then he remembered that Joyce had showed him while she was washing clothes that in all of the inspector's trousers he had a secret pocket only an inch and a half by two inches, where the opening is under his belt. He found that pocket and in it, neatly folded was a crisp one-hundred dollar bill. He put on the inspector's boots and left his own worn-out ones and the blood-stained clothes under the tree.

Carlton was walking up the street toward downtown with renewed vigor, even though the boots were too big for him and he was hungry. A man was riding a bicycle and selling jerk pork. The smell was so enticing that Carton hollered to the man.

"A how yu sell it sah?"

"How is it sold sir?"

The man stopped and took out a piece that would weigh about a half of a pound and handed it to him.

"*Dats ten dolla,*" said the man.

"That is for ten dollars".

Carlton unfolded the one-hundred dollar bill and handed it to him.

"*O, o*", said the man. "*I caa chi-ange dat. Yu a mi firse custama. Goh a de bakery an buy sou bread. Dey wei chi-ange e fe yu*".

"Oh, oh, I cannot change that. You are my first customer. Go to the bakery and buy some bread, they will change it for you".

At the bakery Carlton bought bread, cakes, patties and other goodies for a total of twelve dollars. He got the change and paid the jerk pork seller, then sat down on a street side bench and ate to his heart's content. With a full belly he was ready to go home, but where is home? He remembered where he was living when his mother died four years ago. It was in Kendal and he was the oldest of six children and because there was no one to care for all of them together the five younger ones got adopted by different people and he was left to live on the streets and on his own. He ate from people's trash cans most of the time and slept in abandoned buildings. He had gotten into trouble and was in juvenile court to be sent to reformatory school when the inspector signed to keep him until he reaches the age of twenty-one. At least, that was what he told him. He did not wish to go back to Kendal.

He remembered that a bus by the name of The Lady Champion passes by the inspector's house every morning at ten o'clock sharp, except Sundays. It went in one direction in the morning and again at four o'clock in the opposite direction. If that bus was in Black River he would be in luck, if not he would have to go to the police station and tell them that he was lost, but how can a twenty year-old man be lost? He dismissed the thought. He asked a woman sitting at the side of the street selling baskets where to find that bus. She did not know that particular bus, but directed him to the market gate where all the buses were parked. With great anticipation he hurried to find The Lady Champion. As he approached the bus-park he saw more than a dozen buses, but no bus called The Lady Champion. He walked around reading the destination signs on the front of the parked buses. Some were marked Montego Bay, some were marked Mandeville, one was marked Balaclava, one was marked Treasure Beach and so on. A man saw that he looked like someone lost.

"A wa bus yu a look fa mi fren?" the man asked.

"What bus are you looking for my friend?"

"The Lady Champion", answered Carlton.

"It pawk right de wen it de ya," the man said. *"but now it gane gan service. It wei cum back about tree a'clack"*.

"When it is here it is usually parked right there, but now it is gone to be serviced. It will be back about three o'clock".

Carlton thanked the man for the information and offered him a piece of bread and a patty, which was readily accepted.

The Lady Champion returned to the bus park promptly at three o'clock and people from all directions swarmed into it. Carlton secured a seat just as the bus started to move. The conductress started to collect the fares squeezing her body through the standing room only passage. She stood in front of Carlton's seat, bracing herself on the backrest of the seat ahead.

"A weh yu a goh sah?", she asked him. "Where are you going sir?"

"A inspecta Ham house mam", he replied.

"To inspector Hamm's house ma'am".

"Any bady noh weh inspector Hamm ho-ous deh?" She called out above the noise of sixty or more passengers.

"Does anyone know where Inspector Hamm's house is?"

"Roun de cawna an up de hill, likkle pass Miggle Quata". One man answered.

"Around the corner, and up the hill a little past Middle Quarters".

Carlton paid the two dollars that the conductress asked for.

At Middle Quarters the bus stopped at the round-about intersection. People got off and people got on. The driver and the baggage handler went into the nearby rum bar and within seconds they were served Red Stripe beers. Both stood on the piazza of the bar enjoying them. At the same time there were a dozen or more vendors peddling parched-peppered shrimps to the passengers. Carlton bought a full paper bag for ten dollars. He had never had parched-peppered shrimps, but saw that people were enjoying them, and a vendor had pushed it almost into his face so he felt compelled to purchase a bag.

Around the corner and up the hill Carlton recognized the inspector's house and rung the bell for the driver to stop. As he walked up the long driveway, Joyce and the dogs came to meet him. The first thing she reached for was the bag of shrimps and she started to eat them even without stripping off the shell. She had never eaten parched-peppered shrimps before, but remembered that Prof had promised to get her some as a treat when she turned eighteen. Before finishing the very first one, she handed the bag back and reached for the bread. She had had shrimps before, but not hot-peppered.

They were in the process of washing the hot peppers off the shrimps when they discovered that the vendor had stuffed paper into the bottom of the bag up to halfway. He only got half the amount he thought he had paid for. Anyway, they enjoyed what was left.

Carlton told Joyce all that transpired on the way to the inspector and back, and thanked her for showing him the secret pocket in the inspector's trousers.

"Dis is de bes dey of mi whole life", Carlton said. *"How bout yu Joyce"*.

"This is the best day of my whole life. How about you Joyce?"

"Well", she said. "I don't know of the best day. I know of the worst day".

"Tell mi bout it", Insisted Carlton.

"Tell me about it".

"Mom an dad, they wasn't my blood parents", stated Joyce with sadness in her voice. *"Dem tell me that they adopt me as a baby. Wen I come to have sense they was*

a miggle-age miggle clas faamly. They sen mi to the bes pry-vit school in Mandeville. We have a pretty house an a pretty key-ar an I have a lot of toys an a lot of frens. I was twelve wen they lef to go to Amorica on vakaation. Dem was ongle supos to spen tree mont. Dem never cum back. Mi hear seh dem mussa did dead inna accident. Dem lef mi wid a faamily dat goh a de se-aim church as dem. Mi did goh a de airepout to see dem aff. Mi ne-aily cry mi yeye-ball out. De faamly dat dem lef mi wid ha two big dawta. De gal dem treat mi bad, like mi a Cinderella. A tree time mi run-weh. Das how mi end up inna juvenile cu-out an de inspecta adap mi".

"Mom and dad, they weren't my biological parents. They told me that they had adopted me as a baby. When I was old enough to know them, they were a middle-aged, middle-class couple. They sent me to the best private school in Mandeville. We had a pretty house and a pretty car and I had lots of toys and lots of friends. I was twelve when they left to go on vacation in America. They were only supposed to spend three months. They never returned, and I was told that they died in an automobile accident. They had left me to stay with a family that attended the same church as they did. There were two teenaged daughters in the family. Those girls treated me real bad, like I was Cinderella. I ran away three times, that's how I ended up in the juvenile court and the inspector adopted me".

"Well", said Carlton, in a kind of consoling way. *"At leas yu goh a school fe a while. Mi was twelve wen fe mi madda dead. Befoe dat mi ongle goh a school two maybe tree dey a week. Every adda dey mi ha fe goh a de train station goh pick up de yam an pitata dat fall affa de*

people dem baaskit soh mi madda cudda bwile it fe wei it. Afta she dead mi neva even se de school doa".

"Well, at least you attended school for a while. I was twelve when my mother died. Before that I only went to school two or three days per week. Every other day I had to go to the train station to pick up the yams and potatoes that fell from the people's baskets so my mother could cook them for us to eat".

Wednesday morning it rained long and hard and although the truck from the Creamery was late, there was no milk for them to pick up. Thursday morning both Carlton and Joyce milked the cows, but they only were able to collect ten gallons. However they did not get it to the gate in time for the truck, so again there was no pick up.

Carlton stood at the gate and wondered what to do with all that milk. He thought about feeding it to the hogs, but felt that it would be almost like throwing it on the ground, so he decided to tell everyone that walked by that the milk was free. News of the free milk raced through the neighborhood and within an hour all ten gallons were given away.

Friday morning early Carlton was at the hog pen feeding them when Prof walked up and tapped him on the shoulder.

"I have to touch you to make sure you are not a ghost," he said.

"Why?" asked Carlton.

"Because," said Prof. "I saw the jeep, and no one should survive that wreck. The driver's side is bashed in".

"A noh mi did a drive it", Carlton said. *"A de inspecta"*.

"It was not I who was driving it. It was the inspector".

"Is he dead?" asked Prof.

"No," replied Carlton. *"Im deh a aspital, but im look dead to mi"*.

"No, he is in the hospital, but he looks dead to me".

Both Prof and Carlton milked the cows that morning and they secured the required twenty gallons, but when they took it to the gate for the truck, there was a line of people from the neighborhood with containers waiting for free milk. Carlton had to explain to them that the only reason the milk was free the day before was because the truck had left it. They understood, but left very disappointed.

Saturday came and went without much incident. The milk quota was met. The cattle were herded to the pond to drink water for the second day in a row. Prof and Carlton butchered a pig and all three of the inspector's helpers had an early and sumptuous Saturday afternoon dinner. Just before dark, Prof used the inspector's mule to pull the jeep from the gate to the carport and removed the levers he had installed for the inspector to drive it. Other than the dent in the side it was now drivable.

Sunday morning when the sun was far up in the sky and all the animals were making noises, wanting to be fed, Joyce crawled out of bed to look at the clock on the living-room wall. It was showing a quarter-to eleven. She had never slept that late in the almost six years since her parents left. She looked in Carlton's room but he was not there. She ran outside and called his name out loud. His answer came from inside the house. She ran back in, and noticed that the inspector's bedroom door was opened. She ran in and saw Carlton searching through the dresser drawers. He had already gone through the chest-of-drawers and the night-stands and had opened more than a dozen cardboard boxes that contained bottles of liquors and another dozen boxes of empty liquor bottles.

"Carlton, how did you get in here?" she hollered.

"A got de key fram de inspecta chouses packit a de aspital". Carlton answered.

"I got the key from the inspector's trouser pocket at the hospital".

"Weh yu looking fa now?"

"What are you looking for now?"

"De key to de secrit room", answered Carlton.

"The key to the secret room."

"Gimmie de key dat yu have," said Joyce.

Carlton gave her the key and wondered what she needed it for. Calmly she walked out of the room. Carlton followed to see what she needed the key for. She inserted it into the lock of the secret room and like *se-se-me* it opened. What they saw almost took their breaths away. There were rows of clothes on racks. Most of the clothes were uniforms and cover-all's for the inspector: dozens of girls' dresses of different sizes made of grey khakis, the kind that Joyce herself wore, dozens of boy's shirts and trousers, and on the floor were boots and shoes of mainly three or four sizes.

Blocking the only window were two huge iron safes, one was a gun safe and the other, money safe. They were both locked. Carlton did not tell Joyce about the key or the notebook.

"Dere have to be a book aroun here some place wid de combination numbaz", said Joyce.

"There have to be a book around here some place with the combination numbers".

"I ha de notebook", said Carlton. *"It did deh wid de key inna de inspecta packit"*.

"I have the notebook. It was with the key in the inspector's pocket."

Carlton ran to his room and retrieved the notebook. They searched it through, but could not find anything that looked like combination numbers. However they saw some letters that did not seem to make any sense to Carlton. Joyce studied the letters for a few minutes before she hollered to Carlton.

"A fine it, a fine it," she said.

"I found it, I found it".

Carlton looked at the page that Joyce was focused on.

"Show me," he said.

"Dis is a game we play in school," she said. *"Yu staat fram one an dat is a a, two is be, tree is cee, four is dee an so an"*.

"This is a game we played in school. You start from one, and that is A, two is B, three is C, four is D and so on".

Together they figured out the combinations. The first safe to be opened was the gun safe. It had all kinds of guns in it. There were long guns, short guns, a machine gun and boxes upon boxes of ammunitions. Most of the guns were loaded. Carlton took the machine gun and hid it under his bed and Joyce took a revolver and hid it under her mattress. When they opened the money safe their eyes bulged at what they saw. There were stacks of notes, notes of all the denominations of Jamaican money, plus stacks of American dollars and English money. They emptied the safe and hid the currencies in their rooms. Joyce took the American and the England notes and Carlton took the Jamaican money. They vowed to each other not to tell Prof about it.

There were some things in the money safe that was even more important than the money. A small wooden box with a receipt book, documents for the properties and a Will written and signed by the inspector himself and witnessed by Charlie Hastings, Justice of the Peace. Joyce quickly and carefully looked at each item.

"Wen a yu nex burtdey?" She asked.

"When is your next birthday?"

"Nex mont." He replied, and asked why.

"De Will seh dat if de inspecta dead afta you reach twenty-one yu will get all his prapaty. Ar it wei all goh to de gohvament" She replied.

"The Will stated that if the inspector deceased after you reach twenty-one, you will inherit all his property, if not it goes to the government"

"A weh wei a go du?' asked Carlton. *"Im did look pretty bad wen mi se im laas week."*

"What are we going to do? He did look pretty bad when I saw him last week."

"Mi wei bwile chicken soup an put ginga inna it", said Joyce. **"Yu carry goh feed him every dey. Dat wei mek im live langa. Afta yu burtdey wei caa stop".**

"I will boil chicken soup and put ginger into it. That will make him live longer. After your birthday we can stop".

"Den supoz im get betta an cum home?" asked Carlton.

"Then suppose he gets better and come home?"

"Doan worry we crass dat bridge wen we cum to it", Replied Joyce.

"Don't worry we'll cross that bridge when we come to it".

For the next three weeks, every morning except on Sundays, both Carlton and Joyce were up early. Carlton, as usual, assisted Prof in milking the cows and Joyce made chicken soup. At ten o'clock, on the subsequent days, Carlton got on The Lady Champion bus with chicken soup to the Black River hospital and returned on the same bus at four in the afternoon. On Carlton's birthday was the last day that Joyce made chicken soup for the inspector. On that last day while Carlton was feeding him, a doctor walked up to him and patted him on his shoulder.

"Any day now son, any day", the doctor said. "We've done all that we can do. I think you may have prolonged his life. Not because of the chicken soup, but by being such an attentive son".

Carlton smiled and said thanks.

As the weeks went by the inspector remained in the hospital. Joyce thumbed through the notebook and noticed that at the end of each month the payment for the previous month's supply of milk to the Creamery should be delivered by the truck driver not more than three days late, in cash, also that a telegram to be sent to the cattle buyer that Ten steers, three fated cows, and two bulls are ready for pick-up. Total price, $30,000. She relayed the information to Carlton along with the buyer's name and address, and told him to send the telegram off.

Three months after Carlton had made his last visit to the hospital he and Joyce had a conversation on what to do with the money they had stashed away. It was a lot of money and there was still more money coming in from the sales of milk and of animals. They decided that since they had lived in the community for six plus years and the only person they really knew was Prof, that they would introduce themselves to the district in a big way. They both had different ideas how to do that. They asked Prof as to where and when could they find a wide cross section of the people of the community at any one time.

"Well," said Prof. "If you have to know. One set is at the community center on Saturday nights and another set is at the two bigger churches on Sundays".

That Saturday after Prof had left, Carlton and Joyce loaded two carton boxes of small bills into the jeep and Carlton drove to the community center two miles away. He barely knew how to drive and did not up-shift the gear-box out of first speed for the two miles. That was only the second time in six years that Joyce had been on the public road. The last time was within a month after she had gone to live at the inspector's house when she attempted to run away, but he chased her on his mule, took her back and gave her a severe beating.

They walked into the hall and saw three to four dozen people. None of whom they recognized. Some were playing dominoes, some were playing table-tennis, some were playing cards and some were just standing around. No one seemed to notice them until they started to throw the bills in the air. At first no one moved, then one man took a ten dollar bill up and after examining it closely, he announced,

"Its fa real. Its not countafit".

"It is for real. It is not counterfeit".

Carlton and Joyce stood and watched as people scrambled for the money. Then one teenaged girl walked up to Carlton and planted a kiss on his jaw.

"I know yu", she said. **"You a de bway fram de inspecta house. Yu ghi us de milk de adda dey".**

"I know you. You are the boy from the inspector's house. You gave us the milk the other day".

Carlton felt very elated. No female had ever been that close to him before. On the way home Joyce had a sulky look on her face.

"Wa hapn?" asked Carlton.

"What happened".

"Dat gyal weh cum up to yu," she said. *"A doan like har".*

"That girl that came up to you, I do not like her".

There was no response. That night they had supper and not much was said before they went to sleep.

Sunday morning. While Joyce made breakfast, Carlton fed the chickens, the pigs and the goats, and the two out-fitted themselves with new clothes and boots that were stored in the secret room. Carlton was the first one to be ready and while he waited for Joyce he filled three carton boxes with paper money in ten and twenty dollar bills and loaded them into the jeep. He had backed the jeep out of the carport and sat in the driver's seat waiting.

Joyce came out looking as sexy as any girl could, wearing khaki blouse and skirt with laced-up leather boots. Her hair was plaited and reached her shoulder. That was the first time Carlton had seen her hair. She always wore a tie-head cloth or a cap, and sometimes both. As they rolled down the long drive-way they met Prof on the inspector's mule. He waved for them to stop, but Carlton stepped on the accelerator instead. Prof turned the mule around and galloped after them. Out of necessity Carlton was able to up-shift the jeep's gearbox and it picked up speed, leaving Prof in the dust of the gravel road.

Three miles down the road they stopped and asked for directions to the churches. The closest one was within a half a mile and the second one was another two miles further. They went to the farther church and arrived there as the congregation was praying. Carlton walked in with one box and Joyce with the another. The praying stopped and all eyes were riveted on the two strangers. They placed the boxes on the altar and the preacher stepped down from the podium and shook hands with the two.

"**Dis**", said Carlton. "**Is to share up fe yu people**".

"This is to be shared for your people".

An old man from the pew stood and said, "**Hal-le-lu-yah. Mi pryah is ansad**".

"Hal-le-lu-yah. My prayer is answered".

Then the old man stepped forward, leaned on his walking stick and planted a kiss on Joyce's jaw. The preacher thanked them and asked them to stay. They declined, saying that they had to go to another church.

On the way to the second church on a different road they met Prof on the galloping mule. Seemed as if he had gone to the other church, the closest one and not finding the two there he was heading to the other church. Again he waved for them to stop, and again Carlton up-shifted the jeep's gearbox, leaving him in the dust. Prof hastily turned the mule around and followed after them.

Carlton and Joyce walked into the second church and made their presentation. This time they stayed long enough for the preacher to lay hands on them and prayed for them. Each person from the congregation also thanked them personally while shaking hands with them. From the church they went to the intersection at Middle Quarters and bought parched-peppered shrimps, then they drove around the rest of the neighborhood and waved to everyone they saw. They drove home and were very pleased with themselves. At the carport they alighted the vehicle together. Carlton put a hand on Joyce's shoulder. She looked at him with visible surprise.

"**Dat ole man dat kiss yu at de church**", I **duan like im**", said Carlton.

"That old man that kissed you at the church, I do not like him".

They both smiled without saying anything.

Monday morning Prof showed up a full half an hour earlier than normal. He knocked on Carlton's bedroom window and went to the back door and waited. Carlton opened the door and with one hand was rubbing sleep out of his eyes. He noticed that Prof was dressed in new clothes and ankle-high rubber boots.

"What kind of damn fool thing you have been doing with the inspector's money?" He asked, angrily. "I'm going to Black River hospital right now and let him know what you did, and you better not be here when he comes back".

Prof mounted his mule and headed down the drive-way. Carlton decided that since he would have no help to milk the cows that he would get an early start.

True to his promise, Prof had reached the hospital and was the first visitor to be allowed in at the start of visiting hours. He followed a nurse to the inspector's bedside. That was his first visitor since Carlton brought him chicken soup several weeks before. The inspector was glad to see Prof and he immediately asked,

"How is Carlton doing?"

"Boss man", answered Prof. "The boy gave away all your money. Hundreds of thousands of dollars. Saturday gone he went to the community center and gave away two carton boxes full, and yesterday he went to the top and bottom churches and gave away the rest of it."

It was a full sixty seconds since the nurse had led Prof to the inspector's bedside when she heard,

"Nurse, nurse come quick".

It was Prof who was calling.

The nurse responded right away and saw the inspector gasping. She pulled the curtain and asked Prof to step outside. Prof stood in the corridor and watched medical personnel moving back and forth. The minutes were like hours and Prof wondered if he shouldn't have waited until the inspector returned home to give him the news, but then he consoled himself that if he waits Carlton could give away the animals, the house and the land.

He badly wanted for the inspector to go home. He himself had not been paid for almost four months although he was never short of money. The inspector had given him permission from day one to reap the limes, which he sold and kept the proceeds.

Prof was the first person to be told that the inspector had passed away. He mounted the mule and rode straight to his house.

At two-fifteen a police vehicle pulled up at the deceased inspector's house. An officer informed Carlton of his adopted father's death and handed him some papers to sign so that the police could handle the burial. The funeral was held on the Wednesday. It was solemnized by a Chaplin from the police training school. In attendance were three policemen who gave a three gun salute and by Carlton and Joyce.

On Friday late afternoon a man who rode a bicycle was at the fence where the dogs were barking. Carlton went to him to enquire of his visit. It was a man Carlton recognized from the second church.

"*A cum to waan yu sah*", he said.

"I come to warn you sir",

"*Waan mi a bout wat?*" asked Carlton.

"Warn me about what?"

"*Four man de dung a de square*", he said. "*Dem belang to de Bandana gang fram Kingston. Dem a all escape convick. Dem seh dem hear seh yu ha money a ghi weh, an dem cum fe fe dem. Please sah, dem wei cum te-night doan stay in de house*".

"Four men are down at the square. They belong to the Bandana gang from Kingston. They are all escaped convicts. They said that they heard that you have money giving away and that they are come to get theirs. Please sir, they will come tonight. Do not stay in the house".

"Okay" Carlton said. "*Ride you bicycle a goh call de police*".

"Okay, ride your bicycle and go call the police".

With that information Carlton and Joyce embarked on a plan of defense. They left all the doors in the house opened except the door of the secret room. Then they tied the two dogs near to the gate at the public road to warn them of intruders. At nightfall Joyce locked herself into the outdoor toilet with the loaded revolver, and Carlton climbed on the roof of the house with the loaded machine gun and hid behind the water reservoir.

Within fifteen minutes after they took their spots the dogs began to bark and slowly a little white open-back van came up the drive-way.[1] It stopped at the gate near the carport and four men stepped out.

"Hey you bay an gyal in deh", one of them said. *"Cum out wid yu hand dem up an yu won't get hurt"*.

"Hey you boy and girl in there. Come out with your hands up and you will not get hurt".

The warning was repeated while the other three men took up positions around the house. When they were sure there was no one there they entered the house. They fired gun shots to break the lock of the secret room door. Within minutes Carlton watched from the roof and saw them carrying the boxes of liquor to the van. Then it took all four to carry each of the two safes. The weight of the safes and the liquors weighed down the back of the vehicle and raised the front wheels off the ground. Two of the men jumped on the bonnet to get the front wheels to touch the ground.

As Carlton opened fire he heard the police siren a half a mile away. Two of the four were killed by Carlton's gun, a third was killed by the police and the fourth was apprehended and taken to jail.

Three weeks later Prof went back to work. Carlton was his new boss and they were best friends again. Carlton did not want to keep too much cash in the house so he went to the bank to open an account. They told him that he needed to have a beneficiary so that if anything happened to him the money would not go the government. He went home and told that to Joyce.

"A noh wa wei caa du", Joycee said. *"Yu caa married to me"*.

"I know what we can do. You can marry to me".

"Are you crazy?" asked Carlton. "You are my sister."

"Yes, but look at it this way" she replied. "I know you, and you know me, anyone else is pure gamble. End of story."

Three weeks later they were married at one of the churches. The wedding was attended by almost all in the district. For the reception, which was held at the community center, Prof had help to butcher and cook one steer, three goats, two pigs and more than two dozen chickens. Everyone ate and drank to their hearts' content. Carlton and Joyce lived happily ever after.

Note: Like time, man's power is fleeting.

John-crow no-fly zone.

Maroon Town is not really a town as the definition of township goes. Yes, it has people and a governing counsel, but there is nothing else to qualify it as more than a village. It was one of the two most remote areas in Jamaica that served as refuge for revolting slaves on the island; long before the emancipation of slavery. The areas were so remote that it was said that not even crows flew there. The slave masters did not think twice of not going after slaves who escaped to the areas. At one time all the people looked alike for obvious reasons. No one from the outside was allowed to habituate with the Maroons. There was even an arrangement with the authorities to pay them a reward for the return of any other slave that escaped to the area.

On January 6th every year, a celebration is held in Accompong, the only remaining Maroon village, to commemorate the singing of a peace treaty with the government of many years ago. With this event, visitors from all over the island converge on the community to mingle, enjoy their food, dance exhibit, and as some say; enjoy the best marijuana in the world.

Until recent years, most Maroons only had one name, an African name, and that was based on the day of the week in which they were born; e.g. Sunday = Quashie, Monday = Cudjoe, Tuesday = Bene and so on.

On one of the yearly celebrations, a Maroon by the name of Bene from the Osumu family made friends with a visitor who had just returned from a six month farm worker contract in Florida. He was very impressed with the way his new friend was dressed, the way he spoke with a twang and how he charmed the ladies, so he implored on him for information that would allow him to be like that. A month later the friend secured a Farm Work Invitational Card for Bene and went with him to Kingston to the medical test and interview which was required for the program.

Bene could not read or write and barely understood English. His friend tried to prepare him, but the time they had together was limited, so there were many words that were strange to him.

On the day of the interview, Bene sat in the waiting room at the doctor's office and watched as many fellow Jamaicans went in and out of the examination room. Those that passed the test went through one door and those that failed came back the way they went in. When it was his turn, he energetically walked into the room. The doctor was a white American female. This was the first time that Bene had been so close to anyone else except his fellow Maroons and his new friend. He was very nervous.

She used a very small bright light and peered into his eyes, and then she squeezed his private part and said 'good' before she asked,

"Young man! Do you have any scars on your skin?"

The doctor's accent and the question had Bene totally confused.

"Key-ar ma? No ma'am, no ma'am, not even a bicycle", answered Bene.

"Car mam? No ma'am, no ma'am, not even a bicycle".

The doctor smiled, thinking that Bene was just being comical. Next she told him to "Take in a deep breath and blow".

Bene inhaled and held his breath for a few seconds before he let out a very loud ' Promp promp'.

"I am sorry my friend", said the doctor. "You do not have a car or a bicycle, but you certainly do have a car horn. I cannot allow you to travel to America".

"Wha mek ma'am?" asked Bene.

"Why is that ma'am?"

"Because you are so illiterate that I'm afraid that you would be a danger to yourself and others around you".

Bene left the office very disappointed and distraught. He had told everyone in Accompong that he was going to America, and had even promised his girlfriend to marry her on his return.

For days he wandered around Kingston, surviving by the kindness of strangers for food. One day he walked to the harbor at Newport West and saw a single ship anchored there. He asked where the ship was going when it leaves Kingston, and was told that it was destined for Miami. He bought some Excelsior crackers and with a bottle of water he sneaked onto the ship.

For two days and two nights he hid himself between metal containers in a standing posture and was glad when the ship came to a stop. He sneaked off the way he sneaked on.

On the street, he told himself that Miami looked the same as Kingston. Even the cars seemed to have Jamaican license plates. After an hour walking the streets in the down-town area he saw a man he recognized as another Maroon who visited his family in Accompong every year at celebration time.

"Quamin a Mimba!" he called.

They were glad to see each other and embraced for a while before Bene said;

"Mi neva noh seh yu de a Miami. Mi did tink seh yu de a Mo Bi-ay"

"I did not know that you were in Miami. I thought that you were in Montego Bay".

"Dis yah a Mo Bi-ay", replied Quamin. *"A how yu get yah?*

"This is Montego Bay. How did you get here?

"Mi come pon de ship frau Kingston", replied Bene.

"I came on the ship from Kingston".

"Doan worry", said Quamin. *"Mi come yah de se-aim we-ay. Mi caa get you a jab at de hotel whe mi werk, but fus yu ha fe goh to night school fe larn fe read an write because granulated sugar an salt look de se-ame an ef yu can read de label yu wei use one fe de adda an dem wei fire you.*

"Don't worry. I came here the same way. I can get you a job at the hotel where I work, but first you will have to go to night school to learn to read and write.

Granulated sugar and salt look the same, and if you cannot read the labels you will use one for the other and they will fire you.

Note: Reading is fundamental.

Playing with matchsticks.

There were two friends who were neighbors growing up as children. They attended the same schools and were classmates. They had the same friends and until they graduated from high-school were pretty much inseparable. Eventually, one went to college in Jamaica and the other migrated with his parents to Ghana. They kept in touch by letters through the mail.

Years went by and both got married and by misfortune both their wives died at childbirth. The babies however survived, but both had handicaps. One child, a boy, was mute and the other, a girl, was deaf. They were each raised by their respective fathers. The boy was twenty, a year older than the girl when the fathers decided that they along with their next of kin should visit one another. The father that stayed in Jamaica was the wealthier of the two and they agreed that he would travel with his son to Ghana.

At the Accra International Airport, the boy and girl met for the first time and love light sparked in their eyes. The drive to the home was a long, dusty and bumpy one, but the youngsters hardly noticed as they were busy admiring each other. The two fathers talked among themselves all the way. They reminisced about childhood days and talked about people they knew and places they had been. The boy tried to make signs but the girl did not fully understand him.

At the house the two fathers enjoyed sandwiches and fruit drinks before they went horseback riding to see the estate of the other. The girl prepared dinner while the boy thumbed through old magazines. After dinner the two friends continued their catching up on old times, and the boy and girl were trying their best without much success to engage in conversation. Finally, the girl brought a box with matches.

"Lets' play Chutsy", she said.

The boy made signs to ask what that was. She explained the game to him.

- The object was to use matchsticks to form letters to make words in a conversation, using as few matchsticks as possible.
- Each player would be given twenty-five sticks per turn to start or continue the conversation.
- Both players have agreed to the use of abbreviations or misspelled words.
- The player who accumulates one hundred sticks wins the game.

Nice game the boy thought. No girl should be able to beat him at that. He took the first turn. The sticks he laid out read:

I love u. I L [] V [_] Eleven sticks were used. He saved fourteen sticks.

On her turn, the girl used ten sticks and continued the conversation by adding to what he said:

I love u too. I L [] V [_] T [] [] She saved fifteen sticks.

On his next move the boy used nineteen sticks to form the words; letz go. LETZ [7 []

He saved six sticks, added to his first amount for a total of twenty.

At her next turn she used six sticks forming the word "To". T []. She saved nineteen sticks to give her a total of fifteen plus nineteen equaling thirty-four.

On the boy's third turn he used sixteen sticks to form the word Hotel. H [] T E L He saved seven sticks. He had a new total of thirty-three.

The girl looked at him and shook her head from side to side. She saw the question in his eyes, but she was a little embarrassed to tell him no, and why. Finally, she re-arranged the first and the last letters in the word he formed last; H[]TEL to read K [] T E X. Here she did not use any of her twenty-five sticks, which added to thirty-four brought her new total to fifty-nine. She showed him her total, and emphatically shook her head from side to side.

The boy had little or no knowledge of the female use of the brand of product, so he asked; WHAT, using twelve. He added thirteen sticks to his thirty-three, for a new total of forty-six.

The girl realized the boy's ignorance, used seventeen sticks to write a brand that was new, but heavily advertised. She wrote TAMPAX.

Her new total was then sixty-seven.

The young man realized that he was so far behind and his subtle request was denied because of circumstance, he decided to splurge. He used twenty-two sticks to form; lets kis L E T S K I S. The girl used twelve sticks to form the word Y E S. They stopped counting and fell into each other's arms.

Finally the girl proved how much of an expert she was with the game, she arranged matchsticks to read; STAY FREE.

Note: Never give up.

Sonny Winston

S onny Winston was born in the fall of 1920 on a farm where his great-great grandfather was a slave. All of his father's family from the prior four generations were born there, lived there, died there and are buried there. The living quarters for the property owners and the plantation workers were separated by about two hundred feet. The owner's at the end of the driveway, and the workers' off to the side toward the back of the main house. The driveway to the public road was approximately a mile, all on the same property. Because of this distance and other reasons, children of the workers who were born on the property would never see anyone from the outside other than the occasional visitor and delivery personnel.

At the age of seventeen, Sonny's departure from the plantation was quite unintentional. The truck that picked up the supply of milk six days per week had left the plantation's milk-house on the way to the creamery when Sonny hopped on to it on his way to the grocery shop a half a mile up the public road. Sonny had been hopping on that truck for two years and always managed to get off at the top of the hill in front of the grocery shop, but the last time he got on the truck it was moving too fast, preventing him from getting off.

Fifteen miles away the truck stopped at an intersection for a traffic signal. Sonny quickly got off.

He had one big problem, and that was how to get back home. Cars past at which he waved, but none stopped. Finally, a truck loaded with sugarcane came by that seemed to be going the direction of his home, and it was moving slow enough for Sonny to hop on.

About three miles down the road he seated himself on top of the load of sugarcane and started to enjoy a piece when the truck made a turn unto a road that was not the way to his house. The driver was not aware that he had a passenger and did not seem to hear Sonny hollering for him to stop.

It was after midday when the truck stopped at the scale at the Holland sugar factory and it was more than three hours since Sonny had left home. The driver was surprised to see Sonny climbing down from his truck.

"***Weh yu cum fram bway***?" asked the driver.

"Where are you from boy?"

Sonny vaguely remembered it mentioned that from Luana a person could get to anywhere in the island.

"***Luana sar***," said Sonny.

"Luana sir."

"***Which pawt a Luana***?" the driver asked.

"Where in Luana?"

"***Missa Tomlinsen faam sar***, replied Sonny.

"Mister Tomlinson's farm sir."

"***How yu a get back deh***?" asked the driver.

"How are you getting back there?"

"***Mi noh no sar.***"

"I do not know sir."

"Dere is a red-front Bedford truck dat bring cane here," said the driver. **"If im cum tedey yu are in luck. In de mean time here is sixpence, gadder tree chain an put pon mi truck."**

"There is a red-front Bedford truck that transports sugarcane here. If it comes today you will be lucky. In the meantime here is sixpence. Gather three chains and place them on my truck."

Each truck had a bundle of sugar cane tied with three chains to facilitate the crane picking the load up from the truck' stake body. The chains were big, long and heavy. Sonny collected the sixpence and put it into his hip pocket along with the other sixpence his mother had given to him earlier to go to the shop. He loaded the heavy chains to the truck and the driver seemed relieved that he did not have to handle them himself. As that driver left, another truck came in. Sonny volunteered and retrieved the chains for that truck and the driver thanked him and gave him some coins. He counted the coins. They totaled ten-pence. The time was approaching three in the afternoon and there were no red-front Bedford truck. Three other trucks came in with sugarcane and Sonny retrieved their chains. All the drivers gave him money.

At five o'clock a loud whistle that the locals referred to as *kaachi* from the factory blew to signal the time for the end of workday for some workers, and the beginning of a shift for others. Dozens of people streamed out of the factory and the offices through the gate. Most of them rode bicycles. A few of them were on foot, some were on motor bikes and others were in automobiles. Sonny noticed one man leaving one of the offices who was dressed in white, and wondered what kind of work he did. In all his seventeen years this was only the second person he had seen dressed in white. The first was the doctor who visited the farm just before one of his brothers died.

After five o'clock there were no more sugarcane trucks and Sonny's hope of getting home was dashed. He walked through the gate and headed up the road from the factory to the public road about a mile and a half away. By this time he was very hungry. He had not eaten since breakfast when he had only a piece of cassava bread and a half pint of milk. He had money in his pocket but there was nowhere to buy anything.

As he walked up the dusty road he thought about how worried they at home must have been that he might have ran away. He does have a big brother named Ben that ran away five years before. Ben was seventeen just like Sonny. Mr. Tomlinson had wrongfully given him a sound whipping one morning for something that, as it turned out, he did not do. That night as it turned dusk his mother gave him a change of clothes in a brown paper bag and five shillings and told him to get as far away as he could from the Tomlinson's farm. No one had since heard from Ben, and that was the last time that Mr. Tomlinson took a whip to any of the Winstons' children.

He reached the public road forty-five minutes after he passed through the factory gate and wondered whether to go left or right. He had no idea of the direction to get to Luana. He had never been more than two miles from the farm house before that day, and that was only as far as to the grocery shop. That morning the milk pick-up truck took him to Westmoreland and then the sugarcane truck took him through the hills of Saint Elizabeth. He remembered though that just before the sugarcane truck turned off the public road onto the factory road, he had passed over a river and there were buildings on both sides. From where he was he heard the roar of the river to his left so he turned to the left.

A half a mile later, he saw the buildings. They were two grocery shops, one on each side of the river and a market house close to one of the shops. Calmly, he walked into the nearest shop and bought some wheat flour cakes and a beverage. He ate, drank and was full. There were some men in one corner of the shop's customer area playing dominoes. Sonny stood there and watched them with much delight as that was his favorite game. Time seemed to have moved so fast that he was momentarily startled when the shopkeeper shouted, 'Closing time'. He glanced at a watch that one of the domino players was wearing and noticed that the time was eleven o'clock. Earlier he thought that he would have gotten a ride to Luana, although he wasn't even sure how far or even in what direction that was. After he ate and went to watch the game, his thinking of home left him.

As he stepped onto the side-walk and the door of the shop closed behind him, he noticed how dark it was outside. He thought about walking back to the factory, but that was almost two miles away and he was very tired, not to mention that it was late at night. His last option was the market house. It had a fence around it, but it had waist-high front walls. He climbed over the locked gate and found a stall with dried banana leaves. It did not take long for him to fall asleep.

Sonny might have slept until afternoon or even to the evening if the market custodian hadn't woke him. It was after ten o'clock when he set out to walk the near two miles on the dusty road to the factory where he hoped to wait for the red-front Bedford truck to take him to Luana. Half way to the factory he saw a cloud of road dust moving in his direction. Hastily, he had to take to the far edges of the road to avoid being hit by the trucks that appeared to be racing. The red-front Bedford truck was one of the two trucks that passed by. It had been to the factory and was returning on the way to Luana, or thereabout.

Faced with a new dilemma, Sonny pondered on his options. One: he had some change that he could use to pay his fare to the Luana cross roads, where ever that is. Two: he could go to the factory and hope that the red-front Bedford truck would make a second trip, or three: the change he collected from the drivers the day before was the first time in his life that he earned money, and he was encouraged to stay all day. His thinking was that the next day Saturday, for sure, he could get on a market truck that would take him to Luana. The jingle of the coins in his pocket had an influence on him, so he proceeded to the factory.

At the factory, he picked up right where he left off the day before and at five o'clock he had collected so much coins that he had to secure them in all four of his pockets. There was no red-front Bedford truck returning that day and Sonny was not sure if he was to be happy or sad about it. Just as the whistle blew signaling draw-off time for the day workers, a supervisor sent another worker to call him to the office. On the way there, he was afraid and confused. His worst fears were that his money would be confiscated and he would be sent away.

"I've been watching you for two days now," said the supervisor. "And I saw that you make yourself useful to help the drivers retrieve chains, and you also picked up the scattered sugarcane. You work very well. I am going to hire you to continue picking up the scattered sugarcane; that way I do not have to bring in a machine from the field once a week to scrape them up. Be here at eight in the morning and work till five. Take one hour break from twelve to one. What is your name and how old are you?"

"Mi ne-aim Sonny Winstan sar, an tomarra a mi burtdey sar, mi wei be eighteen sar."

"My name is Sonny Winston sir, and tomorrow is my birthday sir, I will be eighteen sir." Sonny replied. He had a slight lisp in his tongue when he talked.

Sonny thanked the supervisor and joyfully walked through the factory gate with the day workers.

The two mile walk to the grocery shop did not seem as far as it did the day before. He had not eaten all day but he was not hungry. As he approached the market house he saw that it was buzzing with activity. There were vendors selling everything, from both cooked and raw food, to clothing, house-wares and small animals.

His first stop was at the clothes vendor. There he bought a pair of GB athletic shoes, a pair of grey khaki trouser, a long-sleeve plaid shirt and his very first pair of boxer shorts. Next, he went to the food vendor and bought a meal. After he ate, he bought washing soap and went down to the river and under the bridge about a hundred feet from the grocery shop. He took a bath and washed his dirty clothes and his rubber boots. The night was coming on fast as he finished. He hurried and hung the wet clothes on the bridge supports and stuck the boots in the abutment.

Dressed in new clothes and with a full stomach he felt satisfied with himself. He counted what money was left, and was surprised that even after all that spending, he had seven shillings. He entered the shop, and to his delight there was a domino game in progress. As he watched he noticed that the men were discreetly playing for money. Even some who were not playing were betting on those playing. The evening wore on and the losers moved out and fresh players moved in. One man asked Sonny if he wanted a hand and he gladly replied to the affirmative. Sonny was good at playing the game, but he had never played for money.

"***Shilling a han.***" The man exclaimed.

"It is one shilling per hand."

Sonny bowed his head in agreement. He sat at the table and he and his partner won game after game. The losers got up from the table and fresh players sat only to lose as well. This continued until no one else cared to play against them.

At eleven o'clock, the shop-keeper announced the closing of the shop and Sonny walked out. He was hoping that his sleeping place of the night before would be there for him, but he noticed that the market gate was still open and lights were on in the building.

The lights allowed him to count the money he won at the domino game. The total amount of paper currency was thirty-five shillings. The coins were much less. He didn't bother to count them. Some vendors were on top of their goods snoring. One who was awake challenged him by saying,

"Ef yu tink yu a cum ya fe rab wei. Yu betta tink aghen."

"If you think that you are coming here to rob us. You should think again."

"Oh no mam," said Sonny. *"Mi jus staat work ova de factory an mi live too fur fe guh home, an cum back a mawnin, so mi a try fe bonks it in ya."*

"Oh no mam, I just started to work at the factory and I live so far to go home and be back in the morning, so I am trying to find a place to stay."

The stall with the banana leaves was vacant. Sonny secured the paper currencies into his back pocket and put the coins into his new pair of shoes which he put into a corner and then he went to sleep. He thought he was only sleeping for one hour, but it was five o'clock in the morning when a man pushing a wheelbarrow with bunches of green bananas hollered at him.

"Bway yu inna mi spe-ace."

"Boy you are in my space."

Sonny reached for his shoes, but they were not there. He asked the banana man if he has his shoes. The man denied seeing them. Sonny tip-toed to the river under the bridge and retrieved the rubber boots and his work clothes. He remembered that that day was his birthday and his mother would be baking a special carrot cake for him. She made special cakes when her children had birthdays. She even made cakes for Ben's birthdays although he had been gone for five years.

Saturday was a different day in terms of work for Sonny. No trucks came in but there was plenty of work that kept him busy for all eight hours as the crane transferred sugarcane from a storage heap to the mill. That day he picked up so much sugarcane and was so tired that at five o'clock no one was as happy to walk through the factory gate as he was. To walk the two miles to the grocery shop on the public road, he stopped twice to rest.

The market session was over and the gate was locked. Sonny bought some refreshments at the shop and even before the darkness of night set in he climbed over the locked gate and went to sleep in the same stall he occupied the two previous nights.

The sun was high up in the sky when Sonny awoke. He changed into his new clothes which he carried in a bundle, and with his work clothes tucked under his arm, he climbed over the gate into the street. Hunger had set in so he went to the shop to buy something to eat. The shop was closed. He walked over the bridge to the other shop; it was also closed. He sat under the shop piazza not knowing what to do. A newspaper vendor on a big mountain bicycle rode up. He was a boy about the same age as Sonny. His name was James.

"Hey bro, yu have a light?" James asked.

"Hello brother, do you have a light?"

"No mon, I duan sumoke," answered Sonny. *"Do you noh any-whe round here whe I caa buy supm fe eat?"*

"No man, I don't smoke, but do you know anywhere around here that I can buy something to eat?"

"No, not really," answered James. *"Ef yu goh lef is tree mile an ef yu goh right is tree mile. Mi a goh deliva two pe-aipa down de road, ef yu we-ait fe mi a caa ghe yu a ride up de road. A noh dem open."*

"If you go left its three miles, and if you go right its three miles. I am going to deliver two papers down the road. If you wait for me I can give you a ride up the road where I know they are opened."

Sonny accepted the offer and James rode off.

James returned in less than thirty minutes and the two boys rode off toward Lacovia. As they entered the Bamboo Avenue, it started to rain. They found shelter under the bamboo canopy, and there the two boys talked at length about their families. James was the first to speak. His father was an alcoholic and died from the effect eight years prior. His father used to earn a living from bee farming and from renting farming plots. After his death, his stepfather came to live with them. He is the father of his two young sisters, Linda, seven and Lorna, five. Things were going good for a while until he fell off a galloping horse and is crippled until this day. That is why there is no income in the household except the ten shillings a week that he gave his mother and the few chickens that she raised.

Sonny felt sorry for James and wished that he could help, but he felt obligated to tell his own sad story, and so he stated that he too was of lean standings.

"Mi family," he explained. *"All live on de sle-aive-masta lan. At present grand-pa who wei call Taata is in a likkle house by himself. Mom an Dad an one big*

brada, one likkle brada a be-aiby sista an mi live in a two bedroom house. Mi oldis brada, nobady noh weh him de, an mi fifteen year ole twin sista dem live wid mi auntie. Mi brada dat falla mi, dead. Mi faada an mi big brada get pe-aye fe milk cow fe Missa Tamlinsen an fe fix fence, an mi madda wash clothes fe Misses Tee."

"My family all live on the slave master's land. At present, grandpa, whom we call Taata, is in a little house by himself. Mom and dad, one big brother, one little brother, a baby sister and myself live in a two bedroom house. My oldest brother, no one knows where he is, and my fifteen year old twin sisters live with my aunt. My brother that follows me died. My dad and my big brother get paid for milking Mr. Tomlinson's cows and for repairing wire fences, and my mother does washing clothes for Mrs. Tee."

By the time the rain subsided and they reached the intended shop, it was already closed.

"Cum to mi house," suggested James. *"Mi wei share mi dinna."*

"Come to my house. I will share my dinner."

Sonny was reluctant to go. He wanted the food, but he was thinking of his sleeping place for that night and how he would get back to be at work at eight o'clock the next morning. He explained this to James and he assured him that it would be okay with his parents for him to spend the night and that in the morning before he start his paper route, he would take him to work.

It was a long way from the main road, up and down two hills to James' house, and on the way the two boys further discussed their childhood, their families and their plans for the future. James had been out of school for three years and had been on the paper route for a year and a half. He wanted to rent a room near the main so that after the paper delivery he could have time to stroll and pick up girls. His big problem was that he could not afford to rent on a paper-boy's wages. Sonny had never been to school. His mother taught him to read from the old newspapers she used to make wallpaper at their board house. All he wanted to do was to save his money to take home to his parents and to wear a white suit when he does go home. He found out that the man in white suit at the factory is an engineer. Sonny liked that title. He didn't know what it meant, but he harbored thoughts that one day he too would be an engineer.

That night neither of the boys got much sleep. They talked into the night about renting a room together, about their meals, about girls and so on. They agreed that the very next day James would find a place and they split the rent. One thing that they could not find an answer to, or come to an agreement on, was what would happen when the sugarcane crop is over and Sonny would be out of work.

That Monday night they moved into their new abode. It was a single room with two half-sized beds and a chest-of-drawers. Sonny was overjoyed that he had a safe place to stay and it was near the main road.

In the days that followed, Sonny saw the red-front Bedford truck twice. He asked the driver how far he was from Luana and was told that the distance was less than ten miles, but he had no idea where the Tomlinson's farm was. The days of the week passed quickly and on Sunday, Sonny's day-off, he went with

James on his paper route. He had heard about Santa Cruz and was mesmerized by the sights even on a Sunday. Most of the houses were new and pretty with cars in the driveways. Some of the people to whom they delivered the papers invited them to breakfasts. Some gave them coins as tips.

There was one thing that bothered Sonny very much, and that was how to secure his money. He could not trust to leave it in the room. James was always there whenever he was there, but there were times when James was there alone. That would give him time to search and find it. Sonny had seen evidence of that when he packed some old newspapers he wanted to take home and after work one day he found them ransacked.

He used his lunch hour one day to search the scrap metal heap where he found a piece of two inch pipe about two feet long. Next day, he took it to the metal shop and asked one of the welders to make him a piggy bank. That Saturday he took it to the room wrapped in his dirty clothes. On Sunday while he was there alone he used a hacksaw blade to cut a hole into the floor board under his bed. He moved a part of the bed pedestal to cover the hole. His bank was completely safe.

As the weeks went by and the sugarcane crop was winding down, Sonny counted the days to the day that he would be out of work and had to go home. That was bad news for James, because he would either have to find a room-mate or give up the room. The factory would be closed for five months for the mills to be repaired and be ready for the next sugarcane harvest. Sonny would like to come back. He knew that his parents wouldn't oppose, especially when he tells them that he would like to save money to buy them a house.

James was saddened by the thought of moving back to his parent's house. His paper route paid fifteen shillings per week plus the occasional tip. Out of that, he had to give his mother ten shillings for his siblings and on top of that he still owed Sonny his share of the first month's rent. Unknown to James, Sonny went to the landlady and explained the situation to her. She agreed to reduce the rent from thirty shillings to twenty shillings per person for the five months that he would be away. He instantly paid her twenty-five shillings for his part of the five months' rent.

One month before the factory closed, Sonny stopped saving money and started buying things for himself and his family. On the first Friday, he went to the Taylor and had his measurement taken to build him a suit - not just any suit, but a white suit. On the second Friday, he bought dresses for his mother and his baby sister. The third Friday, he bought two pairs of leather boots for his bigger brother Edward and his baby brother. He also bought a leather belt for his father and a box of Cuban cigars for Mr. Tomlinson.

It was the in the middle of July on a Friday when the announcement of the end of sugarcane processing was made. Sonny collected his pay envelope and was told that a bonus would be paid the next week Friday. He thought that his bonus would not be very much because he did not start there at the beginning of the season, and he badly wanted to go home, so waiting around for a bonus, which may only be a few shillings was out of the question.

He bought a half a dozen cigars as a present for James and a bottle of Wincarnis wine for both of them to share that night as a celebration.

Saturday morning at about nine, the landlady who lived on the other side of the house was working in her garden when she saw Sonny all dressed in white standing in front of her with two suit cases. He handed her a ten shilling note as a present.

'*Weh yu going dressed like dat?*" she asked.

"Where are you going dressed like that?"

"*Mi a goh home mam,*" replied Sonny.

"I am going home ma'am."

"How?" she asked.

"*Mi a goh tek de bus to Luana an walk from dere.*"

"I am going to take the bus to Luana and walk from there."

How fur yu ha fe walk?" she asked.

"How far do you have to walk?"

"*About five mile mam,*" answered Sonny.

"Oh no," she said. *Tedeh a Satdey an de bus full a mawkit people, plus yu caan walk five mile wid two suit case inna sun-hat inna white suit. Let mi goh call mi pawsen*">

"Today is Saturday and the bus will be full of market people, plus you cannot walk five miles with two suit cases in the hot sun wearing a white suit. Let me go and call my parson."

The landlady returned an hour later. She told Sonny that the parson was doing visitation and would be there just as soon as he was through. It was another two hours that a black Dodge De Soto pulled up into the yard and the parson stepped out to shake hands with Sonny.

The drive to Luana only took a few minutes and Sonny was most surprised how close he was. However, the distance from the Luana crossroads to the Tomlinson's farm, although a shorter distance, took more than twice the length of time because of the unpaved hill road. It gave them time to converse about Sonny's life, his future and his soul. Sonny could not believe that for all the previous months, he was less than twenty miles from home.

As they approached the entrance to the Tomlinson's farm, Sonny asked the parson to take him to the grocery shop a mile further up the road. There he quickly got out of the car and into the shop. There were a lot of people waiting to be served and Sonny thought it was a mistake to stop as he did not want to keep the parson waiting. Just then the grocer held up a hand to Sonny and said, "Can I help you sir?"

Sonny did not expect that special treatment. No one there recognized him. He made his purchase of sixpence worth of codfish which was what his mother had sent him to get that fateful morning when the milk-pick-up truck took him away.

Mr. Tomlinson was standing on his verandah watching the car crawling up the driveway. He watched with anticipation for the visitor, thinking that someone was coming to see him, but then the car veered pass the main house and stopped at the farm workers' quarters. Sonny stepped out of the car and the dogs made a rush for him, but he called them by their names and they quieted down.

Sonny's father and his brothers were at the back of the house cutting fire-wood and his mother and little sister were inside the house. They all saw the car when it drove up and they heard the dogs barking, but it was when they recognized Sonny's voice quieting the dogs that they all ran towards the car.

Sonny's mother ran up to him. Her eyes swiftly glanced at him up and down several times within a few seconds. She reached up and took his hat off his head. At that moment her knees wobbled and she fell to the ground. Both the parson and big brother reached down at once and stood her on her feet. They all hugged.

Mr. Tomlinson was standing nearby and watched as the family rejoiced. He did not speak. The parson introduced himself to Mr. Tee. They shook hands. Sonny reached into his attaché case and handed him the box of cigars. He took it with a trembling hand.

"Ow much a owe yu sah?" asked Sonny of the parson.

"How much do I owe you sir?"

"Nothing son," he replied. "Just seeing this family's reunion is pay enough for me, but come back and see us when you return."

They shook hands and the parson left.

"Mi pickni, mi pickni" 'Sonny's mother said with tears in her eyes. *"Wei tink yu dead. Mi fret an mi pre-eh night an dey. Wei saw-ach fey u, wei aks fey u, Missa Tee even drive im jeep roun an aks, but mi neva give up. Jesas noh."*

"My child, my child we thought you were dead. I fret and I prayed night and day. We searched for you, we asked for you, Mister Tee even drove his jeep around and asked, but never did I give up. Jesus knows."

"Yes mama," Sonny remarked. *"Mi tink bout oono to. Ow is Taata?"*

"Yes mama, I think about you all too. How is Taata?"

"Oh mi chile," said the mother. *"Im aks bout yu every dey. Yu noh ow much im love yu, but on a whole im is holdin up. Im av bad deys an im av good deys. De head go an cum Sonny.*

"Oh my child, he asks about you every day. You know how much he loves you. But, on a whole, he is holding up. He has bad days and he has good days. His head goes and comes; Sonny."

Everyone was given their presents and they all thanked the Lord and asked Him to bless the hand that gave them.

Sonny and his mother walked hand in hand to Taata's little house.

"Taata," she said. " Sonny."

Taata sat up in his bed. He put a hand over his forehead as if shading his eyes from bright light.

"Sonny?" he asked. *"Mi preh-yaz ansad. Den ow yu soh fancy? Yu noh pen cow tedey?"*

"My prayers have been answered. How are you so well dressed? Do you have to herd the cows today?"

"No Taata," Sonny's mother replied. *"Him noh pen cow fe a lang time. Im jus a cum back fram Hallan."*

"He hadn't herded the cows for a long time. He just came back from Holland.

"*Hallan!*" exclaimed Taata. "*Yu mean yu goh a farrin? No wanda yu look soh spiff.*"

"Holland! You meant that you had gone abroad? No wonder that you are looking so sharp."

They did not wish to further confuse Taata so they left him with his belief.

The family had dinner and Sonny and big brother Ed conversed for hours until everyone else was asleep. Sonny told Ed about his piggy-bank. He did not know exactly how much money was in it, but he was sure that every week for six months he had put at least twenty-eighty shillings into it, and that was a very conservative estimate.

It was then that Ed revealed his own money-making and saving scheme to Sonny.

"*Rememba,*" he said. "*The animal docta, im give mi some ganga seed to plant fe him. Mi plant dem ova de hill weh mi an yu goh shoot bird. Wen dem grow up mi cut dem an sell dem to him. Im seh im use it fe mek animal medcine. Mi av all dat money in a bamboo joint an was wandarin what to do wid it. mi noh wat mi wan to du, but ow to goh bout it was a puzzle until now. De bout a wei money togedda wei doan av to explain to anybady. Mek dem tink you bring it ya*"

"Remember the animal doctor? He gave me some marijuana seeds for me to plant for him. I planted them over the hill where you and I used to go to shoot birds. When the plants grew, I cut them and sold them to him. He said that he used it to make animal medicine. I have all that money in a bamboo joint and I was wondering what to do with it. I know what I want to do, but how to go about it was a puzzle until now. With both of us money together we do not have to explain to anyone. They will think that you brought it all here"

The next day being Sunday, the entire family slept until late except Sonny's father, who had to milk a few cows so both his and Mr. Tomlinson's family could have fresh milk for the day.

After breakfast the boys cut open their money-safes. To avoid an individual count, they both emptied their containers on the dining table and invited their mother to do the counting. Everyone's eyes bulged at the heap on the table. The two younger children straightened out the bills that were crumpled and folded and the mother counted as the others watched.

When she was finished counting, she announced that the total was just over a thousand pounds. They all doubted her and told her to count again, which she did, but the amount was the same.

"Mama," exclaimed Ed. "*We gonoh buy you a house.*"

"We are going to buy you a house."

"*Kip dis quiat,*" said the father. "*Ef Missa Tee get wind of dis, I be out of work an den wat wei all eat? Wei caa eat de house. Beside Mr. Tee woan allow no bady fe sell wei any house. He wei pay dem double any ting we ahfa.*"

"Keep this quiet. If Mister Tee gets wind of this I will be out of work and what will we all eat? We cannot eat the house. Besides, Mister Tee will not allow anyone to sell us any house. He will pay double of anything we offer.

"*Papy, Papy we-ait,*" said Sonny. "*De pawsen seh dat ef im caa du any ting fe help us wei musn hesitate fe mek im noh. Maybe dis is what im caa help wei wid, an wen a was cuming back close to Luana dere is a prapaty wid a for sale sign on it. Wei caa buy it."*

"Papy, papy wait. The parson said that if he can do anything to help us that we should not hesitate to let him know. Maybe this is what he can help with, and on the way back I saw a For Sale sign on a property close to Luana. We can buy it.

"A doan noh," said the father. *"De pawsen is a strainja an I doan chus strainjas."*

"I do not know. The Parson is a stranger and I do not trust strangers.

"But Papy," answered Sonny. *"De Pawsen is a christian."*

"But Papy, the parson is a Christian."

"Missa Tee seh im a Christian," the father fired back. *"An look wah him an im faambly du to mi an mi faambly fram slave deys till now."*

"Mister Tee says that he is a Christian, and look what he and his family had done to me and my family from slave days until now."

"Ernest," hollered the mother. *"Lisn to de boy. Wei caan tan ya fe anada ginaraytion."*

"Listen to the boy. We cannot stay here for another generation."

With that said, Sonny, his brother Ed and their father mounted two mules and went off to see the property. They were quite satisfied with what they saw, even though the entire property seemed to be covered with overgrown thickets, and they did not know the price. On the way back, the plans were made to approach the parson for help. For a start they would offer to donate to the church a plot of the land close to the main road for them to build another church.

Monday morning early, Sonny's father and his big brother went to work as usual while Sonny got dressed to go and see the parson with the proposal. He was not sure of what transportation he would take to get to Lacovia where the parson reside, but he knew that he would have to walk almost six miles to the Luana crossroads, so right after he gulped down a pint of warm milk, he set off on a trot down the drive way.

Mr. Tomlinson was standing at the entrance of his carport watching to see if Sonny would have picked up doing his chores. It was Sonny's part of the operation to clean the milk containers and line them up for the milk to be measured and poured into them for the pick-up truck. While Sonny was away it was Mr. Tomlinson who handled that chore. He saw Sonny running down the driveway and called out to Sonny's father, "Hey Earnest! Is that boy running away again?"

"*No Missa Tee,*" Earnest replied. "*Im jus gaan to see a fren.*"

"No Mister Tee, he is only going to see a friend."

"You tell him," warned Mr. Tomlinson. "That nobody lives on my property that does not work for me."

Turley Tomlinson walked toward the empty milk containers. As he was about to pass Earnest, both men stood face to face. Turley was a full two years younger than Earnest. Both six feet tall with thinning and receding head hair, Earnest was the stockier of the two. They were both born on the farm, but through boyhood Turley had been away at boarding school and as a young adult he attended college in a foreign country. Earnest had never left the farm and was barely able to scratch his name on a piece of paper. However, all through their young lives they were friends. Whenever Turley was home, particularly for the summer holidays, the two boys did boyish things. They played marbles, swam in the streams on the property, hunted rabbits and birds, and so on. All that changed when Turley turned twenty-one. Old man Author Tomlinson out of the clear blue gave Turley the whip and told him, "Whip that boy. Let him know that you are in charge now."

Turley refused. The old man took the whip and gave Turley a hard one right across his backside before he gave it back to him and told him to carry on. After the whipping, Earnest was hurting, but he felt sorry for his friend Turley. He still loved Turley like a brother. It was he who later brought twenty-year-old Darcas to the farm the year before to be care-giver to the elderly Tomlinson's and encouraged Earnest to marry her. Earnest knew that Turley depended on him for the manual labor needed to operate the farm. Once per year, he traveled abroad for three months and would always return to find that Earnest had everything in order. Now, with Sonny being the source of contention, the business he was gone to see about and with Darcas' determination to leave the farm, the eminent separation of these two was near. Earnest spoke first. He tried to be as mild as he could.

*"**Missa Tee**," he said. "Yu an mi noh each adda fe more dan fifty year, an a always du right by yu, but Sonny is mi bwoy an him unda age, soh any weh mi deh*

him haffy dedeh to, unless him waa go, soh tink bout way yu jus seh."

"Mr. Tee, you and I have known each other for more than fifty years, and I always do right by you, but Sonny is my boy and he is under age, so anywhere I am he has to be there too, unless he wants to go. So think about what you have just said."

Mr. Tomlinson was speechless for more than a few moments. He stood there and stared at Earnest as if he was shocked by his length of speech. Never since Turley's twenty-first birthday did Earnest have a dialogue with him on any subject outside of mending wire fences and taking care of the cows. Since that time, his only words were, 'Yes-sah, Missa Tee' and 'Noh-sah, Missa Tee.' When he was satisfied that nothing more was coming from Earnest, he said, "If and when that boy gets back, let us sit down and have a talk."

"Yes-sah Missa Tee," answered Earnest as he returned to milking the cows.

On the way to Luana, Sonny caught up with a woman who was walking briskly in the same direction.

"***Why yu runnin,***" she asked.

"Why are you running?"

"***Mi goin to Luana mam,***" he replied, adding that, "***I am really going to Lacovia, but I doan noh wah transportation goh dere.***"

"I am going to Luana ma'am". I am really going to Lacovia, but I do not know what transportation goes there."

"***Yu doan have to run,***" said the woman. "***De Mandeville bus leave Black River at seven. Ef de bus***

**crew stap at de Lower-works restaurant fe brekfus, den
it woan get to Luana fe annada fauty-five minute, but
ef dem neva stap, den dey pass Luana areddy."**

"You do not have to run. The Mandeville bus
leaves Black River at seven. If the bus crew stops at the
Lower-works restaurant for breakfast it will not get to
the Luana cross roads for another forty-five minutes,
but if they do not stop, then they will have passed
Luana already."

The two walked at a little more than a leisurely
pace and talked about things on a wide variety of
subjects. The woman, named May, said that she lives
in the house behind the grocery shop which Sonny
had been to many times. She was middle aged and the
mother of two teen-aged girls who leave for school in
Mandeville Sunday nights and return on Fridays. She
was very surprised how intelligent Sonny was, having
never been to school. She introduced the idea that her
two daughters could teach Sonny's younger brother
and sister the three R's on Saturdays.

The two got on the bus and sat together. They
continued their conversation and Sonny did not realize
that he had passed his intended stop until the driver
announced the Tombstone intersection as the next
stop. He bade May goodbye and walked back the half
a mile to his land-lady's house.

The landlady was again working in her garden just
as she was two days before when Sonny left.

"Honey! What happened? She asked frantically.
"You are back so soon I wasn't expecting you for
another five or six months."

*"**Well mam**,"* Sonny said. *"**On de way home laas week de pawsen seh dat ef mi eva need help in anyting I mus cum an se im, an mi an mi faamly need some help fe buy a prapaty.**"*

"Well mam, on the way home last week the parson said that if ever I should need help in anything I should come and see him. My family and I need some help to purchase a property."

"Son, that is really good news," said the landlady. "But the parson left this morning for meetings in Kingston and won't be back until Thursday or Friday. You may wish to stay until then. Your roommate will be glad to see you again."

Sonny pondered whether he should return home or stay. If he returned home, he would have to help with the cows and he did not want to work for Mr. Tee any longer. If he stayed, he could spend some good time with James doing as he says, gadding with girls. After a moment of thinking and reminding himself that on Friday would be bonus pay-day, he decided to stay, and right away volunteered to help the landlady to pull weeds from her garden.

The parson returned on Thursday and the landlady, being one of the church's faithful, was the first to be visited by him. He was very surprised to see Sonny again so soon. The landlady explained Sonny's mission to him and offered to help in whatever way she could. The parson was aware that the property was for sale and had discussed with his congregants about purchasing it to build another place of worship. However, he and the church's higher-ups decided that it was too huge a property and church rules prohibited the resale of any church holdings as that would be viewed as speculation, but now the prospect of a part of it could be donated to the church excited him.

Friday morning Sonny and his landlady got into the parson's DeSoto with him for the trip to Barclays bank in Black River. Their first stop was at the factory office. There, Sonny collected his bonus. He was very surprised to see the huge amount of cash that was in the envelope and wondered out loud if they had made a mistake. He had only worked there for a part of the season earning minimum wage. The land-lady explained to him that bonus was earned as a percentage of his total pay to the end of the season and not based on the time he spent there.

The bank accepted the proposal made by the parson on the behalf of Sonny's parents. Sonny could not be part of the purchasing group as he was not yet of the legal age. The bank had four requirements of which one was to be fulfilled that day. That was the deposit of good-faith money which happened to be the exact amount that Sonny had just received for his bonus. The second was a notarized signature of both of Sonny's parents and optionally his big brother. Third, was the down-payment, which was a percentage of the total price, and fourth was proof of employment of the members of the purchasing group.

The three friends got back into the car with the relevant forms and headed to the Tomlinson's farm.

When they got there the milk-pick-up truck had already left and Sonny's father and his big brother were out mending wire fences. Mr. Tee was looking out from the carport and noticed the parson and the landlady chatting with Sonny's mother. He was not the least bit concerned and might have been slightly ecstatic that the parson might be trying to evangelize the Winston's. He thought to himself that that would be a benefit to him. He knew that most Christian people are honest and hard-working. He himself fit that last part very well. The youngest Winston boy ran off to the pasture to get his father and big brother. The papers were signed and notarized by the parson. He and the landlady got in the car to leave.

"Doan leave mi," Sonny called out. *"Mi waa goh a yu church dis Sundey."*

"Don't leave me. I want to go to your church this Sunday."

Everyone was surprised. No Winston had ever been to a church. From the days of slavery until then all religious events that they were ever involved in were held on the farm. Everything from christenings to weddings to funerals was performed there. Sonny ran into the house and came out with his white suit, hat and shoes in an over-night bag. He got into the car and waved goodbye.

Sonny was not aware of the proposed meeting with Mr. Tee nor was his parents aware of the third requirement of the bank. However, they were all in different ways planning to confront Mr. Tee with demands for other reasons that would eventually meet the requirements.

Sunday morning Sonny and the land-lady were the first to be at the worship hall. Sonny, of course, looked as dapper as ever in his white attire. They sat together at the front row of the pew. As people walked in, they stared at the two, particularly at Sonny dressed in white with his hat rested on his knee. Some greeted them with smiles and handshakes. Some just walked passed in slightly mellow moods.

Before the service started, the gossips were in more than just whispers. They all knew that the landlady affectionately called Sista Ida who were in her late sixties, and had been a widow for more than twenty years did not have children. In fact, no one knew if she even had relatives. They reasoned out loud that the young man whom they had never seen before could not have been a suitor as he seemed to still have his mother's milk on his mouth. The guesses as to who Sonny was were endless.

After the first hymn and a prayer, the parson stood at the rostrum and introduced Sonny as his new best friend. The questions were fired at the parson like a rapid fire gun. "Is he a doctor? Is he a lawyer or judge? Is he a cricketer? Is he an engineer?" One teenaged girl asked if he was an angel or a prince.

"Oh no," said the parson. "He is a guest of our dear Sister Ida and part of a family that had just purchased a large property in this parish and, had agreed to donate a parcel of it for us to build another worship center, and I might add that he likes to wear white."

The cheers and hand-clapping were loud and long and after the service the congregants formed a long line to shake Sonny's hand and told him thanks. That afternoon he was the parson's dinner guest before he was taken back to the Tomlinson's farm.

As the Dodge DeSoto departed down the driveway, the Winston family huddled. It was then that

Sonny learned of the impending meeting with Mr. Tee, and the rest of the family was told of the third requests from the bank. Together, they embarked on a strategy to get what they needed from Mr. Tee without letting him know about the property. First, they would show him Sonny's last pay envelope. It was just a plain brown envelope with Sonny's name, date of pay and the amount of pay typewritten on the back. At the top left-hand corner was rubber stamped;

> *Holland Sugar Estate*
> *Middle Quarters,*
> *Saint Elizabeth.*
> *Jamaica, West Indies.*

Then they would ask that from then on, that they each be paid in an envelope with the name, the date of pay and the amount of pay written on the back, and finally for good measure they would ask for a raise of pay.

It was about five-thirty when the entire Winston family, except Taata and the two youngest, approached the big house and was ushered into the parlor by Mrs. Tee. She looked at Sonny up and down as if she had never before seen anyone dressed in white.

Sonny looked around the room. The last time he was there was six years ago. Only half of the floor was polished and shined. He remembered it well as if it was the day before. That day Mrs. Tee had given him instructions to use Spanish-needle weeds to scrub the floor, then to use bees wax to polish it and lastly to use the coconut husk brush to shine it. In the process of performing this task, he had to move a three-foot ceramic vase which already had a wide crack. No sooner than he put his hand on it, it fell apart. Mrs. Tee was livid. She slapped him on the left side of his face with her right hand so hard that he saw star-lights. As he reeled from the pain, she slapped the right side of his face with her left hand that the star-lights multiplied themselves by at least ten. He ran out of the house to his mother. His crying put him in hiccups.

Mrs. Winston took him by the hand and confronted Mrs. Tee who flatly denied hitting him, saying, "The boy is just lazy and does not want to work."

In a tantrum, Mrs. Winston pointed her finger into Mrs. Tee's face and said,

"Don't yu eva, eva put yu han an mi pickny aghen, ar a bun dung de house wid all a oonu in deh."

"Don't you ever, ever put your hand on my child again, or I will burn down the house with all of you in it."

The matter was promptly reported to Mr. Tee that evening by his wife. He stood at the top steps of the big house and hollered, "Darcas Winston! Come up here."

Sonny followed his mother closely, knowing that she was not a yes-sah person like his daddy.

Mr. Tee went close up to Mrs. Winston until their noses were almost touching, and then raising his hand as if to strike a blow, said, "You have been disrespectful to my wife. Make this be the last time or I will take the whip to you. Do you understand?"

Sonny put a hand over his mouth to keep from chuckling as he had done earlier that day. His mother took one step backward and said, *"Maasa Tee, se gad deh, ef yu eva put yu han an mi, a piesen yu an yu whole*

faamly an den a bun dung de house wid all a oonu in deh."

"Master Tee, see God. If you ever put your hand on me, I will poison you and your whole family and then I burn down the house with all of you in there."

Sonny was still reminiscing and did not notice that Mr. Tee had entered the room until he said, "You can all sit. "For a brief moment there was complete silence. Mr. Tee was the first to speak.

"Earnest," he said. "I don't have to remind you that you and I go way back to toddler days and all this time there was just one unfortunate incident which I hope you had forgiven me for."

Everyone looked enquiringly at Mr. Winston, including his wife. None of them knew of the whipping that he got at the hands of Mr. Tee at the command of his late father.

Mr. Tee continued.

"You have been blessed with a family. My only sibling, my sister Theresa eloped as you do know and was disinherited by my father. Both you and I are getting up in age. I am now fifty-three and I have no offspring. If the good Lord smiles at me maybe I'll do another twenty, thirty tops. I am thinking to adopt your last boy Terrence. He is now twelve. I would have his surname changed to Tomlinson and send him to school so when am gone he can take over."

"**Stap right dere**," said Mrs. Winston.

"Stop right there."

"Yes Darcas," responded Mr. Tee.

"When you go into town tomorrow," said Mrs. Winston. "Could you please buy me a bouquet of flowers?"

"Oh sure," answered Mr. Tee. "But what is the occasion?

"Gimmie mi flowas wile mi alive sah," she replied. *"Wen mi dead an gane e noh do mi no good. In twenty ar thirty year dead lef noh no use to Mi.*

"Give me my flowers while I am alive. When I am dead and gone it will do me no good. In twenty or thirty years inheritance is of no use to me."

To everyone's surprise, Earnest spoke next. As he handed Sonny's last pay envelope to Mr. Tee and watched his eyes bulged, he said, *"Missah Tee, dat is sumpm to tink bout. In de mean time wen yu pay mi an mi bway Ed please put each one in a invilup like dis an write de ne-aim, de de-aite an de amount on dem, an ef yu caa se inna yu hart fe gue wei a raise e wei goh a lang way."*

"Mister Tee. That is something to think about. In the meantime when you pay my boy Ed and I please put each one of us pay into envelopes like this and write the name, the date and the amount on them. And if you can find it in your heart to give us a raise it would go a long way."

Mr. Tee studied the envelope and wondered why Earnest and Edward wanted their pay in envelopes. He could not come up with an answer except that to show off to Sonny that they too get their pay in envelopes. He considered that reason childish and dismissed the thought as such, but to please them, he could promise that he would do it.

"Putting your pay into envelopes is not a problem, but I'll have to check my books to see how much of a raise I can afford. There will be something extra in it starting this Friday. And one more thing, your knight here in shining armor can stay as long as you all wish. However, he has to pick up on his task and I cannot pay him what the sugar estate pays."

The Winston's went to their house with smiles, knowing that they got all that they asked for and did not have to give up anything. Around their dining table, the family sat and together they gave thanks for everything that had happened and about to happen to them. Then Darcas gave an opinion and revealed a secret to them.

"Turley," she said. "He thinks he is so smart. It would be good for Terrence to attend school, but not in the name of Tomlinson. If we all get reasonable pay we will be able to afford to send Terrence to school in the Winston name. If his name changes to Tomlinson, Turley would not have to pay him even when he becomes adult. Just last week Mrs. Tee pinched me and said that Turley recently went to his doctor and was told that he had symptoms of the same disease that his father, old man Tee died of. That means that if he lives twenty more years he would be on over time. They are planning to sell the farm and go to live with her relatives in England where the medical treatment is much better. So the sooner we get out of here will be the better, or we may soon find ourselves answering to new and maybe worse owners."

The whole family was stunned. Not only of the news of Mr. Tee's illness, but how eloquently Darcas spoke. No one had ever heard her speak anything but patwa. They all knew that she could read. She taught them all to read; even though just a little from the old newspapers she used as wall-paper in their house. She had, on occasions, attempted to teach her husband, but gave up saying that he was too proud and pig-headed. He did, however, learn from her how to barely write his name and to do some very basic calculations.

The week that followed was like no other week on the Tomlinson's farm. All the Winston's worked with enthusiasm and seemingly new found vigor and vitality. Earnest, Ed and Sonny, in addition to their regular chores, found things to do that normally they would have put off doing.

Darcas and the two youngest ones did extra work at the big house. Everyone was cheerful and agreeable. Mr. Tee noticed the change and remarked to his wife that the parson must have had the whole family converted to Christianity. By Wednesday, he asked Sonny when would be the parson's next visit.

"***Soon sah,***" answered Sonny.

"Soon sir"

Little did Mr. Tee know that they were all counting the hours until Friday for the pay envelopes to be issued. Those pay envelopes were the third part of the bank's request to be fulfilled before the transaction of purchasing the property becomes legal.

Friday morning right after the truck from the creamery left with the day's supply of milk, Mr. Tee handed out the pay envelopes. One went to Earnest and one to Ed. There was none for Sonny as each Friday's pay represented the work for the previous week; Sonny was not there.

First, they noticed that not only were all the information they requested on the envelopes but on the top left corner of each envelope was rubber- stamped:

TOMLINSON'S CATTLE FARM

Hodges Plain,

Saint Elizabeth.

When they opened the envelopes, they were even more surprised. Of course, they were expecting an increase in pay but not more than double what they normally got. Earnest sat on the ground and counted the cash. He did that three or four times. Tears welled up in his eyes.

"***Tek dis mi pickny,***" he said as he handed the cash and the envelope to Sonny. "***Du wa yu ha fe du.***"

"Take this my child. Do what you have to do."

Sonny hurried to their house with the cash and the envelopes from his father and big brother. His mother was at the big house. He hollered for her to come quickly. He showed her the money and the envelopes and while he changed into some clean clothes, she retrieved the rest of the money, counted out fifteen hundred notes and secured it in a small leather pouch for him to take it to the bank. When he was ready to go, his mother made him a sandwich and gave him an extra ten shilling note to keep in his pocket, just in case of any unforeseen thing needed, and wished him good.

Sonny mounted his father's mule and headed down the driveway. He barely knew the way to Black River where the bank was. He had only been there once and that was from a different direction. He did not even know how far it was from the Tomlinson's farm, but he knew the general direction, and he knew that he had to get there before it closed at four. However, it was still morning and the mule was young and strong so he decided to gallop all the way there. For miles, there were no familiar landmarks, just the unpaved road with bushes on both sides. About two and a half hours into the journey, he reached the outskirts of the town. He felt comfortable because he was sure that he was on the right way, but about a mile from his destination the unpaved road ended and the asphalt road began, however, its smooth surface spooked the mule. At one point, a motorist blew his automobile horn as he was abreast of the mule. The animal railed and almost threw Sonny. That was when he dismounted and led it by the reins the rest of the way.

At the bank, Sonny sought out and found the officer that started the paper work the week before. He sat with him in his office and watched him count the cash, then he handed him the envelopes. After a half an hour of the officer typing, stapling, stamping and signing, he shook hands with Sonny and gave him a large envelope with papers for him to take to his father.

As Sonny walked out of the bank, he was happy just thinking how happy his mother is going to be when he gets home and deliver the papers to them. At the doorway out he glanced at the fence where he had tied the mule before he entered the building. The mule was not there. He made an alarm to a man on the street. The man pointed him to a stable at the back of the building where the bank customers hitched their horses. The mule was not in the stable so he went into the bank and told the attending officer that someone had stolen his mule. The officer told him that first he had to see if the mule had left dung where it was tethered, and if it did then he had to go to the police station to see if it was impounded.

The dung was there as Sonny suspected, so he asked for the direction of the police station and ran there. The constable at the station desk told him that he must first go and clean up the mess then return and pay five shillings before he could get his mule back. It was then the thought hit Sonny that his mother must be an angel, for how could she have known that there would be unforeseen circumstance to give him that extra ten. He cleaned up the mess, paid the fine and before he left the town he walked into a florist's store and with the remaining five shillings he bought the bouquet of flowers that Mr. Tee never got. When he got back home he was tired and hungry, but he and the rest of the family was happy.

The next day, Saturday, the entire Winston's household with the exception of Taata was up an hour earlier than usual. The milk was ready for the creamery truck a full forty-five minutes before the usual pick-up time. At the light of day Mrs. Winston and the baby-girl had set off on a donkey to their new property. They did not know exactly where it was but was confident that based on the direction given them by Sonny, it would not be hard to find. She was standing under a tall tree that a "FOR SALE" sign was nailed to when Earnest arrived on his mule with baby-brother holding on behind him. Earnest dismounted and took the sign down. All four waited for Sonny and Ed who travelled by foot and arrived fifteen minutes later.

They started to clear a path from the road with their machetes. It was a very slow process as the shrubs and young trees were a thick growth. Four hours had passed and they were only able to clear about three hundred feet of an eight-foot wide path. This frustrated them quite a bit because they were able to see through the bushes a part of the old farm house, but knew that they needed to clear the bushes all the way there to explore it. They were very cautious in going forward as the property had been unoccupied for many years and the further from the road they got the more wild cats, dogs and hogs they saw, and worse of all, was not knowing what other wild things were there.

At two o'clock the parson pulled up in front of the Winston's house. He remained in the car and watched as the dogs circled around it. No one came out to greet him as the previous times. After about a five-minute wait, he jammed the car in reverse and accelerated it to the front steps of the big house. The dogs followed, so again he stayed in the car. Mrs. Tee came on the verandah as he rolled his window down.

"Good afternoon Mrs. Tee," he greeted her. "I am here to see the Winstons."

"Good afternoon sir," she replied. "This time of the day the men are working in the pastures, but Mrs. Winston and the two young ones are there. They are always there."

The parson was sure there was no one there. He thought to himself that they might be gone to see their new property, so he waved to Mrs. Tee and headed down the driveway. Mr. Tee's jeep was not in the carport and for a brief moment, the parson wondered if he was with the Winstons, but he could not find a reason why he would be, so the thought was quickly dismissed. He did pass by the property on the way but it didn't come to mind that any of them would be there.

The parson reached the area and parked his car under the big tree at the entrance. As he stepped out, he noticed the freshly cut pathway and proceeded to follow it. He heard the sounds of machetes chopping and faint voices that he recognized to be Sonny and his family. One of the little ones saw him first and ran towards him. The others followed. They greeted each other and the parson congratulated them on their purchase.

As they gathered around him he said, "There are two very important things that I am here to see this family about. The first one is that a month from this Sunday my church will have its' Bi-annual Confirmation service, and for the first time we do not have candidates. It is to the eternal benefit of this family that God be entreated and thanked for His blessings toward you. Moreover, there are certain favors that the church grants for its members and I think this family would be grateful for such."

Everyone was silent, and each person gazed intently at each other until Earnest spoke.

"Pawsen," he said. *"Mi neva goh a church in mi life, Sonny is de ongle one who ha church clothes, none a wei caa read de bible cep Darcas an how we a goh get deh an cum back?"*

"Parson, I have never been to church in my whole life. Sonny is the only one who has church clothes.

None of us can read the bible except Darcas, and how are we getting there and back?"

Earnest thought that he had more questions than the Parson could answer.

"Mr. Winston sir, please," said the parson. "There is a first time for everything, and I guarantee that you will not regret it. On the second point, there are a number of tailors and dressmakers in our church. Sister Ida is one of them. They will all be happy to be of service to you. Thirdly, there will always be someone to read and explain the bible to you, and in time you may even learn to read. On the last point, I will personally come to get you at ten o'clock. The service lasts for two hours, after which a luncheon is served and you will be back home by three in the afternoon."

"Okay Parson," said Darcas. "Please go ahead and arrange it."

"Whats' a confirmation?" asked little brother.

"A confirmation is a testament that you love God" answered his mother.

"Whats' a testament?" asked little-sister.

"That is to tell someone that you love God," replied Sonny.

"Any more questions or concerns?" asked the parson.

There were no more questions.

Satisfied that his invitation was accepted, he paused for a short while before he said, "My second reason for coming here to see you is to tell you the history of this property. I made some inquires and was told that it was owned by the Sharp family of Essex, England. That is why it was called the Essex Farm.

They grew cocoa and caster beans and a variety of fruits and vegetables up until twenty-five years ago when the last kin went back home. From then, twenty years, and no real-estate tax was paid.

Five years ago Barclays bank paid the arrears and took title to the property. They have been trying to sell it ever since. There were no slaves on this property and the only structures were a barn and the family house. There is still a good market for these produce and the entire twenty plus acres was at times past was fully cultivated. Now with all that said, I will arrange with the relevant church members to come by and get your measurements for some new clothes for the big day. And do not worry about the cost. The church will finance everything."

The following week Wednesday between five and six o'clock in the evening, Earnest and the two bigger boys were in the front of their house making smoke from the fire of dried cow dung and green bushes. It was the rainy season and the smoke was needed to drive the mosquitoes out of their house before they closed the windows and doors to enable the family to sleep without mosquito bites. They were quite attentive to the fire and did not notice the parson's car until it was close to them. The dogs did not bark. Either they were afraid of the smoke or they might have gotten used to seeing the car. They had tucked themselves under the house floor.

The parson stepped out of the car and fanned the smoke from his face. Behind him were Sister Ida and two men. After the greetings and introductions were made, one of the men opened the car trunk and retrieved two folding tables, measuring tapes and five or six huge rolls of cloth. Each person of the Winston's family including Taata was measured for new clothes, and the Parson and his party left.

As the weeks passed, there were very few verbal interchanges between the Winstons and Mr. Tomlinson. As a matter of fact, both Mr. and Mrs. Tomlinson were given the silent treatment by the entire Winston family. They, the Tomlinson's, knew something was different and tried in very subtle ways to find out what. They tried extra hard to be nice even to the point of offering to pay Sonny full pay for three hours per day work. Mrs. Tomlinson surprised everyone one day when she, who was never known to have culinary skills, baked a corn pudding and took it to Taata. That provided many laughs for the Winston's, because they knew that Taata did not know anything about the purchase of the property. Through the duration of Mrs. Tomlinson's visit, Little Brother hid and eavesdropped, and the only information that Thaata volunteered was that "*Sonny goh a farrin an cum back, an de two young uns tell mi dem a larn to read an write. Every Satdey dem goh to de grocery shap to de shap keepa dawta dem fe lessen.*"

"Sonny went to foreign and return and the two young ones are learning to read and write. Every Saturday they go to the grocery shop to the shop keeper's daughters for lessons."

Six days a week Earnest, Edward and Sonny milked the cows; however Sonny would always hitch a ride with the milk-pick-up truck to the public road. Mr. Tomlinson was curious as to where Sonny went in the mornings after he got off the truck, so one morning he followed a short distance after the truck. Sonny was at the roadside waiting for three young men that he hired to help him to clear the new property. When he noticed that Mr. Tee was watching him, he and his three companions went to the piazza of the grocery shop and played dominoes all day. The following day was the same thing.

The week before the confirmation Sunday, the parson and his crew brought the new clothes. Everything fitted well. The parson's crew and the Winston's held hands forming a ring in the front of the house and they sung a hymn and prayed. Both the Tomlinson's were on their verandah a hundred and fifty feet away looking on. After the prayer, the parson walked up to them and informed them of the Winston's intention to be confirmed as members of the Anglican Church.

"We would be delighted to have you in the pew," said the parson. "The service starts at ten-thirty sharp and concludes at twelve-thirty."

"No, thank you," replied Mr. Tomlinson. "We are both Roman catholic and we attend Mass in Black River every Sunday morning at eight."

Sunday morning at nine o'clock the whole family of Winston's, including Taata, were dressed and waiting to be transported to the church. The parson arrived at about twenty minutes past. It took very little time for all seven Winston's to fit into the DeSoto.

As they started down the mile-long drive to the public road, everyone was in a good mood. They had clearly passed the half-way point when the Dodge

DeSoto and the Land Rover Jeep were front bumper to front bumper, almost touching. The driveway was only one lane. It is common courtesy for the up-hill vehicle to reverse to a clearing and allow the down-hill vehicle to pass. For a full minute, none of the vehicles moved. The parson lightly tapped on the horn which produced a sound that was very much like some adult saying the word PROM. What followed was the ear piercing high frequency PEEEEEEEP sound of the Land Rover's horn that even Taata, who couldn't hear so well, had to put his palms over his ears. The sound lasted for more than thirty seconds until the parson jammed his gear-box into reverse. He backed up about two hundred feet to the nearest wide area to allow the Jeep to pass.

When he was ready to go forward, the car was stuck. Everyone alighted except Taata and the parson. They pushed and pushed, but the car was too heavy, and a part of the under-carriage was hitched to a rock in the ground. The men were beginning to sweat; even Mrs. Winston had to wipe perspiration from her face, and not to mention that everyone's patience was on edge.

Sonny ran back to the house and got his father's mule. They tied a rope from the mule to the front bumper of the car and while Little Brother pulled on the halter, Sonny, Edward and Earnest lifted the back of the car to get it going again.

They entered the public road and the parson apologized to the family and cursed the devil who he said was into Mr. Tomlinson.

That started a series of questions from Baby Sister. The first thing she asked was, "Is Mr. Tee pregnant?"

Then, "Do we have to come back?" And on and on she went, right up to when they entered the church yard.

It was a full fifteen minutes after the service was scheduled to be started when the parson led the family down the aisles to a pew reserved for them. As they proceeded gingerly, Sonny heard his name just a little louder than a whisper. He turned his head in the direction of the sound and was glad to see his friend James. They exchanged smiles. Sonny had just sat when he felt a tap on his shoulder. Before he turned around to see who it was, his mind started to race to find a face; any face that he might have met while working at the sugar factory.

Yes the face was familiar, but not from the sugar factory. The face was that of May, the woman he had met a few weeks earlier. They had travelled on the same bus from Luana to Lacovia. May was sitting between two teenaged girls, and although he was seeing them for the first time, they totally fit the descriptions that his younger brother and sister gave him of them. They were the same two that were teaching his siblings to read and write. Right away, he wished that they could also teach him to read and write.

He smiled at May and then at the girls, prolonging his not so discreet glance on each. He had some immediate questions. May was mulatto, one girl looked half Chinese and the other looked half Indian. Was May their real mother and they have different fathers? Who was the elder? Would any of them be interested in him? Are they even ready for dating? He had never dated anyone so how would he go about it? He decided that he would talk to his mother. He assured himself that he could talk to her about anything; after all she reads a lot and she was much smarter than his father. The first chance he got he approached her, and she told him that the girls were adopted.

The service was thoroughly enjoyed by all and was so expressed after the conclusion by the smiles and embraces of members and visitors alike.

The next stop was at the parson's residence for dinner. A table was prepared under a tall mango tree with chairs to seat thirty people. Sonny guessed that only a few people of the more than two hundred that attended the service were invited, and wondered if May and the girls would be among them. It did not take him too long to find out. He stood beside his bigger brother in the yard watching as guests arrived and servers moving in and out of the kitchen with food to the table when he noticed what looked like a brand new Buick Roadmaster station-wagon drove up. It stopped at their feet and the driver, a grey haired man, beckoned to them to open the rear door. Sonny released the latch and momentarily held the door open. The first girl, whom he later learned was Diana, stepped out and brushed herself against him. He almost lost his breath. He was making himself to stand steady when the second girl stepped out. The rim of her hat touched his forehead.

The table was impromptu, made of long rough boards, but covered with white cloth and beautiful flowers, and food enough for at least fifty people. The seating was arranged so that the driver of the new car sat at one end across from May. Next to her were the two girls and across from them were Sonny and

Edward. Little Brother sat beside Sonny and across from him sat Little Sister. Darcas Winston sat beside her little girl and Earnest Winston sat across from her. Taata sat beside Earnest and Sister Ida sat across from him. The parson and his wife were at the head of the table and the other guests occupied the rest of the seats.

There was a buzz around the table like the sound of bees until the parson stood. He gave a speech and said a short prayer then beckoned for everyone to dig in. Some of the buzz continued, but most of the sounds were that of the utensils and the plates.

None of the Winston's had ever used knives and forks to dine with and it became noticeable when some knives were literally flying to the ground. Taata did not attempt to use his. The parson noticed the clumsiness and so as not to let anyone feel too embarrassed, he himself picked up a chicken thigh between his thumb and fore-finger and tore into it. No one at the table used a knife after that.

Everyone was having a conversation with the person sitting across from him or her except for Sonny, Edward and the two girls. Sonny badly wanted to say something, but to begin with, he did not know what to say, secondly he was afraid that whatever he would have said would sound awkward and stupid, and thirdly, he would not wish for anyone else, particularly May, to hear what he had to say.

It was the greatest of relief to Sonny, half way through the meal, when one of the girls spoke.

"We heard that you guys are the new owners of the Essex farm."

"Yes, we are," replied Edward.

"Must be a lot of fun restoring the old buildings," the other girl mused.

"I would rather a new house," the first girl said.

"We can do that," remarked Sonny, trying to say as few words as possible so that his grammar wouldn't show.

"Would you? Promise," she blurted.

"Of course," replied Sonny.

"My name is Diana, this is my sister Ceilia, and you are?"

"Sonny, Sonny Winston."

"That's a cool name," she said softly.

She whispered something that Sonny only knew because he read her lips. "Mrs. Diana Winston."

She smiled and Sonny smiled at her.

"Where did you go to school," she asked.

"I didn't," replied Sonny.

"You mean you were home schooled?" She asked.

"You can say that," replied Sonny.

"Cool, we can be pen pals," she said. "I will write to you from school. Check at the Fyffe's Pen Post Office next week."

The parson asked everyone to stand and he again gave thanks for the meal. As the guests started to leave, he called the Winston family into his study. After handing each of them a certificate of Confirmation and church membership card he told them that in gratitude of their intention to donate a plot from their property, the church had agreed to pay off their mortgage.

"*Wat margidge*?" asked Taata.

"What mortgage?"

"We'll tell you about it later," replied Darcas.

The drive back to the Tomlinson's farm was very gleeful for all except Taata. He sat in the front passenger seat with a stone face, neither looking right nor left. Going to the church was only the first time in his eighty-three years that he had been in an automobile. It was also the first time that he had been off the Tomlinson's farm, and it was very obvious that as the car moved along the public road, his head was moving from side to side as someone would when watching a tennis match from side court. It was very clear that he did not want to miss any of the scenery, but on the way back he might have as well had his eyes closed.

The parson's car stopped at the Winston's front door and the family alighted. After good-byes were said and the parson left, Darcas could not hold back from finding out what was ailing Taata.

"Taata, why is it you are so silent? She asked. "You haven't said a single word since dinner."

"Well dawta," Taata said. *"Mi tink mi was de head a dis fambly. Wha kine a margidge de pawsen a talk bout? Mi naah lef ya. Fe mi granfaada bawn ya, him live ya, him dead ya an him bury ya. Mi faada bawn ya, him live ya, im dead ya, an him bury ya, mi bawn ya, mi live ya, an mi a dead an bury ya.*

De Tee dem always geh wei every ting wei need. Wei neva even ha fe goh a road."

"Well daughter, I thought that I was the head of this family. What kind of mortgage is the parson talking about? I am not leaving here. My grandfather was born here, he lived here, he died here and was buried here. My father was born here, he lived here, he died here and was buried here. I was born here, I live here and I will die and be buried here. The Tees always give us everything we had need of. We do not even have to go to the road."

Everyone was silent until Earnest spoke.

"*Taata, nobody is telling you to move, but everybody wha se how much caan pudden Misses Tee gwine geh yu.*"

"Taata, no one is telling you to move, but we all want to see how much corn pudding Mrs. Tee will give you."

Taata did not respond. He hobbled to his one room house fifty feet away.

Around the dining table, the whole family was gloating over their new Christian life and the blessing it had brought them. They started to make plans as to their spending power and their priorities. The clearing of bushes on the property was going fairly well, but could be much advanced with more man-power. A new survey needed to be done so that the plot for the church could be fenced and made official. The rebuilding of the house and barn could begin at the earliest possible date. They all agreed on the things to be done, but couldn't agree on the order except that the land clearing would continue.

They next turned to figuring out the source and timing of money for the projects. There was some money in the bank. It was earmarked as emergency for one month's mortgage, but since there was no mortgage, that money would remain as just emergency. The weekly earnings of Earnest and Edward was enough to pay the three fellows who worked with Sonny clearing the land. The sugar factory would not be re-opening for another three months for Sonny to earn some money. By that time, the land-clearing would be completed, and the earnings of Earnest and Edward could be spent elsewhere.

Edward did not and could not reveal his marijuana earnings from the animal doctor which was more substantial with every delivery. Only he and Sonny knew of that. In the mean-time, as the land was being cleared, Sonny planted a vegetable garden and was selling callaloo and spinach to market vendors. In addition, some of the fruit trees like citrus and mangoes had enough to sell. The two brothers decided that they would merge the proceeds of the produce and the marijuana and tell their parents that it all came from the sale of produce. It worked, and repair work was ordered to be done. First on the list was the survey, then the repair of the barn along with the construction of a latrine.

Something was bothering Sonny. He could not figure out how Diana knew that he and his family were the new owners of the Essex property. As far as he knew, only the parson and the bank outside of his family should have known.

Sonny could read a lot better than he could write, and with his family a newspaper serves three main purposes: for information and entertainment as it was intended, for wallpaper, and as toilet tissue. It was typical that with any poor family, they would have kept a small tin can of water and some newspaper in their latrines. The water was used to dampen the paper to make it soft. Sonny was sitting on the latrine seat and going through the paper that was discarded by the Tomlinson's. It was already a week old. He glanced at a column that captioned LAND SALES.

He carefully read it two or three times. It stated:

'*The once very fruitful Essex property near Luana in Saint Elizabeth was recently sold for an undisclosed cash sum to the wealthy Winston family of the same parish.*'

Sonny was shocked. His first thought was, had the Tomlinson's seen it? The paper had made two mistakes. The first was that the property was sold for cash, and the second was that it was sold to a wealthy family. But those were good mistakes, because had the Tomlinsons seen it, they knew that Sonny's family was far from being wealthy, and they definitely couldn't pay cash. He showed the paper to his mother. She laughed out loud.

"This puts you and your brothers in the limelight my son," she said. "Now you do not have to go looking for girlfriends. They will find you. I will have to work harder with you especially, for you to learn to read better and to write properly so you can communicate intelligently and effectively."

Sonny always enjoyed the close relationship he and his mother shared. After his eldest brother left home, Edward stuck close to Earnest as if to be protected from a whipping like his brother had, but Sonny stayed close to his mother. She was especially glad to have him near her because her child that followed him had died and guardianship was given to her sister for the twin girls that followed that child. Sonny was also the full-time baby sitter for the two younger ones.

During the bereavement period, coupled with having to give up her twin daughters for their own good, and having had to send her first born child into an unknown world, Sonny became truly bonded with her. Baby brother Terrence was a full six years Sonny's junior, so Sonny spent quite a few years holding on to Darcas' frock tail, during which time she taught him to read from old newspapers, and she spoke proper English with him on several occasions.

Much of Darcas' days were spent washing clothes for her family as well as for the Tomlinson's. House cleaning and cooking for both families, taking care of the two last children and to a large extent Taata too, plus doing her own back yard gardening made her days full. Up until Sonny was twelve, when he started to spend more time with his father, he was mama's helper and go-fer. That was how she was able to teach Sonny to read, but there was never enough time to sit with him to teach him to write. What he could write was what he basically taught himself.

The weeks went by and Sonny remained busy with his helpers clearing the land and planting the garden. He had only been to the Post Office once, which was the week that he was expecting the letter from Diana. He was only half expecting her to write anyway, so he wasn't too disappointed not receiving it. Normally, the Winston's only receive mail once or twice per year and that would have been from Darcas' sister who was caring for the twins. If and when such mail arrived at the Post Office it would be collected by Mr. Tee and delivered by hand to Darcas.

The first week in December and the land-clearing project was completed, and so was the repairing of the barn and the construction of the latrine. The rebuilding of the house was well underway. The following week Monday, Sonny would be reporting to work at the sugar factory.

That Saturday, his little brother returning from his lessons with Ms. May's girls, brought him a note. He quickly unfolded it and read out loud:

'Why haven't you answered my letters?'

He ran to his mother and said, "Look ma, one of Ms. May's girls sent letters. Did you get them?"

"No, but I bet Mr. Tee got them," she replied. "But I told you this would happen. You are not the only one who reads the newspapers."

Sonny jumped on the bare-back of his father's mule and raced down the mile-long driveway. In less than ten minutes he was hitching up the panting mule at the side of the grocery shop. He knocked at the gate of Ms. May's house and within seconds she appeared at the front door.

"Did your siblings get home alright?" She asked.

"Yes mam, but I need to speak to Diana"

"Diana? What for, may I ask," she said with a stern face.

"I just need to tell her that I did not get her letters," Sonny replied.

"Letters? What letters?

"Her pen-pal letters mam," he replied unapologetically.

"Oh," said Ms. May. "Just for your information young man, I'll tell her, but please bear in mind that she is only fifteen and not yet ready to date. You don't want to go to jail, do you?"

With that said, she turned into the house and slammed the door behind her.

He rode back to his house sad, but glad that she had written. Not trusting that Ms. May would deliver his message he made a promise to his little brother to bring him something extra special when he returned from the sugar factory.

"What is it?" asked Terrence. "*You know mi wei du anyting fe yu, present or no present.*"

"You know that I will do anything for you, present or no present."

"Okay, next Saturday when you see Diana," Sonny told him. "Tell her that I will be gone for seven months and when I get back I will start building the house so she must wait."

Sonny had hardly finished saying the word wait when Terrence ran off hollering, "Mama, mama Sonny is going to build a house. Sonny is going to build a house."

Sonny told his mother the whole story that started around the dinner table at the parson's house.

The relationship Mr. Tomlinson and the Winston's took a turn for the worse right after Sonny left. The milk production had increased beyond the point where Earnest and Edward could keep up, so Mr. Tee had to hire outside help who was very unreliable. On top of that, Mrs. Winston refused to let twelve year old

Terrence help out. The week before Christmas, the clothes and haberdashery vendor who normally visited once per year and had served the Winston's for years at the Tomlinson's expense did not show up.

Two days before the New Year, a Sunday, Darcas took her two younger children, their clothes, her pots and pans, and some bed linens and moved into the partly refurbished house. That night all three huddled together on the floor. Early next morning Edward brought her all the proceeds from his last marijuana sale and told her to go to Black River and buy whatever furniture was needed. He told himself that it wouldn't matter if she knew the source.

Earnest and Edward continued to work for Mr. Tomlinson and would only sleep at the new house Saturday and Sunday nights. After about three months of that routine, they bought a mule for Edward and the two rode back and forth from their home to the Tomlinson's farm six days a week. It was about the same time that Sonny bought a motorcycle and travelled from his home to Holland six days a week.

True to his word, after the seven month sugarcane season, Sonny and his brother Edward, who saved most of his money from the marijuana sale plus his weekly wages, started the construction of a duplex residence a short distance from their main house. It took three years of on and off work to complete.

One Sunday evening Sonny was sitting on the latrine seat, and going through the Sunday papers. He remembered that the sale of their property was announced in a previous issue, so he decided just for the fun of it to look into the LAND SALES column.

What he saw was a big surprise:

The hundred and eighty acre dairy farm at Hodges Plain in Saint Elizabeth, formally owned by the Tomlinson family was recently sold to the Ministry of Agriculture. The government plans to auction the livestock, and to sublet the land to the local farmers in five acre lots.

Sonny showed the paper to his mother. She laughed that cynical laugh that her family was accustomed to.

The completion of the brothers' duplex coincided with the completion of the church which took only a year to build, but neither would be occupied for another three months. Invitations were being handed out for the double wedding of Sonny to Diana and for Edward to Ceilia. The weddings would be the first functions to be held at the church.

Note: All is well that ends well.

The Half-wit Brother-in-law

A young man from Montego Bay had just returned home from attending college in the United States. He and his childhood sweetheart wanted to get married, but their parents who were neighbors and also long standing enemies were bitterly opposed to the relationship. The two lovers were not to be denied. They eloped and after they tied the knot they went to live at the other end of the island.

The husband landed a very good job, and for the first few months their lives became fulfillments of years of dreams. When they realized that the wife was pregnant, she was in her third month. They were both ecstatic about it, until a few days later, the husband was chosen by his job to go to the U.S. on a six month study program. They were distraught about the separation, even though it would be temporary. They figured that if everything went well the husband would return in time for the birthing.

The wife was not looking forward to being alone, so she went back home and arranged with her elder brother with whom she had always had a very close relationship. She asked her brother if he would come and live with them. The husband was very happy with this arrangement, however, there was just one problem; her brother was slightly deranged.

The husband had completed two months of study, and everything was going just fine. The two talked on the phone almost daily. He even occasionally spoke with his brother-in-law. The pregnancy was in the fifth month when ultrasound revealed that twins were on the way. There was no need to be overly concerned as both mother and babies were well.

Two weeks before the husband's scheduled return, both he and his wife were on a count-down of the hours.

On Sunday the wife and her brother were fixing the babies' room, preparing for their arrival when she had a fall. She was taken to the hospital in an unconscious state. The babies, a boy and a girl, were delivered by Cesarean section. Her brother kept an almost constant vigil at her bed side, and only went home to eat and wait for the regular time when his brother-in-law would call.

When the babies were five days old, the mother was still unconscious, and the hospital authorities asked the brother, as next of kin, to name the babies. He was happy to do so.

That night when his brother-in-law called he was very excited. He relayed that his sister was still unconscious. His brother-in-law was puzzled that in spite of the condition of his wife, his brother-in-law was so happy, so he asked him what else was going on.

"Well, they asked me to give the babies names," he answered.

"Did you give them the names that your sister picked out," asked the husband.

"No, I didn't like those names," was his reply.

"What names did you give them?" was the next question.

"The girl I gave the name De-niece," he answered gleefully.

"Nice name," said the husband. "You are not as half-witted as they say you are. From now on I will have to think of you differently. What did you name the boy?"

Giggling, the brother-in-law answered. "De-nephew."

Note: It takes time to know one.

Games people play

Lascelles Ledgister was a very wealthy man, who gained his wealth through years of hard work mostly raising animals for slaughter. He did not smoke, as he referred to that as burning money; neither did he drink any alcoholic beverages in public, because his father was poisoned as a result. He was not really liked in the area of the parish where he lived and worked, particularly because of a remark that he made at a community meeting. The occasion was for honoring the locals for their achievements. He was awarded a plaque and was asked to give a speech.

"Any man who can read and write and is not rich by the age of forty is a cruff", was his awkward remark.

"Any man who can read and write, and is not rich by the age of forty, is good for nothing."

This remark angered a lot of people, and consequently, no one over forty worked for him. All his employees except women were young men.

Lascelles was the younger of two sons. His elder brother Lloyd had just graduated from high school, when their father was out celebrating Lloyd's achievement, when someone who had a grudge against him, dropped poison into his drinks.

Sadly, Lloyd followed in his father's footsteps and became a heavy drinker. Lascelles, however, with the help of his mother who worked as a housekeeper, finished high school. His mother's boss, Mr. Almaros was a German who settled in Jamaica and was a big time cattle farmer. Upon Lascelles graduation from high school, Mr. Almaros hired him on a part-time basis to assist him in record keeping of farm activities.

Within a year, Lascelles had saved enough money to buy ten female goats. But before he made the purchase; he asked his boss if he could use a hilly part of the farm that was not suitable for the cows, to raise some goats. His request was granted and he started out with ten ewes and on ram goat. Lloyd, in the meantime, was employed by the Public Works Department and got more and more into drinking. He was living on his own and would only visit his mother about once per month, usually in a drunken stupor. The two brothers rarely spoke to each other.

Rearing goats was much harder than Lascelles had anticipated. First, he had them tethered with ropes, which required his daily attendance, and then, he had to transport water three miles on a daily basis by donkey for them to drink.

Five months after he started, six of the ewes had kiddies, all within a one week period, and in one night wild dogs ate all the kiddies. Lascelles was heart-broken and devastated. There were four more ewes expecting to have kiddies within a week. The ewes were too heavy to walk three miles to where he shared a rented house with his mother, and the land-lord would probably not allow a herd of goats on his property anyway.

Lascelles went to his mother and to Mr. Almaros with the problem. His mother wept, but had no solution. Mr. Almaros told him that, that was a test to see if he would become a man or remain a boy. He offered him two weeks off work. One week with pay and one week without.

His mother was terrified when he told her of his plans to stay in the wilderness with the goats at nights. She nevertheless supplied him with blankets to keep him warm and a kerosene oil lantern for light. He went to the animal market and bought two dogs, and then to the general store and bought an axe and food for himself and the dogs.

During his first night on the hill, he made a big fire and slept on the ground with the goats and the dogs around him. At the sign of daylight, he set out cutting logs. For hours, he continued and only stopped briefly at mid-day to feed the dogs, and himself had something to eat. By mid-afternoon, he had enough logs to build a hut. At sunset the hut was completed, thatched roof and all.

On the second night, he used his blanket to make a hammock and retired to sleep. He awoke in the middle of the night to rain-fall. The fire he had made late that evening was gone, but he and his two dogs were dry in the hut.

The next three days, Lascelles worked from dawn to dusk cutting logs. In the meantime, his mother was very worried about him. He had told her that the wild dogs only roamed at nights, but he had been gone already four nights. She enquired of Mr. Almaros as to the direction of the hill and he told her not to worry, and that it would take three, maybe four hours to get there and back, but if he is not back by Sunday he would go looking for him. She was not consoled, however, she decided to wait. That day was only Thursday, and she had not seen her son since Monday.

"Doan worry yusef," said Mr. Almaros. *"You odder boy is in mo danger everyday an you not worried bout him."*

"Do not worry yourself. Your older boy is in more danger every day, and you are not worried about him."

Saturday early afternoon found Lascelles putting on the last set of logs on a twenty-four by twenty by six foot fence for his goats. He tied the two dogs at opposite diagonal corners, and left enough grass in the enclosure for the goats to feed until his expected return the following Monday. By six o'clock he was home waiting for his mother. She was so glad to see him, and in no uncertain terms she let him know how worried she was about his safety. She was expecting that he would return in the day-time and only spend the nights watching the goats, but when he explained to her what he had done, she congratulated him.

Sunday Lloyd came by; drunk as usual. His mother told him of his brother's misfortune and what he had done to avoid a similar occurrence. He offered to spend a night or two on the hill with his brother, but was told that the hut and hammock was only suitable for one person at a time. He withdrew his offer.

Monday morning Lascelles left home with fresh supplies of food for himself and his dogs. His plans were to build a separate enclosure for the expectant goats, and to enlarge the existing one for more goats.

On nearing the top of the hill where he thought of as his base; he heard the bark of only one dog, and hurried to see if the second one was knotted up. To his dismay, he discovered that thieves had stolen his ram goat and one of his dogs. That week he cut the logs he needed and the Saturday he went to see his mother and Mr. Almaros. He bought supplies and returned to his base to watch his goats before it was night.

As the months went by, Lascelles' had to limit his time on Mr. Almaros' job to a mere four hours per week. His herd of goats was increasing at a very rapid pace. He had bought more ewe goats and he continued to expand the enclosures. His first sale was a truck-load of young rams that he had castrated and fattened. The sale was by weight to a vendor, and the proceeds were an enormous amount of cash, all of which he brought to his mother.

The years went by, and Lascelles continued to work part-time during the days for Mr. Almaros and to take care of his goats full-time. For more than four years he spent every night in his hut. His mother begged him to sell his stock and use the money to attend college.

He thought about it but argued with her that if he continue selling goats, he could retire at age thirty, whereas if he spend four years going to college; he would have to work until he reach fifty-five to even earn the money that he could save in less than five years.

He was going home one morning when he noticed a freshly painted FOR SALE sign at the main entrance of Mr. Almaros' property. Quickly, he removed the sign, hid it in the bushes and ran to the big house where his mother works. She was as surprised as he was, and together they confronted Mr. Almaros.

"Yes the property is for sale," said Mr. Almaros, "but, only a part of it. I plan to give the hill to you Lascelles so you can continue raising goats. Mrs. Almaros and I intend to return to Germany and we will need money from the sale of the land and the stock of cattle to live off."

"What is the price of the land?" asked Lascelles.

"The bank will evaluate it and sell it at a fair price," replied Mr. Almaros. "I had authorized them to take fifty percent deposit and the rest on installment just in case they were not offered cash."

"We'll buy it," shouted Lascelles.

Mr. Almaros took one step backwards and stiffened his neck before he uttered a figure.

"Sir, if you give us one month we will have that money ready for you," Lascelles said.

"Okay, I'll go to the bank and tell them to stop the sale."

Within a month most of the cows were sold and title to the land was transferred to the names of Lascelles and his mother. Arrangements were made for the installment to be sent to Mr. Almaros in Germany every three months.

As Mr. and Mrs. Almaros moved out of the house, Lascelles and his mother moved in. Mr. Almaros had left all the household furnishings, a few cows and his old Land Rover Jeep for which Lascelles was very grateful.

His first task was to move what was left of his goat herd close to the house, and for the first time in four years he slept on a bed. Over the next five years the cattle and goat herds grew. Lascelles got married and started a family. His first child Lawrence was nine years old when there were only four quarterly payments left on the property.

Lascelles made a sale of most of the livestock and took the money and his family including his mother on a vacation in Germany, at which time he gave Mr. Almaros the final payment.

Although he was somewhat familiar with the map of Germany, on his travel agent's advice, he flew into Frankfurt, only to find out that he and his family could have gone to Dresden, which is closer to where Mr. Almaros lived. He left his family at a hotel and travelled two days by bus to a little town called Niffus to meet with his former boss.

It was a Sunday when he got there and was intending to leave the following morning. Mr. Almaros was happy to see him, but was disappointed that his family was not with him.

Mr. Almaros had spent thirty-five years in Jamaica and liked the patwa dialect very much, but it was always a joke when he spoke more than one sentence of it. He mispronounced and misinterpreted words. His English wasn't all that good either.

Mr. Almaros was driving Lascelles to the bus terminal for his return trip to Frankfurt when he said, *"An falo mi to ze bank so me put away zis money you brought me yesterday."*

"Follow me to the bank, so that I can deposit this money you brought me yesterday"

They stopped at a Mercedes Benz car dealership and Mr. Almaros stepped out of his car saying that he would be right back. He was gone for quite some time and Lascelles wondered if he would be on time for his bus. On Mr. Almaros' return to the car, he beckoned for Lascelles to follow him to an office in the show-room.

"Me send auto parts to friend in Jamaica. You sign now and sign in Jamaica eh."

"I am sending some automobile parts to a friend in Jamaica. You sign for it now and again when it gets to Jamaica, Okay?"

Lascelles trusted Mr. Almaros so he did not read the invoice. He quickly signed it and handed it to the clerk.

One week after returning to Jamaica, Lascelles received a telegram from Mr. Almaros. It read:

'Car had been shipped. Please have it parked in your garage until further instructions'.

Lascelles considered it strange. He remembered that Mr. Almaros had him to sign for car parts for his friend. He was busy catching up on a backlog of work and did not spend time thinking about the car.

The next day was his thirty-fifth birthday and he had promised his wife that he would be home from the field early to spend time with the family and enjoy the children's favorite; ice cream and carrot cake. It was a quarter-to-four when he pulled into his driveway in the old Jeep. The garage door was closed and he wondered why. They always leave it opened so that he could drive in. He appreciated that very much, especially when it rains. He stepped out of the vehicle and started to walk along the side of the house towards the back porch. Half way there he was met by his nine year old son and his seven year old daughter.

"Happy birthday daddy, we have a surprise for you," one of them said.

"I already know," said Lascelles. "It's ice cream and cake. We do that for everybody's birthday."

"No daddy, it's bigger than that," shouted the girl.

Just then he saw his mother all dressed up sitting on the porch reading the newspaper.

"Go clean up son, and don't keep me waiting," she said.

Lascelles walked into the kitchen and was disappointed, because the usual smell of cooked food was not there to greet him. He really felt like grabbing a morsel of meat on his way to the shower. He peeped into the living room and was surprised to see his mother-in-law sitting on the couch. He waved and continued through the passage to the bathroom.

While the cold water ran over his body he told himself that his mother-in-law's visit must have been the surprise the children mentioned. She had never before been there for his birthday.

As he turned the water off, his wife handed him a towel and he noticed that she had in her hands his most fancy leisure suit and a pair of dress shoes. He also noticed that she too was dressed.

"Hurry up, it will be dark pretty soon," she said.

"Where are we going," asked Lascelles.

"For a drive out in the country side," was the reply.

"That Jeep is messy," Lascelles remarked. "You are all dressed up. It will take me a half a day to clean it up."

He still had his shoes to put on when he was physically dragged toward the passage door to the carport. It was dark in there, but the form of a large object was slightly visible. One of the women opened the side door. Another one opened the doors to the outside, and the cover of an automobile with the Mercedes emblem became clear that it was draped over the car.

The younger Mrs. Ledgester pulled the cover off the object and said, "Thad-daah."

It was a brand new red Mercedes Benz. In the glove compartment was a birthday card from Mr. Almaros. It read: 'A birthday gift. Enjoy'

Note: Hard work and sacrifices paid off.

The broom seller.

A wealthy couple who lived in one of Kingston's most affluent neighborhoods had an only child, a son they named Jeremiah. From kindergarten through to the mid-elementary school years Jeremiah was the brightest child in his classes, although that was partly due to the private tutors his parents hired to push him along.

Both parents had occupations that required them to spend more time away from home than normal, and sometimes they only see Jeremiah on weekends and on holidays. Trouble started for Jeremiah in his first teen-age year. Up until that time he was always bringing home plaques and prizes from school for academic achievements. The private tutoring stopped because the two facilitators complained that Jeremiah was being disrespectful to them, and he told his parents not to waste their money paying them because he was as smart as they were. The parents had no idea that their son was truant, and when he did attend school, he was late.

The school administrators gave him notes to take to his parents to inform them of the situation, but got no response. None of those notes reached home. The teachers made frequent telephone calls, but no one was ever home to answer. There was one class, however, that Jeremiah had never missed and was always punctual, and that was the Physical Education and Athletics class. He brought home trophy after trophy for achievements in that class.

At the end of the school year he failed the examination that would allow him to advance to the next level of classes. This situation required him to repeat the class, but by school rules, the parents needed to meet with the administrators before that could happen. It was then that they became aware of their son's deplorable grades. His excuse was that the teachers do not like him because his parents are rich, and remarked that the only good teachers were those of the Physical Education and Athletics classes who gave him passing grades.

The couple loved their child and wanted for him to be a success, so they moved him to another school. Jeremiah had an aunt who resides in the vicinity of the new school. The aunt signed for him at the school as his guardian, and the arrangement was made for him to stay with her during the school weeks and return home on weekends. The problem was that this aunt lived alone, worked as a nurse and had long and varied hours away from home, so Jeremiah was again alone after school.

For the first year at the new school everything went fine. Both parents and the aunt made regular visits and called to the school administration to check up on Jeremiah's status. For that first year, one parent or the other would be prompt in picking him up and taking him home on weekends.

As time went on, his parents began to trust him to take the bus home when they were too busy to pick him up. Little by little, the condition deteriorated. He found excuses for not going home when he was supposed to. When the parents visited after school he was never at his aunt's house. The telephone was locked away from him because of the excessive calls he made, so for weeks his father was only able to see him once when he paid a surprise visit to the aunt's house one night very late.

Things went from bad to worse. Jeremiah had dropped out of school and none of his relatives knew where he was. For a while the aunt thought that he had gone back to live with his parents, and the parents thought that he was with his aunt. He was reported to the police as missing, but nothing was done to find him.

One Sunday evening the telephone rang at the parent's house. Anxiously, the mother picked up the receiver and said, "Hello."

"*Ma-drin, dis a yu son-drin Jahmiah I.*"

"Mother, this is your son Jeremiah I Rastafari."

"Who?" asked the mother frantically. She recognized the voice, but could not help herself asking 'Who'.

He mentioned his real name, but in a very hushed tone that sounded as if he did not want anyone near him to hear.

"Where are you? And why haven't you been home in five weeks?"

She had questions, and wanted answers, but he spoke over her voice.

"*Ma dump some dunny in I man account. I man a dwell wid some I drin an a try fine I man self.*"

"Mother, deposit some money into my account. I am living with some brethren, and I am trying to find myself."

The telephone was abruptly hung up at the other end.

"You look very surprised. Who was that?" asked the father.

"A sick friend in Harbor View," answered the mother. "I plan to go and visit her next week."

As it turned out, the mother did have a sick friend living in Harbor View whom she had planned to visit the following week. On the day of the visit she did not drive her car, as on her last visit she parked it on the street and someone broke a window and stole her umbrella from it. She took a cab.

The two friends were happy to see each other and the sick one even managed to make it out of bed into the living room for the first time in more than a week. They were each enjoying tea when they heard a broom seller down the street. The voice was a loud, clear and a repetitive BREWUUUM. It could be heard from a half a mile; even behind closed doors.

The friend asked her visitor to go to the gate and buy one of the brooms. At the gate Jeremiah's mother saw the broom seller on the other side of the street one block down and approaching in her direction.

She waved to make sure that he saw that she wanted to buy a broom. As the person came closer to her, she noticed that he was wearing onion bags. One bag layered over another. It was plain to see that he wasn't even wearing underwear. He was wearing sandals made from used automobile tire. The knitted hat on his head looked like he had a soccer ball under it. Suddenly, the person on recognizing her, walked very fast in the middle of the street past her. She opened the gate and ran up the street after him. As she caught up with him their eyes met and she realized that the broom seller was her son. She fell to her knees. He took the fifty dollar bill from her hand and left two brooms.

Note: Life is full of choices.

The Preacher from afar.

Clarendon, Manchester and Saint Elizabeth are three neighboring parishes that stretched from near the middle of Jamaica toward the west of the island. During the late fifties and up to the early seventies at least four large Bauxite and Alumina companies built factories in those parishes and processed the bauxite ore and alumina silt for export. Work was plentiful, and men from all over the island flocked to the vicinities in search of employment, to trade, and some even to gamble. Most of those who got employed managed to find temporary housing in the areas and travelled back to their homes on weekends.

One man from Saint Thomas had a physical impediment (fin hand). His friends called him Finny. He went from site to site, but no one would hire him. From time to time, some workers gave him money, but he never had enough to eat, pay for his lodging and to travel back to his home, so for weeks he was stuck in Saint Elizabeth.

One particular weekend he found himself flat broke, as all his friends had gone home to be with their families. What made it worse was that the following Monday would be a holiday and no one he knew would be returning before Tuesday morning. That Friday,

Finny could not even pay for his lodging and had to sleep at a shop piazza with some drunkards. It was a long night for a sober man.

Early that Saturday morning he went and washed himself in the nearby river, and put on his best clothes that he carried with him. He then entered the home of one of the locals and told them that he was a travelling preacher who got robbed the night before. The residents felt sorry for him and fed him breakfast. While he was eating he was thinking about his next move. When he was full he asked to borrow a bible and a folding table. His request was granted.

He walked about a mile to the town square, and set up his table in front of the market house.

As quick as he set the table up, he opened the bible and set it on it; he then put his hat upside down under it. One by one, people stepped up and put money into the hat.

Before mid-day the hat was full of money and Finny had to empty it into a carton box he carried around with him. People started to gather around and he started to preach. Every time he raised his voice to a crescent the crowd shouted, 'Ha-le lu-yah!'. This continued for hours and Finny barely had time to empty the hat, only to have it filled again.

He was about to bring his preaching to a close when he saw a familiar face in the crowd. It was one of the gamblers from Kingston. Finny himself had gambled with him more than once. He thought to himself that he must have been down on his luck why he hadn't gone home. Knowing that the gambler knew that he was not a preacher, he once again got the crowd into a frenzy. Just about everyone was saying Ha-le-lu-yah. Then at the top of his voice Finny said,

"Man from afar, who see me an know me. Houl thy peace and I will see thee later."

"Man from afar, who sees me and knows who I am. Hold thy peace, and I will see thee later."

Only the gambler knew what he said. The crowd thought that he was in the spirit.

The Ha-le-lu-yahs got even louder, and there were calls for 'MORE, MORE'. It was difficult for Finny to leave. He beckoned to the gambler to pick up the table and his bible while he clutched the carton box and shuffled through the crowd.

The two became a team, and every week they travelled to a different site. From then on Finny was able to go home during the week and be present to preach every Saturday.

Note: Stick with what works.

Barking dog.

Alton Daley was eleven years old when his family moved to the other end of his parish, causing him to change schools. He was shy and did not make friends right away. The school-bully was a twelve year old named Lad Wilson. Lad was big for his age, as he was the same size as some fifteen year olds. He immediately noticed Al's shyness and started to pick on him. Every school day Lad ate Al's lunch and threatened to beat him up if he mentioned it to anyone.

After a few weeks, Al found out that a boy named Pete from another class was also new to the school and was also the victim of the bully. The two new-comers stuck together every chance they had, and for a while that kept the bully away.

Al and Pete were very surprised one day when they were called into the principal's office. As they entered the office they saw Lad standing in a corner. He had tears running down his face and his clothes were muddy.

"Al Daley and Peter Brown," the principal said. "As of today you are both being suspended from your classes for two days. Lad had reported that you two boys jumped him. This type of behavior will not be accepted in this school, and if it happens again I will have no choice but to bar both of you from ever attending this school, or any other in this parish."

The boys did not have a chance to defend themselves as the Principal ushered them straightway out the door. He gave them notes to deliver to their parents. Al told his parents that Lad had lied because he and Pete were always together so that he couldn't pick on them. His parents believed him, because they knew that he always tell the truth, but blamed him for not reporting the first incident to them. They went with Al to see the principal and the suspension was reduced to one day.

For the next three years Lad pestered both Al and Pete, but he picked on them separately, and when no one was watching. Because of age limitations, at fifteen Lad had to leave school. Al and Pete decided that they would meet him on the street and get their revenge since the principal no longer could protect him. It was in the summer when all three met on a lonely part of country road. The two younger boys attempted to carry out their plan, which resulted in Lad beating both of them bloody.

Their parents took them to the police station, and made a report, and then to the health clinic to have their cuts and bruises attended to. The police searched for Lad, but he managed to evade them, and the next morning he got on an out-of-town bus, never to return.

The following year both Al and Pete started high school in different areas, but they remained close friends. Whenever they met, their conversations would always include reminisces of the bad experiences with Lad. They desperately wanted revenge, but to begin with, they did not know where he was, and even if they could find him, he was, and would always be physically bigger than they were, or hoped to be.

Both boys graduated from high school and Pete immediately entered Seminary saying that was the only way he could forgive Lad. Al joined the Police Force, but his parents were very disappointed because they wanted him to become an attorney. He was very adamant about his decision saying that he would see the criminals before the lawyer does. His real reason was to use his police influence to find Lad.

Within six months of graduating from the Police Academy, Al had worked on different shifts at different stations all around Kingston. The work was very dangerous and demanding, and for a while he had forgotten the real reason he joined the Force. As a rookie cop he was mostly assigned to the graveyard shift in the most dangerous parts of the city.

One night, Al and his partner were on foot-patrol when they spotted some men utilizing the lights at a shop piazza to gamble. Both policemen rushed the group. They all ran in different directions, but Al and his partner were able to catch up with one. The gambler fell to his knees and begged for mercy. The sound of his voice and his giant-like statue made Al realize that the man was his long time nemeses. He whispered to his partner that he knew the man, but the man did not recognize him, so he was going to play some tricks on him.

*"**Dis time a night**,"* Al said, holding his baton over the kneeling man's head. *"**Only police, street-sweepas an dawgs soppose to be on de street. It obvious dat yu not***

a police. Yu knaa wear unifaam. Yu not a street-sweepa. Yu noh ha noh broom, so yu must be a dawg. Declare yu self."

"This time of the night only police, street-sweepers and dogs are supposed to be on the street. It is obvious that you are not a police, because you are not wearing uniform. You are not a street-sweeper. You have no broom, so you must be a dog. Declare yourself."

"Mi a dawg sah, mi a dawg," answered the man.

"I am a dog sir, I am a dog."

"Well since yu a dawg, let mi hear yu bawk," said Al's partner.

"Well since you are a dog, let me hear you bark."

The gambler began to bark Har,har, har.

"Wha kine a dawg bawk like dat?" asked Al.

"What kind of dog bark like that"

"A mongrel sah," he answered.

"A mongrel sir."

"A mongrel? Gi mi a pitbull bawk," said Al.

"A mongrel? Give me a Pitbull bark."

The gambler barked, 'Wow, wow, wow' like a Pitbull dog.

"Now gi mi a German shepherd bark".

"Now, give me a German Shepherd bark."

The man barked, 'Wuff, wuff, wuff' like a German shepherd dog, and on and on it went until neither police knew of any more kinds of dogs for the man to imitate. They told him to crawl on all four and to pretend that he was trying to catch his tail with his mouth. They had the laugh of their lives. Finally, at about four o'clock they cuffed him and took him to jail.

Al's shift ended at eight that morning, but before he left the station he went to the jail cell and revealed himself to Lad, and made him a deal to drop the charges if he would go the elementary school in the area with him to tell of his ordeal so that school bullies could learn not to victimize other children.

Note: Beware of what you dish out.

Mad, and mistaken to be mad.

Two preteen boys, Lon and Ted, were next-door neighbors. They were the closest of friends. They did everything together. They even had slight resemblances of each other, of which, no one could explain, but they didn't mind and were on many instances mistaken for twins by people who did not know them.

Both boys were avid fans of Western style movies and comic books. Sometimes they dressed themselves as the characters and played the parts.

One hot summer day they were in an open field near to their houses playing a game of Cowboy and Indians. Lon was playing the part of Cowboy and Ted was playing the part of Indian. They reached the part where Lon was the cow-boy who's' gun ran out of bullets and he was being chased by Ted, the Indian with a spear. Something snapped in Lon's head and he got delirious. He was taken to the hospital where he remained in that condition for several weeks.

When he regained consciousness, he was not his usual self and the doctors recommended that he should be kept in a controlled environment, because unpredictably his illness could escalate, and he could become a danger to himself and anyone around him.

He was admitted to the asylum. Over a four year period of therapy and different medications, he was evaluated and determined to be well enough to go home.

On Lon's return home he and Ted were just like old times, although both sets of parents watched them as closely as possible for any sign of Lon returning to insanity.

One day Lon was outside his house waiting for Ted to come out and play. While he was waiting, he used a machete to sharpen a piece of stick that was about four feet long to look like a spear.

When Ted came out to play Lon held up his spear and told him to run. Ted feared for his life and ran as fast as he could through the open field that was their playground. He was almost out of breath when he fell. He thought that, that would have been the end of his life; to his surprise, Lon helped him to his feet, gave him the spear and told him that it was his turn to chase him.

Ted was reluctant to chase his friend with a spear, but Lon reminded him that that was how they have always played the game. Knowing how delicate Lon's brain was, Ted obliged and started to chase him. The chase had just started when both sets of parents emerged from their houses and noticed one boy chasing the other with the sharpened stick. They called out to Ted, but apparently he did not hear. One of the fathers ran and grabbed him from behind, threw him to the ground and tied him up with his belt. Ted tried in vain to tell them that it was just a game. Even Lon told them so, but they paid him no mind.

The police arrived and immediately put Ted into a straitjacket, and took him to the asylum.

His parents visited him every day, but the only thing they got from him was; 'I am not mad'.

The asylum staff tried to give him medications which he would put into his mouth and held under his tongue only to spit out as soon as they turned their backs. He purposely would not respond to any therapy.

His parents had a meeting with the doctors to discuss his condition and while they were in the doctor's office Ted was waiting in an adjoining room. He put his ear to the closed door and listened intently to the conversation. What he heard from the doctor was, "your son has presented me with the biggest problem I had ever faced in this facility. From the day he was admitted here his condition has been immeasurable. As it is, we do not know if he is coming or going. Medicines have no effect and his only utterance is '**Mi noh mad**'. 'I am not mad'. We would like to release him, but only if we see change from a bad behavior to good."

With that information, Ted embarked on a plan to show the administration what they needed to see so that he could be released.

There was an insane man in the unit who was also a known sex offender. He had no room-mate. Everyone was afraid of him. Ted went to the warden and asked to be the man's room-mate. His first request was denied, because of concerns for his safety, but he insisted day after day until his wish was granted.

It was near curfew time that he was ushered into the room. He sat in one corner and the insane man into another corner. When the lights were turned off for the night, Ted sat on the toilet, and in the dark he daubed his own feces all over himself and then went to bed. He had not laid down a full minute before the man made his move on him. When the mad man discovered that Ted's naked body was covered in feces, he hollered for the guards.

"***Tek mi out yah,***" he said. "***Tek mi out yah. Dis bwauy is mad. Tek mi out yah.***"

"Take me out of here. Take me out of here. This boy is mad. Take me out of here."

The mad man was removed and Ted washed himself off and went to sleep.

The next day words reached the doctor of the occurrence and he ordered solitary confinement for Ted. After two or three days Ted asked to see the doctor and was taken in restraint to the office. The doctor was very surprised how intelligent Ted was. They talked about politics, about religion and just about everything else. The laughter of the doctor was heard outside of the office as Ted told him of the behavior of the inmates and wardens of the facility.

The two conversed and joked for hours until finally Ted told the doctor the whole story of how he got admitted to the asylum. That evening the doctor drove Ted to his parents and apologized for his admittance and detention.

Note: The end justified the means.

One, two, three.

In the old days, before the late nineteen twenties and early thirties, most Jamaican rural communities were very isolated and remote. This was partly due to the lack of transportation coupled with the bad condition of the roads. The main means of transport was the mule and dray, and the horse and buggy. The only paved roads were in the middle of the cities. People who lived in sections of both east and west of the island only needed to travel to Spanish Town, the island capital then for most of their merchandise, entertainment, shopping for their other daily living needs.

Quite a lot of in-breeding took place because of the isolation of the communities, and only business men and the wealthy normally travelled out of their districts to find mates. Any man or woman who was lucky to get paired up with a mate from the outside were always well honored and well respected.

One man who was fairly wealthy and wanted to marry someone to whom he was not related searched the entire eastern section of the country for years without success. He heard about a place in Westmoreland; a hundred miles away, with plenty of young women available for marriage. Marriage there required none of the usual courtship, just acceptance by the girl's family and a substantial monetary gift. The money was not much of a problem, but he was past middle age and was concerned about age difference.

For months the man made preparations to travel to Westmoreland which was almost a hundred and some miles away.

One sunny Sunday morning he left home on his dray with three mules and the necessities for the round trip that would possibly take two months. On the way he made some unexpected extra money transporting market people to points he had to pass. He did not tell anyone about his mission for fear of getting robbed.

At the designated district, he discreetly advertised himself and his mission, and within a week was seen by many families, but none accepted him. He became very distraught and was about to return home unmarried when he was chosen by a middle aged widow named Sue.

The wedding was quite a fanfare. The money that he would have had to give to the family of a young girl was spent on the wedding and given to friends of the bride.

With his wife he set out on the long journey back to Saint Thomas. He was anxious to get home to consummate his marriage. He drove the mules relentlessly. He only stopped when he wanted to sleep, and often that was not more than a few hours at a time. Those were the only times the mules rested and were fed.

One day while going up the Spur Tree hill, the mules became tired and agitated. The lead mule was his eldest, a five year old he named Doris. Doris started acting up. The man stopped the dray and went in front of the mule. He fiercely grabbed the reins and said; *'Doris das one'*. 'Doris! That's one'.

The mule quieted down and the journey was continued. A few miles up the hill, and again the mule began to act up. Again the man stopped the dray, went in front of the mule, fiercely grabbed the reins and said; *'Doris das two'*. 'Doris! That's two'.

Again the mule quieted down and the journey continued. Not more than a half a mile later, the mule repeated the antics. The man did not speak. He stopped the dray and his wife looked at him with an enquiring look. Slowly, he reached behind his seat, got his rifle and shot the mule in the head. His wife began to rant and rave.

"Why did you do dat?" she asked. *"You could a sell dat mule an by the tings a wife need. Blah, blah, blah."*

"Why did you do that? You could have sold that mule and buy the things a wife needs. Blah, blah, blah."

On and on she ranted and raved, until finally the man looked at her and said; *"Sue, das one."*

"Sue that is one"

He buried the dead mule by the side of the road, and they rode the rest of the way in silence, and lived happily ever after.

Note: Three strikes and you are out.

Look like a police or look like a criminal.

A single mother lived in Kingston with three pre-teen children. A boy named Cole twelve, and two girls, one ten and the other eight years old. She became single when her husband of fourteen years left for America on a farm work contract. For the first two months of his absence he sent her money by Western Union. He did not write or telephoned, and she had no way of contacting him.

The money he sent was barely enough to pay the rent and buy the necessary things for the family, so at the end of those two months the mother had to seek assistance from relatives and friends. She managed to get a part-time job as a domestic helper, but the wages was far from being enough, so she moved into a smaller place in order to pay less rent. This new place was not convenient for the three children and herself, so she arranged to send the boy to live with grandparents out in the countryside.

The grandparents themselves were poor and could not afford to send the boy to school. Although the boy was very big and tall for his age, he was not used to hard work and none of the farmers in the area would hire him even part-time. He made friends with some street boys, some of whom were run-aways. They all had the grunge look, because they had no one to care for them, and their tattered clothes were all that they could afford. They earned money mainly on market days when they helped the women to carry their baskets from the market to the bus station. Whatever money Cole earned, he would take a part of it to his grandparents, and they were always thankful. At the Christmas season, his mother sent him new clothes and shoes which he sometimes sold and secretly sent the money to his young sisters.

Because of his Kingston accent and his size and height, he unwittingly became the leader of the boys that he hung out with. They were a gang, but they did not do bad things other than being truant. They helped people on the streets whenever their assistance was needed and they never asked for payment.

After a couple years, Cole and his buddies managed to save enough money to have a fleet of custom push-carts made. The carts were rigged to look like sleighs. The boys formed teams and operated the carts to do short-distance transportation of everything that could fit in them and needed to be moved within the town. They made most of their money on rainy days when the streets were flooded and people needed to go from block to block without getting their shoes wet. These passengers were completely satisfied to pay them less than what the taxi-cabs would have charged. It was a blessing in disguise!

As time went on, people loved the Grunge Boys, as they were called. Their biggest fans were the teenage school girls who were often the recipients of lavish presents from them. But the Grunge Boys also spent money on themselves. On Sunday evenings and on holidays they could hardly be recognized as they were all dressed in the latest fashions and looked as sharp, if not sharper, than the so-called privileged boys around town.

A full three years after Cole went to live with his grandparents he turned fifteen, but he looked every bit eighteen or nineteen. He received a letter from his mother stating that; *'I will be paying your fare on the country-bus for you to come and visit me and your sisters for the Christmas season. We do not want for you to grow out of sight and become unrecognizable to us'.*

He replied in a return letter:

"I will pay the fares for all three of you to come and spend the Christmas season with my grandparents and myself. I would here emphasize that it had been many years since you had seen my grandparents, and you certainly would not want for them to die and not to see you and especially the girls. Mom, I am the lead-man on my job, and it's our busiest time of year. It would be extremely difficult for me to leave at this time".

Enclosed in the letter was a postal money order that was more than enough for the round trip for all three. The mother felt guilty and compelled. She had for three years wanted to go and visit, but especially since her husband left, she could not afford the fare for herself and the two girls, and she could not trust leaving them alone, so her thoughts were that it would have cost less for Cole to visit.

She read the letter several times and wondered what kind of work her fifteen year old boy could be employed in. She assumed that whatever of a job it was, it had to be part-time, because he had to be in school, but, what kind of work could he do to pay him so much? She had never had a report that Cole was not in school, and she remembered that her parents were very strict with her when she was growing up and going to school, so she didn't expect anything to change.

Two days before Christmas and Cole had no assurance that his mother and sisters would visit. The buses were full of people coming into town from the cities for the holidays. All day and into the night Cole took jobs that kept him near to the bus station, so that he could see the arriving passengers, but his mother and sisters never came.

The next morning, Christmas Eve, he told his grandparents that he would be hanging out with his friends that night, and not to expect him. That day, business was very good. Cole had taken his mind off seeing his relatives, so whatever job came along, far or near, he was on it.

At about two in the afternoon one of his buddies tracked him down.

"Come now bwoy," his friend said. *"Is yu mama an sistas. Dey jus de way yu desdcribe dem. Wei all refuse fe tek dem bag. Wei tell dem dat a special transpout coming fe dem."*

"Come boy, its' your mama and your sisters. They are just the way you described them to us. We all refused to take their bags. We told them that a special transport is coming for them."

Cole raced to the bus station. His sisters were well aware of his occupation. Whenever he sent them money he made sure to remind them not to tell their mother anything. As he rushed to where they were standing, the girls had their backs turned and did not see him. Hurriedly, he started to put the bags on his cart.

"Young man!" his mother said, not recognizing him. "Don't you touch those bags. I have a special transport coming for us."

Just then the girls turned around and saw Cole. They rushed and hugged him.

"Cole! Is that you?" asked his mother. "And why are you dressed like that in those, those grungie clothes. Are you not afraid the police might mistake you for a criminal and shoot you? What happen to all the nice clothes I sent you?"

"But mom," answered Cole. "First of all, if I am dressed up, I would be broke. Secondly, if I am dressed up the criminals may mistake me to be a police and shoot me."

Note: damned if you do and damned if you don't.

From one who was there.

After World War Two, Europe had a lot of structural rebuilding to do. Labor, both skilled and unskilled was very scarce. English tradesmen were very good and fast, but they were few in number, and the neighboring countries France, Germany, and Italy which were also rebuilding, lured them with better wages. The British had little choice but to recruit workers from the colonies. Jamaican, Trinidadian and Barbadian workers were the most preferred because of the language similarity, and their tolerance for hard work.

Jamaica at that time was very progressive especially for the skilled workers. The export industries of banana, sugar and logwood were at their peaks. The natives were building more and better houses. Cuba was recruiting sugarcane cutters, and America was recruiting contract farm workers. The typical Jamaican worker had his choice of work, and a lot of them were leery about travelling, because decades before, many had relatives who went to work on the Panama Canal construction and died there from the mosquito-transmitted plague. Many died with the accompanying high fever.

There were newspaper advertisements and politician encouragements about special bonuses for couples and about helping the Mother Country. The first set of immigrants who entered England in the late nineteen forties and early fifties were all well received. They were given free living accommodations, transportation to and from work and other treats to make them comfortable.

Words got back to Jamaica that the life in England was good, and before long, workers by the ship loads were entering the Mother Country from the little island. There were no special requirements other than the show of a birth certificate by each person to verify being a British subject. England was overwhelmed by the numbers. The treats were discontinued, and employment for new arrivals was few, primarily because most of them were unskilled.

Many of them wandered the streets before being rescued by the YMCA. They were taken to different locations within London. Men were in one warehouse and women in another, sometimes on the same compound. These were not really warehouses in reality, but were rather bomb shelters in Brixton, and other such areas.

The accommodation was crude and unusual for them, but they had no choice. Housing was in an underground shelter, where water was scarce, toilets were pit latrines, and heating was antiquated. Some had borrowed money from friends and relatives back home with promises to return the same with interest soon. Since they were unskilled workers, as work was not as fort-coming as it was for the skilled, therefore they were not able to fulfill their promises to repay their relatives as they had planned.

On weekends, the Jamaicans who first migrated brought the new-comers food and other necessities. The women however, got hired as domestic helpers and cooks surprisingly quickly, as words got around about their cleanliness and their culinary skills. The men who were unskilled, on the other hand, had hard lives. Some of them desperately wanted to return home, but could not afford the fare, and even if they could, they were too ashamed to return broke. Their main source of income was sporadic. The Labor Lorry would be at the warehouse at six every weekday morning for twenty or twenty-five men to do street sweeping and garbage pick-up. Those chosen would be gone for a ten hour shift, and got paid in cash at the end of the shift. When the lorry left with twenty or twenty-five men there would still be about a hundred left at any one of the shelters. They would spend the time sleeping, playing dominoes or both. There were never any guarantee of more than one day work, and very seldom did any one man work four or five days straight. Jamaicans, on a whole, were always kind and considerate of each other and those who were lucky enough to accumulate some cash helped the others, so that they all could eat.

As time went on, some would pool their monies and rented Flats outside the camps, but as some left others arrived, and this continued for many years. Incidentally Brixton was the only community that would rent housing to foreigners.

The Jamaicans who arrived earlier, particularly the skilled ones earned good wages and were able to have their loved ones join them, and when they visited relatives and friends back home, they wore expensive clothes and jewelry that gave everyone else the impression that England was the place to be.

At one of the camps there was a man named Joe Metcomb. He was about five-feet-six of medium built and was always friendly with everyone. His father was a Caucasian English man whom he never knew and his mother a Jamaican mulatto. He was often recognized as white, and he in fact looked like an over-tanned Caucasian.

Joe was from Kingston and before he went to England he made his living as a 'Sweet Boy'. (He had never worked a full day in his life.) He never made any effort to get on the Labor Lorry, and always complained of one type of ailment or another whenever the lorry arrived. He had one thing going for him, and that was he was a very good cook. Because he made meals for those that worked, others in the camp felt sorry for him and gave him necessary things like cologne, soap and whatever little money they could afford.

There were other men in the camps who did not earn enough money to live off, nor to have anything much to send home. Some of them stopped writing home after three months and the relatives back home assumed that they were dead. Anyone back home who received a so-called 'empty letter' would curse the sender and wished they were dead, but Joe was always sending letters home. He had also written many letters for some camp buddies who couldn't read and write, and scammed them of monies that were supposed to be posted in those letters.

None of Joe's camp buddies knew that when they went off to work, Joe went off to a gambling house where he spent the days gambling. He gambled on everything, from soccer games, to horse racing to bicycle racing, and was pretty good at it, but he always pretended to be broke. This went on for at least a couple of years, and when he was found out at one camp, he moved to a different one, and by that time all the old-timers knew about him, a new batch of workers came in and not knowing his bad habits they treated him kindly.

He bought a bicycle, and on Sundays he rode around down town London to familiarize himself with the area. He spent a lot of time at Piccadilly Circus and at Trafalgar Square. That made him popular with the ladies, particularly those who rode bicycles on Sunday evenings.

Two weeks before Christmas nineteen-sixty-two an Over-seer for the camps informed the campers that they were all invited to the wedding of Joseph Metcomb and Lorraine Simmons to be performed at the Community hall at four o'clock in the evening on Christmas day. To most of the new-comers, the names did not mean anything, but welcome the news as this would allow them to get out of camp, particularly on that day. The old-timers partly recognized the name of the groom as that of Joe, but he had left camp months before, so they couldn't be sure.

Christmas day in the early afternoon, all the immigrant workers from the camps went to the hall. The seating was arranged so that an aisle was between the pews, with an altar at one end of the aisle. All the immigrants timidly sat on one side. Joe and his entourage of six men, all dressed in snug-fitted tuxedos marched up the aisle. Soon after that the bride and her party of six arrived. Each of them looked like they had just stepped off the pages of a metropolitan fashion magazine.

After the ceremony, Joe and his bride shook hands with all the attendees and disappeared.

For months after that, none of his Jamaican buddies heard from him until they saw his picture in the newspaper. Under his picture was the caption: 'London's most elusive pick-pocket finally captured'.

Two of the old-time immigrants went and visited him in jail, and the following story was related to them. 'His wife was a devoted Christian and did not approve of his gambling habit. She insisted that he get a respectable job, but he had no marketable skills, and he flatly refused to do common labor work. Day after day he would get dressed and went down town job hunting, but no one would hire him. Old habits die hard, so he went back to what he was good at from Jamaica, picking pockets. As fast as he brought home money, jewelry and other expensive trinkets, his wife, the good Christian woman that she was, took them to the police station.

The police knew the items were stolen, but had no proof. The items were each time kept at the station in the Lost & Found department for thirty days for the owners to claim them.

Joe was careful that his victims were visitors to London and were not around to claim their valuables. After thirty days of not being claimed, the items were returned to his wife. Month after month, money and valuables were returned to her.

A plain clothes detective was assigned to trail Joe when he was on his prowl. Joe noticed that he was being followed, so he disguised himself as a tourist and approached the officer, pretended that he was lost and asked for directions. The officer patiently tried to understand Joe's patwa dialect and to explain directions to him and did not realize that he was the pick-pocket victim.

The following day Joe was in a pub having a few drinks, and was boasting to his friends how he had picked the badge of an undercover officer who was trailing him. Over-hearing the conversation was another undercover officer who promptly arrested him. The charge was 'stealing from the Crown'.

Note: A fish has to open its mouth to get hooked.

The King Family.

There was a Jamaican man whose last name was King. He was so very proud of the name that he tried to involve the word king in all his dealings. For instance, at the fish market, he would ask at the top of his voice, "What's the price of king fish?" When he was told the price, he would say, "Thy kingdom come."

His first name was Doctal, but he would insist on being called Doc. Doc could hardly read or write, so he tried desperately to always use simple one syllable words. He was always eager to introduce himself to strangers. His favorite sentence was, "Hi, my name is Doc King."

He married a woman named Mabel, and in a short time the 'bel' was dropped. He affectionately called her Ma, even though they were yet to have children.

Ma eventually became pregnant, and the two set out to find names for their offspring. Doc was hoping for a boy and Ma was hoping for a girl. They poured over a lot of names but none suited Doc. One day he was travelling on a country bus when he noticed a sign inside the bus above the windshield. The words of the sign spread across an area that included the access door to the destination sign at the front of the bus. To a normal person, the sign read 'no smoking', but the access door was out of alignment causing a part of the sign to read 'no smo', on one section and the other section to read 'king'. Doc reached into his pocket for pencil and paper, and wrote in one word or one non-word, as it was, 'nosmo'. On the same piece of paper, he had the letters 'tal' written, which was the last syllable of his first name.

About the fifth month of Ma's pregnancy, the doctor told her that she had detected more than one heartbeat, so the family should prepare themselves for twins. She relayed the news to her husband. Doc intensified his search for names. When it was close to the time of birthing, Ma asked him if he had settled on the names for the babies. "Yes," he said. "For girls and for boys."

He handed her a piece of paper. On it were syllables, except for the first non-word, 'nosmo, were, tal, coo, lac, brea, dec, trac, and a dozen or more others. None made any sense to her. She handed the paper back to him, but she had in mind what she wanted to name her children.

Ma's labor pains started, and the midwife was called. Much to everyone's surprise, instead of twins, as was expected, Ma had triplet. The first two were boys and the third, a girl, of course. The ordeal was too much for Ma, she passed out after the boys were born.

After hours of waiting for her to revive, the midwife needed to leave to another call. She asked the father for the names, so she could record them. He handed her the same piece of paper. "What do I do with this?" she asked.

"Just pick from it," answered the husband.

She did, and the children's names were, NO SMOKING, TALKING AND COOKING.

Note: Stay in school.

The Iguana and the Snake.

Whoever had said that one must be wise as a serpent and be harmless as a dove could be right about the dove part, but the following certainly raised doubts about the wisdom of the serpent.

Before the emancipation of slavery in Jamaica, there were a lot of snakes slithering on the land. Many of them had poisonous venoms that killed not only slaves, but land owners and others.

Different methods including manually hunting and killing the snakes were tried, but they proliferated faster than they were being killed. Agriculture was being hampered, not to mention the loss of lives.

Finally, sets of mongoose were brought in from India, and within a few years, the snake problem was well under control. The mongoose and the snake are arch enemies. The snake eats the young of the mongoose and the mongoose eats the eggs of the snake. They also fight each other, and the mongoose would always win. By its' agility, the mongoose tempted the snake to strike at it, and it missed every time. Each time the snake strikes and misses, it expels venom, and when its supply of venom is exhausted, the mongoose grabs it by the throat.

But with the dwindling of the snake population, came the rise of the mongoose in numbers.

There is nothing that the mongoose loves more than eggs; snake eggs, lizard eggs, alligator eggs, and fowl eggs. Most households in the Jamaican country side raise fowls for meat and eggs, and so the mongoose is a pest to the residents. Other than the snakes, the mongoose has no real enemy, except humans, who make traps, and train dogs to catch them.

One day, a young boy and his dog were in an open field searching for mongoose holes. The dog suddenly rushed to a clump of bush and barked profusely. The boy rushed to see what his dog had seen. What he saw was a snake struggling to swallow an iguana. The front section up to the belly of the iguana was in the mouth of the snake, with the hind legs and the tail hanging out. The iguana's tail was wriggling, and the snake was gasping. The boy ran back to his house.

"Papa, Papa," he hollered. *"Run come se. A sin-ake an a ig-wana faasen."*

"Father, Father. Come, run and see. A snake and an iguana are fastened to each other."

"Weh yu a talk bout bwoy? Asked the father. *"Sin-ake an ig-wana a bawn enemy."*

"What are you talking about boy? Snakes and iguanas are born enemies."

Reluctantly, he followed the boy with machete in hand to see what he was talking about. When he got there, the iguana was dead, but the snake was twisting about. The body of the iguana could neither go in nor out of the snake's mouth. Father, son and dog watched as the life ebbed out of the snake.

The father went back to his house, saddled his donkey and with a carton box, he secured the dead animals and travelled to the town square. In the shade of a tree, he erected a sign to exhibit the spectacle. For every person that went to see, he collected a fee. People from far and near went to see the aberration. This continued every day for two weeks, until the carcasses started to stink. The health inspector then ordered that it be disposed of.

Note; Do not bite off more than what you can chew.

Hard Luck

Rudolph was twenty-one, and still a virgin. There were two reasons for this; one, he was so ugly that no girl in his home town wanted to be seen with him, much more to sleep with him. Two; he could not afford to pay the prostitutes even though he offered them more than what he thought was the going rate.

He read the newspaper column for '*Pen-pals Wanted*', picked out some names and addresses, and wrote to a number of girls all over the island. He sent them money and asked them to spend time with him. They all took his money and denied his request. These money offers lasted almost a year before one girl replied, and invited him to her house for an up-coming holiday. She sent him a picture of herself and asked him to send her one of his by mail before she visits. He was ashamed to send his picture, so he asked one of his male friends for one of his, and sent it to the girl.

At the appointed time of the visit, Rudolph with his bicycle boarded the only bus that passes within three miles of the girl's house. He left on the bus at two in the afternoon, and would not get there until after five. He was hoping that it would be dark enough that the girl at first sight of him wouldn't notice that he looked different from the picture he sent her.

It was still daylight when the bus reached where she had directed him to get off. He rang the bell, and the driver stopped right where two teenage girls were standing. Rudolph got off, secured his bicycle, and as the bus drove off, he went to the girls to ask for directions to his friend's house. He did not know that one of the girls was his pen-pal waiting there for him with her best friend. She had showed the picture to her, and they were there waiting for the person on the picture.

"A who yu be," "Who are you?" asked one of the girls.

Rudolph replied, and explained his mission.

Promptly, the girl pulled out the picture, and asked him who it was. Rudolph was ashamed and embarrassed. He tried to explain, but both girls called out, ***Cunu-munu, cunu-munu, teef, re-ape murda"***. "Ugly, ugly, thief, rape, murder", as they ran from him.

Some men who were playing dominoes under a tree in the back of a grocery shop, heard the girls screaming, and saw them running with Rudolph in chase. They beat him severely, and bent his bicycle wheels. He was rescued by a passing motorist, who watched him as he walked away with his bicycle on his shoulder.

In the scuffle he lost his wallet, but he dared not return to search for it. He walked all through the night and most of the next day; more than thirty-five miles to his house. When he got there, his feet were swollen and he was tired and hungry. He vowed to himself that he would stay a virgin the rest of his life.

The months went by, and Rudolph stopped writing letters. Then out of the clear blue he received a letter from one of the girls he had written to more than a year before. She sent a picture of herself that he had requested when he sent her money. She asked for him to send her his picture. He remembered what happened with his friend's picture that he had sent a girl earlier, so he decided to be honest with this one. In his reply to her he stated that he was too ugly to have his picture taken. He also remarked that anyone who tried to take his picture would have their camera broken. There is a common saying that ugly people break cameras.

This new girl was only about ten miles away, so armed with her picture he decided to play sleuth to find out who she was before they meet. He sure did find out that she was as pretty as her picture, and she worked as a live-in maid for a government civil service couple.

Over the ensuing months the letters went back and forth, and he eagerly wanted to get to meet her. Finally, he insisted on not only meeting her, but for them to spend time together. She told him in one letter that her employers spend one week-end every month at a north coast hotel, leaving their house Saturday morning and returning Sunday night. She thought this would be a perfect opportunity, if he could get to her by Saturday mid-day, so they could have some fun before nightfall. He wanted to make sure that she did not see his face in daylight, at least, not the first time they met. He replied that he would be there on the appointed Saturday, but that he might be arriving a little late.

It was between seven and eight that Saturday night when Rudolph got to the girls place, and he was glad that the kerosene oil lamp was dim, so that she could only see the outline of his face. He insisted that they turn out the light and go to bed right away, but she was determined on enjoying the ice-cream he bought her. He stripped down to his boxers and jumped into the bed.

"I wouldn't do that," she said.

"May I ask why?" Rudolph said, wryly.

"Mi bwoyfren caa come anytime", she said. ***"Im know when mi bosses dem gone. Das why mi tell you fe come early, so dat wei caa ple-ay befoe night come."***

"My boyfriend could be here at any time. He knows when my bosses are out of town. That is why I told you to be here early, so that we could play and you leave before nightfall."

Before she could finish talking, a car pulled up into the carport right across from the maid quarters' front door. In a rush she opened the window to the back of the building and told Rudolph to jump. He did jump, wearing only his boxers. He told himself that he would wait until his rival leave, and then he could return to what he was about to do, but up to midnight he was still waiting, and the mosquitos played a number on his bare skin. Finally, he walked home, half naked.

Again, Rudolph vowed to himself that he would stay a virgin for his whole life.

One Christmas season a girl in her late teens moved into his neighborhood to spend the holidays with relatives. Rudolph wasted no time in offering the girl twice what the prostitutes were charging.

Although she was not one of the so-called working girls, she gladly accepted the offer, and a date was set to be Christmas Sunday when she would be home alone.

The week leading up to that Sunday, Rudolph started to prepare himself for the rendezvous. For four days straight he had turtle soup, laced with White Rum. He bought Chinese-brush, Spanish-fly and Coolie-ring. On the Saturday he inveigled a horse stable helper to sell him some horse tonic that the locals called 'thanatology'.

Some of the boys in the neighborhood got wind that Rudolph was preparing for a woman. They badly wanted to know who she was, so that they could have one up on her, or scandalize her.

The Saturday all day and into the night they watched him discreetly. Nothing happened. None of them suspected that it would be the new girl, whom many of them also had eyes on. However, this girl had tricked Rudolph, because while he was dodging in the bushes, waiting for the family to leave for church; he noticed that the girl also left for church with them.

Later that day, some of the same boys had to take Rudolph to the hospital for him to get medical care to relieve his penis of a phenomenal erection. All his extremities were also stiff. He remained in the hospital for three days to enable medication to bring him back to normal.

Again he was disappointed and repeated to himself his vow.

Note: If it wasn't for bad luck, some people wouldn't have any luck at all.

Godmother and Enid.

For nearly a century, from the late eighteen nineties to the early nineteen seventies, Jamaica enjoyed unprecedented growth compared to the other West Indian countries. The capital, Kingston was a melting pot. People from all over the world were taking up residences there. Along with the island's lovely climate, cost of living was very low and many of the new residents enjoyed the island hop to Cuba for fanfare and gambling.

The island's people fared well, because of the need for added housing and other amenities, especially in Kingston where there was plenty of employment.

Early in the twentieth century, the black man, third, fourth and fifth generations of emancipated slaves were virtually shut out of the employment opportunities in the big city. There were many reasons for this. One; the Chinese controlled the grocery stores, the laundry and the bakeries. The Indians controlled the transportation system. The English and Irish controlled the building and road construction. The Jews ran the banks and the jewelry stores, and on and on it went. Each of those nationalities brought their own people to work with them and only needed to hire the natives mostly for common labor work. The black man was relegated mainly to agriculture, which most of them were satisfied with, because, they were their own bosses, and they worked where they lived in the country side.

With the black woman however, it was a different story. To begin with, many of them marry men of those other nationalities, and others had jobs as cooks, domestic helpers, store clerks, dress-makers and so on. One such woman was Iris. She was a clerk at a woman's apparel store in down town Kingston, and she was the Godmother to her best friend's baby girl named Enid.

Iris and Enid's mother Mary were the same age and were next-door neighbors and close friends from childhood days.

Enid's mother got pregnant at age seventeen by a Deep Sea fisherman named Phillip, and married him just before Enid was born. The christening took place when baby Enid was three months old and Iris was chosen as her Godmother. Within months after that she went to live and work in Kingston.

As time went on, Mary had another child, a girl she named Pam. Life was good for Phillip and Mary. With proceeds from Phillip's fishing, they were able to buy a piece of land and started to build a house, which they moved into with only two of the five rooms finished.

Enid was fifteen and her sister Pam twelve when Phillip drowned at sea. His body was never found. His partner, Darrell took over the business. Mary struggled to raise the two girls, and often had to seek financial help from Darrell, and pretty soon he moved in to live with her. Rumors spread that Darrell had killed

Phillip to get his wife. Mary was aware of the rumors and promised herself that as soon as her daughters were grown she would end the relationship.

Enid dropped out of school and went to learn Dress-making with Mrs. Gooden. She was a Scottish immigrant who lived in the area. The payments for Enid's lessons, were for her doing house-hold chores for Mrs. Gooden and her family two days per week.

When Mary wasn't cleaning fish for Darrell, she would be working in her vegetable garden from which she sold or traded to help make ends meet.

Iris was aware of her friend's situation, and every Christmas season she would visit with presents, especially for her Goddaughter.

Enid had not too long ago celebrated her seventeenth birthday when Mary noticed that Darrell had eyes on her first child. (making sexual advances) That night she sharpened her deceased husband's machete that she had hidden under her mattress. She then waited until her man was in bed fast asleep before she rubbed the back of the machete across his neck. Darrell awoke, almost frightened out of his wit.

"Ooman," he said. "Are you mad?"

"No," answered Mary. ***But ef yu mess wid mi pickni dem, nex time mi wei use de machete mout, an mi nah rub. Mi a chap***".

"No, but if you mess with my girls, next time I will use the sharpened edge of the machete, and I am not going to rub it. I am going to chop."

That night Darrell slept in the storage room adjoining the detached kitchen, and had made that his sleeping quarters ever since.

That Christmas, Iris paid her usual visit, and Mary reported the incident to her.

"Pack har tings," said Iris. *"She is going to Kingston wid mi. A noh a lady who need a live een helpa. Har ne-aim is Mrs. Wright an she is de wife of de Presbyterian minista. E wei be easia fa yu to watch dat you noh wat wid one chile."*

"Pack her things. She is going to Kingston with me. I know of this lady who needs a live-in helper. Her name is Mrs. Wright. She is the wife of the Presbyterian minister. It will be easier for you to watch that you know what with one child."

Two days later, Enid was on the Diesel train with her Godmother to Kingston, and the day after that was taken to see Mrs. Wright. When Mrs. Wright heard that Enid could sew, she was very elated. Enid liked the job very much. She would be getting a weekly wage of fifteen shillings, and she didn't even have to buy her own food. Immediately she made plans to send ten shillings per week by the market vendors that bought vegetables from her mother to her.

Within days of being at her new place of abode, she met the boy next door. He said his name was Reds, but that was what he was called, because he was of German descent from Saint Elizabeth. Reds worked as a gardener for the neighbors, and had been there for almost two years. That first day, they talked for hours, he on one side of the fence, and she on the other.

For the first three months, Mrs. Wright brought Enid dress materials and measurements and had her make dresses for just about all the women in the church. Sometimes she gave her dead-lines that caused her to stay up late at nights sewing. Enid did not get any days off, but was thankful that she could use left-over material to make clothes for herself and her sister. Once per week she visited the market and gave the traders clothes and letters with money to deliver to her mother and to her sister.

One day out of the blue, Mrs. Wright visited the store where Iris worked. Iris was surprised to see her. She hadn't been there since Enid started to work for her. She wondered if she came as a customer or just to say hi. There were no thought about Enid, because Iris spoke to her by telephone the day before, and all was well.

"Good morning Iris!" said Mrs. Wright.

Iris replied in kind.

"I want you to come to my house today after work. I have to speak to you and your niece together."

With that saying, she walked out. Iris did not ask her about what. She could not contact Enid by telephone, because she knew that she had no access to the phone when Mrs. Wright was out of the house. It was a Tuesday, and Iris wished that Mrs. Wright could have waited one more day, because the down town stores are closed at mid-day every Wednesday. Now she would have to get off work at five, take a bus up-town, and get another bus to Stony Hill to Mrs. Wright's house. For sure she would have to take a taxi from Stony Hill back to her house, because no bus runs there after six o'clock. That would cost her five shillings that could go towards something else. That upset her.

Iris arrived and saw Mrs. Wright sitting in her parlor waiting. Enid was summoned, and the three sat facing each other. She was very surprised to see her Godmother. She hadn't seen her since she went to live with Mrs. Wright, and wondered what the occasion was all about. She was about to find out.

"Glad you could make it," said Mrs. Wright.

Iris nodded in acknowledgement, and showed her anxiety about the meeting by her restlessness in the chair.

"Well, I have no children," continued Mrs. Wright. "But over the years I've employed quite a few young ladies here, so I've gained enough experience to recognize when some are in the family way."

Both Enid and Godmother looked at each other with the most surprising looks ever. Enid had suspicions that something was not normal, but needed more time to confirm her fears. She had never had sex before she met Reds, and every time since that first time she had insisted that they use protection.

"Did you come here with it?" asked Godmother.

"No mam," answered Enid.

Iris was relieved that the damage was not done by Darrell, but she wanted to know who, and hoping that it wasn't the minister. As she asked the next question, she braced herself for the answer.

"Well, who did this to you?"

"Reds mam," answered Enid.

"Reds, who the hell is Reds?" asked Iris, furiously.

"The gardener next-door," answered Mrs. Wright.

All three were quiet for a long while. Enid held her head down, and Mrs. Wright looked at Iris enquiringly.

"Do Mrs. Wright," Iris said, pleadingly. "Since it is not showing as yet, please let her stay here a little longer, and then I will take her. You see mam it would be so shameful for her to go home like this. They would laugh her to scorn."

"Okay, she is a nice girl, and a willing worker," said Mrs. Wright. "But I will have to cut her pay to ten shillings, now that I will have to feed two, and she will have sick days."

With the reduction in pay and the prenatal care expense, Enid could no longer afford to send the usual ten shillings to her mother, she continued however to write to her sister. They had made a pact that when little sister gets out of school that she Enid would have her own place in Kingston, and they both stay together, so she would assume that big sister is saving money towards that end. Enid asked Iris not to tell any of the country folks about her pregnancy.

Month after month, Mary had written to her daughter Enid and got no reply. Enid refused to write to her mother, because one; there was no money to send, and two; she knew that at some point the subject of pregnancy would come up, and she would have to tell her. Mary had warned Enid just before she left for Kingston that if she ever have to have sex before she was married to make sure she used protection, so she would definitely feel let-down, because that is how mothers feel when their daughters go off to Kingston to work, and within a short time period they return expecting babies. Mary did write to Iris to enquire about Enid, and Iris replied that she was okay, but was having some slight money problems, and that they would both be visiting for Christmas.

The baby, a bouncing boy was born in October at the new Kingston Jubilee Hospital. Iris took Enid and the baby to live with her three days after the birth. She was very proud of Enid and the baby that she took that week off work and had a party at her house, and boasted to the neighbors that she had a grandson. She was given presents and money.

Enid kept up the correspondence with her sister through the mail, but did not tell her of the pregnancy, nor the baby, although she had mentioned Reds in most of her letters, and told her that she would be bringing someone special that is related to Reds to meet her.

As the weeks went by, the two women made their plans for the Christmas season trip.

Four days before Christmas, on a Wednesday, Enid, her Godmother and the baby boarded the westbound Diesel train at Darling Street ten-thirty in the morning. Wednesdays are usually the best day to travel on the train, because the next day Thursday is not a market day, therefore there were no market people with food baskets to contend with. But because of the holiday, the train was packed like sardines in a tin with school children going home for the Christmas season.

By the time they got to Spanish Town, because of the clustering of people in the coach section where Enid and Godmother were with the baby, he was crying uncontrollably.

Iris asked the conductor to up-grade their tickets to the first class section where it was less crowded. He did, but at the cost of what it was from Kingston. They were glad for the opportunity, but Iris complained about the cost well after they were reseated.

A man in the seat behind her asked her what the extra charge was for.

"Five shilling sah," replied Iris. *"A whole five shilling. Yu noh hu much bread five shilling caa buy."*

"Five shillings sir. "All of five shillings?" Do you know how much bread five shillings can buy?"

The man gave Iris a ten shilling note and told her to put the change into the baby's piggy bank.

A woman who was sitting beside the same man gave Iris a two shilling piece and said, *"Put dis wid it."*

"Put this with it."

Another man who was sitting in the same row of seats, across the aisle, got up, took his hat off, and in his drunken stupor said;

"Come on everybody. Let's help out grandma here. Its' Christmas, lets spread the joy."

He walked up and down the aisle collecting money. Some people put money in hurriedly just to get him and the smell of rum from their faces.

When he handed the hat to Iris it was full and heavy. The paper currencies in all denominations were on top of the coins. There were gold coins, silver coins and copper coins. Enid picked up the baby from the basinet and Iris emptied the contents of the hat under the blanket. All the passengers clapped and sang Christmas carols the rest of the way.

Six hours and a hundred and nine miles after Enid, her baby and her Godmother boarded the train, the conductor announced; 'Three miles to Catadupa'. They collected their luggage and waited for the train to stop. As the train crawled into the station, Enid noticed her little sister peering intently into the coach cars as the first class section of the train moved pass her. She stepped off the train with the basinet in hand. Godmother was behind her with the baby and paying close attention to the man handling their suitcases.

Enid tried to get her sister's attention, but she was in the middle of the crowd of people getting off and getting on the coach section of the train. Finally as the crowd thinned and the train began to move, little sister looked toward the front of the train and saw Enid. Her face went from a frown to an ear to ear smile as she ran to meet big sister.

The two sisters hugged and laughed for a while. Little sister did not see Godmother with the baby. She looked at her sister from head to toe and said; "Sis you look thin. Are you sick? And where is this special person you said you were taking to meet me? Show him to me so I can help him with the luggage.

Enid pointed to Godmother whose back was turned. Little sister had the most puzzling look on her face. Just then Iris turned around.

"Jesas," shouted Pam.

"No, not Jesas," said Enid. "He is your nephew, and he is the special person.

Pam lightly kissed Iris and grabbed the baby from her.

Iris hailed for a taxi. It was the last one on the stand, and it was an old two colored Austin Cambridge that was teasingly called 'Mayreach'. The two sisters and the baby sat in the rear seat and Iris seated herself in the front passenger seat. Some boys who were standing around gave the car a push, so it could be started. The car smoked the entire three and a half miles to Cho Cho Gulley. Not just ordinary automobile exhaust smoke, but big clouds of black smoke.

They pulled up at the gate, and Darrell approached the car. The baby was sleeping, probably being drunk from the exhaust smoke of the car. Pam rushed with him into the house to avoid the mosquitoes buzzing around in the yard.

"Don't just stand around," said Iris to Darrell. "Get the suitcases. Where is Mary?"

She paid the driver and he drove off.

"Mary gone fe get de goat dem," answered Darrell, as he balanced the two heavy suitcases, one in each hand.

"Mary is gone to get the goats."

Pam had secured the sleeping baby under a mosquito net and was getting the kerosene oil lamps lit as darkness was setting in. Mary and the goats arrived and she locked them into a fenced area before stepping up on the verandah where Enid and Iris were standing.

They greeted each other with much excitement. Then Mary looked at her daughter. Up, down and up again.

"Gyal, a how yu soh mawga?" she asked. *"Dem noh feed yu weh yu ben deh?"*

"Girl, why are you so meager? Don't they feed you where you were?"

Before Enid could respond to her mother, the baby awoke and made a short discomforting sound.

"*A wa dat mi hear soun like duppy,*" said Mary.

"What is that I hear that sounds like a ghost?"

All three looked at each other, and for about ten seconds there was complete silence. It was as if they were waiting to hear the sound again to verify whether it was a ghost or not. Pam had finished lighting the lamps and picked up the baby. As she walked through the doorway with him in her arms to the verandah a ray of the lamp light shone on his red face.

"Jesas Cryice," shouted Mary.

"No Mama," said Pam. "He is your grandson."

Mary spent the next few minutes weeping uncontrollably before she said;

"**Gad bless mi eyesight. Phillip look dung ya. Yu have a gran pickni.**"

"God bless my eyesight. Phillip, look down here. You have a grandchild."

She hugged both of her daughters, and chided Iris for not telling her of Enid's pregnancy.

Mary did not leave dinner for her visitors. She was not expecting them until Friday. Pam however had gone to the train station every day since Monday, and every evening she left the greater portion of her dinner for her sister, plus she had roasted sweet potatoes and yams she had hidden. Darrell milked some goats and they all ate and retired for the night. The two friends sat up talking into the night and so did the two sisters.

At the light of day, Mary went out to the kitchen to make breakfast. Darrell had already left. He and his partner would be gone all day and all night, and return early Friday morning to catch the Christmas-eve grand market with their catch of fish. Mary also needed to procure produce from her garden in time for the traders, who usually show up between nine and ten in the morning. She was anxious to talk to Enid about the baby's father, about marriage, and about saving money for Pam to learn to sew and to get a sewing machine. Also the house building needed to be completed. No work had been done on it since Phillip died, and Darrell refused to spend any money on it until Mary is married to him. Her thoughts were full of what she wanted to say and to know.

Iris, the girls and the baby were up, had freshened up and ate by the time Mary had finished her chores. Mary called for them to sit around the kitchen table with her.

"I have a lot of things to talk about," she said. "But, first things first."

"Yes mama," Pam interrupted. "First things first. While you two were up gallivanting last night, and Enid was asleep, I took the liberty of counting the money that was in the baby's basinet, and guess how much it is. Nine hundred and thirty-five shillings."

"Laud mi Gad," said Mary. *"Weh all dat money come fram. Teekya oonu mek police come come tek weh all a wei.*

"Lord my God. Where did all that money come from? Take care you all don't cause police to come here and take us all away."

"Godmother," called Enid. "Please explain to her quickly, before she gets a heart attack."

Iris explained the incident that happened on the train. Mary was relieved.

"Now back to wa mi wawn noh," she said. *"De be-aiby is tree mont ole. A time fe im chrissen, an Sundey a come is Chrismus Sundey. Dere is no betta time. Every Dick Taam an Harry wei deh deh. Wei caa kill two guout an a pig an mek all de neighbor dem come nyam. Mi proad seh mi pickni neva dash weh belly like some a dem weh gaw a Kingston fe goh look wok. Instead dem goh look man."*

"Now, back to what I wanted to know. The baby is three months old. Its' time for him to be christened. Sunday coming is Christmas Sunday. There is no better time. Every Dick, Tom and Harry will be there. We can kill two goats and a pig and let all the neighbors come and eat. I am proud that my child never had an abortion, like some of these girls that go to Kingston to look for work. Instead they go looking for men."

"Stop Mary," Iris yelled. "The child is already christened. His name is Phillip James Peter Eubanks. Mrs. Wright is his Godmother."

"Enoh mek no difference," retorted Mary. *"Im caa chrissen aghen. Nutten wrang wid a double duouse of blessen. Wei ha fe goh ahead wid de plan. Mi wawn everybody to noh dat mi proad a mi pickni."*

"It makes no difference. He can be christened again. There is nothing wrong with a double dose of blessings. We have to go ahead with the plan. I want all to know that I am proud of my child."

The arrangements were made and on Sunday the baby was christened again. People from far and near attended the service and brought presents for the baby. Mary was surprised to see some of Phillip's relatives at the reception. Ever since he had married Mary, the family ostracized him, because he married out of the Indian race. Now they brought gifts of chicken and young goats for the baby. The girls were happy to see them, as this was the first time they were meeting most of them.

Monday the twenty-sixth, was celebrated as Christmas, and Tuesday was celebrated as Boxing-day. That day Iris and Enid boarded the train and travelled to Kingston, leaving the baby to be taken care of by Mary and Pam. The following day Iris went back to work and Enid started on a new job at the Children's Clothing Store next door to where her Godmother worked.

Over the ensuing months Enid would visit Mrs. Wright on some weekends in pretense so that she could see Reds. They had no telephone contact, so they both looked forward to her visits. Occasionally when he got a Sunday off, they would meet at a hotel near down town, but it was always Enid who had to pay the ten shillings for the room. On one such meeting, the subject of marriage came up. It was then that Enid realized that, one; Reds could not read or write, two; that he was only earning twelve shillings per week despite working seven days at two adjoining homes which belong to the same family, and three; out of the twelve shillings, he had to send ten to the country for the support of his fatherless siblings.

Enid was earning an average of twenty-five shillings per week, but that was not enough to pay rent for them to stay together and with money left to send to her mother for the baby, and for work to be done on the house. She explained the situation to her Godmother.

"If you are serious about this, then I applaud you both," said Iris. "Here is my advice. First you have to prepare yourself to see this through. It might be a better idea to rent a cheap room for him, say fifteen shillings a month. Have him register in two of the free government programs that will provide both literacy and skill. He could also get a weekend gardening job to provide money for food. If his head and heart are in the right place, in six months he'll be earning good money. I did the same thing for my ex-fiancé"

"For real, Godmother?" asked Enid. "I didn't know you had a fiancée. You never talked about him."

"No, we split, because he wanted a family and I was not able to get pregnant."

In the mean-time Mrs. Wright was of the opinion that Enid and the baby was living with Iris. One day she visited Iris on her job and enquired about Enid and the baby. She was on the way out of the store when she turned around and said;

"By the way, lately there has been something that is weighing heavily on my mind, and sometimes I stay up all night thinking about it."

Iris was bewildered by the complaint, and wondered if Mrs. Wright was blaming herself for Enid's pregnancy, or if she doubted who the baby's father was. She had not seen the baby, since the christening and could have doubts about the Minister's involvement. That was not a worry for Iris.

"Oh Mrs. Wright," said Iris. "I am so sorry. Please tell me about it and if there is anything at all that I can do. I'll be glad to do it."

"My dear, this is not easy for me," said Mrs. Wright. "I would love to have your niece to come back. The first time I did not treat her right. All those dresses that I had her to make for my church sisters, I did collect a reasonable price from them, which I should have shared with her, but I did not. Now I want to give her half of that money that was due to her, if she comes back. If I can sleep half the night, I would be contented."

The two women shook hands, and Iris promised to talk to Enid, but she knew that Mrs. Wright wanted to make money off her, besides the job at the Children's Clothing store paid well.

By the baby's first birthday, Reds had completed the Skills program and had secured his first real job as a carpenter's helper. He continued in the Literacy program. The wedding was planned for the Christmas Sunday at the same country church where Enid's parents were married.

Note; You can get there from anywhere!

Lafey

Lafayette Charles first visited Jamaica when he was twelve years old. He had gone there with his Mom and Dad for a one month vacation. His father was born on the island, but went to live with his father in England at the age of six. His mother was a French citizen, studying medicine in England when she met and married Lafayette's father, Carl who was a classmate.

Her Caucasian parents did not approve of the marriage, primarily because her husband was half-white, so they stopped supporting her education. To make matters worse; she became pregnant within months after the wedding. To support the new family, both the newly-weds dropped out of school, and got employment; he as a medical assistant, and she as a waitress.

They migrated to the United States when Lafayette was six, and the family settled in Hartford, Connecticut. The husband continued to be employed as a medical assistant, and his wife continued as a waitress.

Lafayette did not know any of his relatives, other than his parents. His father's father had died before he was born, his father's mother died in Jamaica at a young age. The story told to Lafayette was that his French relatives could not be located and his Jamaican relatives were all distant cousins. He had heard so much about Jamaica from his school buddies, and especially one of the neighbor's boy his age who was a Jamaican immigrant, that he often pretended to be a Jamaican, and even learnt some Patwa words and phrases.

Every year at vacation time he begged his parents to take him to Jamaica, and finally they booked the flight on his twelfth birthday so he could spend time on the island, and also because the fare for children under twelve was half price.

Their accommodations on the island was at a luxurious hotel in Montego Bay. The room had two beds, and a sleeper sofa. They were happy with the service, the food and the amenities.

The day after they arrived was Lafayette's birthday, and the hotel facilitated by providing cake and ice-cream, candles, and some of the staff to sing Happy Birthday. Before the singing was over, the hotel manager went to Mr. Charles and said;

"Sir, we need to adjust the figures on your account."

"What for, may I ask?" retorted Mr. Charles.

"You see sir," answered the manager. "The rules are that children under the age of twelve, stays for free. Now that your son is out of that category, you will have to pay more."

"Oh, I see," said Mr. Charles. "Tomorrow he is leaving to stay with relatives."

This was quite unexpected, because the funds were limited, and it would be difficult to pay a higher hotel fee, particularly at that hotel, and it would not be any cheaper to cut their vacation short. The Airline fare was non-refundable, and the hotel would only refund fifty percent, so moving to a cheaper hotel was out of the question.

There were little or no plans to find relatives. Mr. Charles had left Jamaica almost thirty years before, and there had been no contact with anyone there. He vaguely remembered his mother on her death bed, writing to his father in England for him to come to Jamaica and get him.

'If he doesn't come' she said. 'You will have to go to the Cockpit Mountain in Trelawney and stay with some cousins'.

He had one thing going for him. He remembered that on the plane going to England his father showed him a photo of his mother, and told him that her name was Mary Edgecombe. Although the picture was in black-and-white, and a little bit crumpled, he recognized her as the very pretty woman of fair complexion and with freckled face that he knew only as Mommy. She was a hotel maid, and they lived in the servant's quarters on the hotel grounds. He remembered also that she was very ill and was taken to the hospital before his father came and got him.

The next morning the family got up earlier than usual. They each had Continental breakfasts served by the hotel, before they hailed a taxi. Mrs. Charles was not too happy to accompany them and had to be promised that they would be back before three o'clock so that she could keep her appointment on the tennis court.

After much enquiry along the way, they reached a village that was supposedly where some Edgecombe's used to live. It was no surprise that no one there knew of anyone by the name of Mary Edgecombe.

Mr. Charles started to make contingent plans. One; both he and his wife were wearing expensive watches that they could sell and probably get enough money to pay for their son's stay at the hotel. But the watches were of great sentimental value. Instead of rings at their wedding ceremony, they gave each other gold watches. Two; Mrs. Charles could probably get a job as a waitress at one of the restaurants within walking distance of their hotel. She just couldn't tell them that she was a tourist. He did not like any of those options.

It was just past mid-day when they stopped at a roadside grocery shop and bought some refreshment. While they were on the piazza enjoying their light lunch, a young man in his twenties approached Mr. Charles, rather discreetly, and asked;

"Do you wanna buy some weed?"

"Do you want to buy some marijuana?"

"Only if he or she is related to Mary Edgecombe," replied Mr. Charles.

An old man about in his late seventies, or early eighties was walking out of the shop and turned around quickly when he heard the name. He was wearing old and tattered khaki clothes, and sandals made from used automobile tire. Under his armpit he had a roll of twisted tobacco leaves that he had just purchased from the shop. He looked at the Charles family members one by one, and up and down, then he transferred the tobacco from his armpit to a trouser pocket before he extended his right hand to Mr. Charles.

"Sar," he said. *"I noh hea dat ne-aim fe toh-ty supm yeas. Gad bless yu. An a who yu be sah."*

"Sir, I hadn't heard that name for thirty something years. God bless you. And who are you sir?"

"Just someone who knew her thirty something years ago," replied Mr. Charles.

"Yu look kine a young fa har," said the old man. *"Anyway she was a very pretty gal, ongle she ha freckle. Freckle fe-ace dem always tease har. De Edgecombe did'n want har. Very prejudice breed dem was. See dem was well-to-do. Grow a lot a coffee in dem mountin. She was raise by har maddaz faambly, de Henry dem, because har po madda die at chile burt. Den she goh aff to Mo Beay an come back wid a white man. Nex ting she goh a obeah man fe get rid a de freckle. De damn ginnal tek har money, an give har piesen loution. Kill aff de po gal."*

"You do look young to have been her suitor. Anyway she was a very pretty girl. Only that she had freckles. Teasingly they called her Freckle Face. The Edgecombes didn't want her. They were a very prejudiced set. They were wealthy people. They grew a lot of coffee in those mountains. She was raised by her mother's family, the Henrys'. Her mother died at child's birth. Mary went off to Montego Bay, and came back with a white man. The next thing was that she went to a voodoo man to get rid of the freckles. He scammed her and gave her poison lotion. That killed the poor girl."

It was with much anticipation that Mr. Charles asked the next question.

"Are any of these people around today?"

"De Edgecombe dem all dead out, an wid no picknie to claim de lan, de govament tek e, but de Henry dem til de bout," said the old man. *"A whole villige a dem deh bout two mile dung de road."*

"The Edgecombes are all dead, and with no offspring to claim the land, it was reverted to the government, but the Henrys are still around. There is a whole village of them about two miles down the road."

Mr. Charles gave the old man a U.S. ten dollar bill and told him thanks.

The taxi rolled slowly down the road as all eyes gazed outside for the bamboo-railed gateway that they were directed to turn to find the Henry's village. It was on the right, exactly two miles as the old man had said.

The car was not air-conditioned so the windows were rolled down to allow breeze to pass through as the car moved. The driver slowed to a stop at the gate and the heat of the mid-afternoon summer sun played a number on the tourists. Mrs. Charles was perspiring profusely, but she was plainly more upset about missing her tennis match, than she was about the heat.

The driver got out and opened the gate. He then got back in and moved the car slowly through the narrow space before he returned to close the gate. He got back into the car just as a large cow was running toward him. The road was a dirt track in the middle of a pasture. The car inched slowly up a hill, and from the top, the view was spectacular. The tops of fifty or more small houses could be seen. They were all corrugated zinc with a kaleidoscope of colors. All the houses were within a few feet of each other, with the biggest in the middle, and the others spread out in circles around it.

As the car moved close to the group of houses, another bamboo-railed gate was in sight. The driver visibly showed his disgust as it became obvious that he would have to get out of the car to open that second gate. Some cows that were following the car gathered around it. If he was praying, then his prayer was answered when a man came galloping on a mule. He opened the gate and went to the driver's window and asked what his mission was. Mr. Charles poked his head out the window and said;

"My name is Carl Charles. I am the son of Mary Edgecombe."

"Oh my, my," said the man. "I haven't seen you since you were two or three. We were very disappointed when we saw her at the hospital, and she told us that your father took you to England. We wanted you, but now you are here. Come follow me."

The man rode off toward the complex of houses, and the taxi followed.

The roof of the big building in the center that was seen from the top of the hill was not really a house, but more like a marquee. The man on the mule rode up toward the center, and the taxi driver followed and stopped beside a small pick-up truck.

A crowd of about sixty people of all ages from infant to seniors gathered as the visitors alighted the car. The man who rode the mule stood in the middle of the crowd and announced himself as Mr. Charles' grand-uncle. He was a six-foot muscular red man in his late sixties, or early seventies with large lamb-chop side burns, handle-bar mouth stash, and curly red head hair.

"Faamly," he said. *"Dis is our son dat was loss fa thurty yeas. Now hes back. Lets welcome him home."*

"Family, This is our son that was lost for thirty years. Now he is back. Let us welcome him home."

The crowd cheered, and one by one they shook hands and hugged the Charles.

The taxi driver enquired if he should wait or leave. Mr. Charles said for him to leave, and Mrs. Charles said for him to wait. Both at the same time. After some consultation with the grand-uncle whose name was Henrique, the taxi driver was paid and he left.

Under the big roof was a huge kitchen and dining area, a produce storage area, a farm tool storage area, a carpenter work shop, a laundry area, a mezzanine floor that seemed to serve as a worship area, and other partitioned areas for various purposes. All the small buildings in the complex were merely sleeping quarters or animal shelters.

A feast was being prepared. By the time it took to show the Charles around the residential part of the compound, family members had butchered a goat and some chickens, and the smell of meat cooking was emanating from the kitchen.

The meal was served and everyone sat at a table that was no less than twenty-five feet long. Henrique said a grace and told everyone to dig in. Half way through the meal Mrs. Charles spoke, amidst the clatter of utensils and dishes;

"This is by far the best meal I've ever had, and before I leave I am begging you to give me some lessons. I would love to prepare this at home for my family."

"My dear," said Henrique. "Part of our secret is that the only thing from the outside is the salt, but you are welcome to stay as long as you wish. I am sure that my ladies will be glad to share the family recipes with you, and you can come back anytime"

Lafayette whispered to his mother; "Mom, the neighbor back home, Rufus' mother, she cooks like this all the time, and she got everything from the supermarket, but remember she is Jamaican."

After the meal, the clan split into groups. Some teen-age girls and young women went to the kitchen, some young adult males went to attend to animals, the older men including Mr. Charles went to relax and chat on the mezzanine, and the adult women including Mrs. Charles remained in the dining area. Lafayette and about ten boys near his age were in an area sorting out parts and choosing teams for an indoor game when there was a frightening cry from the dining area. It was from Mrs. Charles. Everyone in the building ran close only to see her bent over in her seat. None of them knew what had happened. Surprisingly Mr. Charles and Lafayette remained calm. They had seen that scene before.

Within a few seconds Mrs. Charles held her head up and said;

"I am so sorry. I have this ailment that takes me without warning, and its' very painful, but it only last for a few seconds. I had forgotten to take the medication before I ate."

"Oh you poor dear," remarked one of the elderly women. "We have to take you to the mountain to get rid of it."

"To the mountain! What mountain," asked Mr. Charles.

"Oh honey," said the old lady. "The Cockpit Mountain of course. People come from all over the world and got cured for everything except death. We'll take her there tomorrow."

The next morning before dawn one of the teen age boys, Mr. and Mrs. Charles left in the pick-up truck to travel twenty-eight miles to the foot of the mountain. They got to a parking area which was as far as automobile could go. It was still dark and there were about a dozen other vehicles parked there. Some men with donkeys for rent approached them and advised that without their donkeys they could not reach the Guzzu-man at the top of the mountain before noon, and by then it would be too late. Mr. Charles complained that the donkey rental rate was exorbitant, but his relative encouraged him to pay the fee. Neither Mr. Charles, nor his wife had ever been on a donkey, so they were both given lessons on how to stay in the saddle. The teenager walked the distance. He would bring the donkeys back for other renters, and would return for the Charles in the evening.

In the dark the donkeys climbed the very narrow pathway toward the home of the Guzzu-man.

The sun was just coming up at the horizon when they reached the edifice at the top of the hill, and both the Charles's were surprised to see such an opulent and huge structure in such a remote area.

They dismounted their rides and were ushered to a waiting room. There they saw about twenty people, including children, seated on overstuffed upholstered sofas. Some of them looked healthy, and others very sick to the point of constant groaning. The people in the room were as varied as any twenty people could have been. Some looked and spoke like tourists. There were black people, white people, Chinese people, Indian people, men, women, children including infants, and there were also people of different languages. Mrs. Charles recognized French, German and Spanish, all of which she herself spoke fluently.

At exactly ten o'clock, on a first-come first-served basis, people in the waiting area were shown into an inner room. They emerged through a different door fifteen minutes later looking drunk and sleepy. Each was led to an area with military style cots where they went to sleep.

At a quarter to twelve it was Mrs. Charles' turn to enter the inner room, and Mr. Charles accompanied her. The Guzzu-man was a slender five-foot six copper colored, Indian looking with a thin goatie beard. His accent was more like a Trinidadian than a Jamaican. After he heard Mrs. Charles's complaint, he gave her a pint tumbler with a dark colored liquid, and told her to drink.

"Wait a minute," blurted Mr. Charles. "I demand to know what kind of concoction you are ordering my wife to drink."

"You want she cure or what," asked the Guzzu-man.

"Do you want her to be cured or not."

"Yes, I want her cured, but just yesterday I was told that thirty years ago some quack doctor gave my mother a potion that took her life. I do not want the same thing happening to my wife; besides don't expect that I am going to pay an arm and a leg for something that doesn't work or make her to be sicker."

"Relax me fren," said the Guzzu-man. *"An since you waan noh. Dere is about a dozen difran bush in it. De main one is ganja an nooni an moringa. De ganja an de nooni cheap, dem grow hea, but de moringa is very dere. Mi have to goh a India an bring it back. De treatment is guarantee ar yu bring har back far annada dose an you will pay far it wedda she drink it ar not."*

"Relax my friend, and since you want to know. There are about a dozen different types of bushes into it. The main ones are the marijuana, the Nooni and the Moringa. The Marijuana and the Nooni are cheap. They grow here, but the Moringa is very expensive. I have to go to India to procure it. The treatment is guaranteed, or you bring her back for another dose, and you will pay for it, whether she drinks it or not."

With some coaxing from her husband, Mrs. Charles swallowed the insipid liquid.

No sooner than the last few drops escaped down her throat that her eyes rolled in their sockets, hiding her pupils, then she slumped over in her seat. Two men rushed in, and one on each side of her walked her to one of the cots. Mr. Charles got up to follow, but the Guzzu-man stood before him and said;

"Money mi fren. Yu wife will be okay when she we-ake"

"Money my friend. Your wife will be okay when she wakes up"

"How much money?"

"Tree undred dallaz."

Mr. Charles' eyes bulged, and for a few seconds he was speechless.

"Three hundred dollars! I don't have that kind of money with me'.

The Guzzu-man gazed at Mr. Charles' wrist watch.

"Who much you were expecting to peay?"

"How much were you expecting to pay?"

"Fifty dollars. Seventy-five tops."

"Gimmie mi de seventy-five an you watch an yu have sevin deays to come back far it."

"Give me the seventy-five and your watch. You will have seven days to reclaim it."

Mr. Charles complied, then went back to the waiting room and sat with his head in his hands.

At two o'clock a neatly dressed young lady offered the waiting guests roasted beef and hard-dough bread sandwiches and fruit juice. Mr. Charles ate the sandwich, but refused the drink.

At three o'clock he noticed that all the people that were there when he arrived had left. He asked an attendant to see if his wife was awake so that they could leave. The attendant returned in a few minutes and told him that it might take another hour or two.

"Why so long," asked Mr. Charles.

"Because sir," answered the attendant. "When the doctor gives a guarantee he made sure the guest do not return."

When they finally walked out of the building the sun was at the horizon going down. The teenage relative was waiting with the two donkeys. Mrs. Charles did not speak for the entire journey back to the village, and Mr. Charles wasted no words in his regret of the trip. Although he could have only imagined the pain and embarrassment his wife had suffered all the years, he told himself that he could live with it.

They arrived at the village and Mrs. Charles went straight to bed.

The next morning immediately after breakfast the same teenage relative drove them to their hotel in Montego Bay. Lafayette returned with them, but only to pick up his clothes and toys.

The weeks passed quickly for Lafayette, but slowly for his parents. There were days when Mrs. Charles did not get out of bed, despite the urging of her husband. The once vivacious and outgoing bombshell did not even keep up with her personal hygiene on some days. The one good thing she found out while she was neglecting herself was that the Guzzu-man's potion worked.

When it was time to leave it was Mr. Charles who returned to the Henry's village to get their son.

On the way from the village to Montego Bay Lafayette could not stop talking. He told his father that all the children wanted to play with him; from the time he wakes up in the mornings to the time he went to bed at nights. Early every morning they would shake him out of his sleep, saying 'Lafey, Lafey lets go play'.

He wanted for the family to spend every summer in Jamaica so that he can be back to the village. His father promised him that if his grades are good he could return when he gets to be fifteen.

On the plane home Mrs. Charles was lively and her husband was glad to see her being happy, but she was only putting on a show so that their son would not see the hurt she was feeling. It wasn't until that first night back home when Carl Charles tried to be intimate with his wife that she told him that she was raped by the bush doctor and needed to see her own doctor the next day.

"Why didn't you say something to me?" He asked, in a rage.

"Because honey, she replied. "I was afraid they would hurt both of us. He has some goons working with him."

"Okay, that's' it for me and that country. They killed my mother, and now look what they've done to my wife. Our son will never set foot down there again. I promised to write to my relatives, but now, forget it."

"Its' not the whole country honey," said his wife, consolingly. "It's just some very bad people there. Please do not let our son get wind of this."

Over the succeeding three years, Lafayette became a high school student and did exceedingly well. His friend and neighbor Rufus had moved across town to the Bloomfield area and they exchanged visits every other Saturday. His father continued on his job, but his mother stayed home to, in her words, 'to write a book on her life'.

Lafayette celebrated July fourth at his friend's house in Bloomfield. He was looking forward to his fifteenth birthday in five weeks, and also looking forward to travelling to Jamaica to spend the rest of the summer. He had done exceptionally well in school and in his mind there was absolutely no reason why his father would not fulfill his promise.

A week before his birthday he started to pack his clothes and the presents he had bought to take for his relatives. He asked his father if the ticket had been bought.

"No," he said. "Something had happened and you will have to cancel that trip."

"What is it Dad?" Lafayette asked.

"I can't talk about it."

Lafayette went to his mother to find out why he wouldn't be going to Jamaica. She was standing at the kitchen sink when he asked her, and without answering she started to cry and rushed to her room. He went back to his dad who was working on the family's car at the side of the house.

"Daddy, Why is Mommy upset when I mentioned Jamaica to her," he asked.

"I told you that something had happened and I cannot talk about it," replied Mr. Charles.

Lafayette was upset, disappointed and perplexed. He was upset for not knowing why his parents were upset. He was disappointed because he had gotten the good grades and his father had reneged on his promise, and he was perplexed because he knew nothing of what happened.

Rufus's mother was surprised to see Lafayette at her house on a Thursday.

"Lafayette what are you doing here today?' She asked, "You were here last Saturday, and Saturday coming is Rufus' turn to be at your house."

"Yes mam, but my parents are upset, and I do not want to be around them when they are like that."

"Are they upset at you?"

"No mam."

"Oh, they are upset at each other"

"No mam, they are just upset."

"How did you get here?"

"I rode my bicycle mam."

"Isn't it dangerous for you to ride this far."

"Maybe, but I was real careful.

"Okay, I'll call later and talk with them," said Rufus's mother. "In the meantime make yourself at home. Lucky for you that school is out or I wouldn't have you here."

The call was made and Lafayette's mother gave the okay for him to stay.

Rufus's father runs a Jerk-chicken Joint and was first very apprehensive when the boys offered to do daytime delivery in the immediate neighborhood. The arrangement was exactly what Lafayette wanted. He had plans to save enough money to buy his ticket and have money for spending in Jamaica.

The summer went by, and from his share of tips he saved seventy-eight dollars.

At the beginning of that school year he went back to school as a junior, and by the first reporting period his parents noticed that his grades had dropped off. They contacted the school only to find out that he had failed one class. After further investigation it was revealed that he did not attend his class on Fridays after the lunch period.

After much prodding, he reluctantly told them that Friday afternoons are the times when Jerk-chicken customers gave the most tips. His father agreed to add half the amount of tips that he normally made to his allowance, so that he stays in school.

By the beginning of the following summer Lafayette had saved enough money to buy his ticket.

He told his parents of his intentions, and asked for additional money for his pocket.

"Son, I would advise you to save your money for college," said his father.

"But Dad," retorted Lafayette. "I had my mind set on it, besides you promised, and as soon as I can save enough money I am going, whether you like it or not."

"Son! There are some very bad people in Jamaica, and we are trying to shield you from them." Mr. Charles was calm in his remark.

The following year Lafayette graduated from high school, and by this time he had enough money for his trip. But there were two obstacles; one his parents were still adamant about him not to go to Jamaica, so they hid his passport, and two; he was not yet eighteen to apply for a new one without the consent of a parent or guardian.

He moved out of his parent's home, and for the first few weeks they were not overly concerned about him, thinking that he was with Rufus. It wasn't until Rufus went to them to find out where he was that they realized their son had disappeared. They searched the neighborhoods, reported his disappearance to the police, and even offered a reward for information leading to his whereabouts.

A year had passed, and Mrs. Charles was just getting over her double-dipped bout of depression that she was able to return to work.

One evening she opened her mailbox and found a letter from Jamaica addressed to Mr. and Mrs. Carl Charles. The sender was one of the Henrys' but the writing on the envelope was distinctly that of Lafayette. Hurriedly, she opened the envelope and read the short note. It simply stated; 'Sorry, but I need money. Reply to the sender quickly'.

She contemplated on what to do, knowing that her husband was still very disappointed in their son. She wrote a note; 'Get to a public phone and call collect, any evening after six or anytime weekends. Love you still'. Then she went to the nearest Convenience store and bought a one hundred dollar money order, and mailed it off.

Her husband got home late that night, and she waited until the next morning to show him the letter.

"I am not going to send him a dime," said Carl. "It was partly for his benefit that we went to Jamaica in the first place so that he could know relatives. All what happened wouldn't have happened. Let him stay there and rot."

Two weeks later, on a Sunday afternoon, Mrs. Charles was in the kitchen preparing dinner, and Mr. Charles was out at a community meeting when the call came in. She picked up the receiver and recognized her son's voice.

"Son, I love you and I want you home," she said.

"Mom, its' a long story."

"I know son, but tell me anyway."

He explained to her that he had disguised himself as a female and paid someone to marry him as such, and then with the marriage certificate he applied and received a passport. When he got to Jamaica his great-uncle Henrique had died and a younger family member named Ernell took over the leadership of the tribe. Most of the boys who were there when he first visited had moved out, primarily because they could not get along with Ernell. Things went well with Ernell and himself for a while, until a few months ago when Ernell caught him with one of his girlfriends.

"It was the day after I updated my ticket and made reservation to come home," said Lafayette. "The poor girl was just giving me a send-off so that I would remember her when I get home. He beat her severely. I felt sorry for her. He burned my passport and my return ticket and drove me out of the village. Since then I had been staying with friends here and there, but now I am ready to come home. The problem is that I have no passport or money."

She was very distraught to hear of his predicament, but was very glad to speak with him and to learn that he wanted to come home.

"Okay," she said. "I'll buy your ticket, and I'll send your passport and some money by registered mail. Please come home."

"Thanks Mom," he replied, and hung up the phone.

She listened to the signal on the phone for a while until an automated voice came on saying;

'If you would like to make a call please hang up and dial the number'.

She ignored the suggestion and did not hang the phone up until the beeping busy signal came on that was too much for her ear.

The next day she made the reservation and paid for the ticket, and then she mailed the itinerary, the passport and some money to the name and address that Lafayette directed her to.

On the day the registered letter arrived Lafayette only had one full day left in Jamaica before the flight. He and his friends decided that they would spend that last day smoking marijuana.

Previously they had been to a place in Saint Elizabeth where they purchased a lot of marijuana for very little money, but part of that purchase money was counterfeit bills.

The marijuana sellers did not know them, but they remembered that they were a party of two red boys and one white boy from Montego Bay. They were expecting them back for the cheap stuff, and they would be in for a surprise.

There is a vine bush in Jamaica that the natives called cows-itch. The scientific name of this hated plant is Mucuna Pryreins. The leaves has microscopic fibers that when in contact with the human skin it causes an agonizing itch for which only elapsed time and or sea water can relieve.

The three arrived at the sellers' place, and they were fed a lofty meal, after which they joined them and smoked a round of the good stuff. The sellers mixed the take-away portion with the cows-itch leaves and then gave them some friendly advice;

"Ef de police tap yu on de way, shub de stuff in yu brief, dey woun fine e'."

"If the police stop you on the way, put the marijuana into your briefs. They will not find it."

They were on the main road close to Montego Bay when they came up on a police road-block. The police ordered them out of the taxi they were in. Quickly Lafayette pushed the package into his briefs. No sooner than he did that, he started to jump like a child on a trampoline. The police retrieved the package and noticed that the cows-itch leaves were mixed with Marijuana.

Lafayette's friends were faced with the incongruity of the situation, but could do nothing to help. The police decided to add more havoc to the matter, and told Lafayette that the itching will stop if he defecate and rub it all over his testicles. He was glad for the advice, because not only was he in obvious torment, but because of the rush of blood in that area of his body, it caused him to have an enormous, and visible erection. His penis was as straight horizontally as a spear and just as hard.

He went into the nearby bushes and did what the police told him to do. Five minutes later he returned to the laugh of the police who then told them that they were free to leave. The taxi driver would not let Lafayette back into the car. "Run," he said. ***An jump in de ocean.***"

At first Lafayette thought that the taxi-man was making fun at him like the police did, until one of his friends nodded yes to him. The nearest shore of the ocean was three miles away.

He took off running, and the taxi followed behind at twenty miles per hour.

The next day he arrived at the Bradley International Airport in Hartford, and as soon as he alighted from the plane, he kissed the ground.

Note; There is no place like home!

Newman Thompson

In the Jamaican country side that Newman lived, he was known as the village lawyer. Many of the folks in the area affectionately called him Barrister. Some even thought that Barrister was his real name. The judicial court days were always on Wednesdays, and Newman would be in the court room whether he had a trial or not. He was well versed with the British court system in England. He had many run-ins with the law there, and because of his oratory skills and fast talking he had managed to stay a step or two ahead of the authorities.

He was the ring-leader of a scam organization that Scotland Yard was tracking when he boarded a ship for Australia, but disembarked at Casablanca, took another ship to Panama before flying to Jamaica.

Newman was forty seven years of age in nineteen-fifty-seven when he landed in Jamaica. He had been away from the island since he was fifteen. His parents were both English, but lived in Jamaica when he was born. They were both Caucasian, and so was Newman. The only ties he had in Jamaica, other than it is the land of his birth was a half-sister, which was his father's child, and three years his senior.

He was as broke; as the locals say; as a cote bird, when he landed at the Kingston International Airport. His sister had to pay the taxi that transported him to her house from the airport. He brought with him from England a sizeable trunk of his own clothes. Many were suits of mohair, wool, tweed and silk fabrics, and over the first few months of his return, he sold some for just enough cash for his pocket money. He was always well dressed, although some folks laughed at him for wearing woolen suits in July, the hottest summer month, but he never seemed to sweat.

His sister Gretel was a widow. She wasn't really poor, but neither was she wealthy. She had Real Estate, and earned her living from the annual crops of Allspice grown on her property. She made it clear to him that he would have to get a job to support himself, but he did not tell her that he had no marketable skills, at least none that was legal. It did not take long for Newman to find a lucrative way of earning money. Whenever someone in the vicinity had a court case, he would offer himself to them as a witness, and demanded that the payments should be a percentage of the awards. He guaranteed his clients that if they lose their case, they wouldn't have to pay. No matter what the cases were, Newman would convince the court that he was present at the occurrences, and he would be able to produce documents if necessary, to support his client's claims.

After only three years of his illegal law practice Newman Thompson became the owner of Real Estate, live-stock, jewelry and other valuables. He had a huge house custom built on the top of a small hill near the main road, and he would spare no expenses in throwing lavish parties.

Whenever he went to the downtown area, he would walk into a rum bar and ordered drinks for everyone present. When he had them tipsy, he would call for them to gather and listen to his world travel stories. At times he demanded that they pay him to tell his tales, and the more he was paid, the taller were his tales.

It was a rainy September day, and Newman was in a crowded rum bar, with dozens of men around him. They had already listened intently to two of his stories, and they decided to put money in a hat for him to tell more. Because of the rain, no one was in any hurry to go anywhere, so he felt compelled to entertain them.

"I was a British soldier for two full years, and hadn't been further than the base where I had done my training", he stared off. "Of course my troop had been on field trips and 'Exercise Exchanges' all over England, but none lasted for more than a fortnight. I was always fascinated by the stories told by soldiers returning from abroad. I was on one of those Exchanges when I made acquaintance with a soldier who was deployed to Australia for a year. He told me about an area in the interior of the country to the Northeast where gold nuggets lay on the bottom of a river just waiting to be picked up. He showed me some nuggets that he brought back, and had already sold the biggest of the lot.

Well, I got the necessary information for a voluntary deployment to Australia, and I signed up behind two thousand soldiers who may or may not have heard about the gold nuggets. I was very surprised when within two months the order came in for me to join troops being dispatched to the country. On the very day I entered the base in Queensland, I discreetly enquired for any soldier with like intentions. It took about three weeks to find Rupert Spence. He was on his second tour of duty there. I told him that I had heard about the river of nuggets, and he replied that he too had heard about it only weeks before the end of his last tour, and volunteered to return only because of his intention to go there. I felt comfortable with him as I was two ranks below his sergeant status.

Two weeks later we were granted three days of leave off-base. Rupert had the Army's Land Rover Jeep all fuelled up, and we left with a change of clothes each, some trinkets that he said were presents for the Aborigines we may encounter, and both of our service revolvers. We followed the map, and the first day we drove on winding paved roads. We had travelled more than three hundred miles that we figured by our map, we only had another hundred or so to get to the river of nuggets. That night we slept at a Bed-and-Breakfast operated by the last Caucasian Australian I would ever see for the next fifteen years.

At day break we set off, and within minutes came to the end of the paved road. We continued on in the same direction on a dry sunbaked clay road. That lasted for a few miles, and then we were driving through bumpy open fields with sparsely grown trees as well as shrubs and cactus. We had refueled at the last petrol station before the end of the paved road, plus we had two five gallon jugs filled, so we were not worried about the fuel to get there and back. It was my suggestion that we bought biscuits and some confectioneries to disperse to the natives, and Rupert agreed.

It was a very cloudy morning, and the sunrise glow was hidden, but we followed our compass and drove in a northerly direction. All was going fairly well until it started to rain, and the clay soil which allows slow drainage became slippery. As if that wasn't bad enough, the rain water formed puddles, and we couldn't tell which was deep, or which was shallow, and getting stuck was not an option.

We pondered whether to continue, or to turn around. 'It can't be far from here', Rupert said.' I can smell the gold. Let's get to those hills on the East of us to bypass the puddles'.

Well, it was one hill after another, and in our minds we sang the praises of the Land Rover Jeep four-wheel-drive. It went over tree stumps and boulders as if they were marbles in a child's play pen. By midday we were on the top of a hill with a river in sight through our binoculars. We hoped it was the nugget river, but in the distance, and close to the river was a village.

On the way the day before, Rupert told me some dreadful stories about a tribe of Aborigines who lived near the river, but nothing to worry about he said, because he spoke their language, and we had presents for them. Little did I know at that time that there were more than five hundred tribal languages in Australia.

As we drew close to the village, we saw a pathway through the shrubs, and we followed it. Unknown to us, we were headed straight into a trap. The villagers had set spikes in the ground that flattened all four of the tires of our Jeep at the same time. We dismounted the vehicle to inspect the damage. As I pondered what to do, I heard Rupert hollering, 'Run for your life'.

I barely had time to grab my bag and my revolver. We ran toward the North away from a mob of villagers chasing us with spears and machetes. Rupert fired his revolver, while running, and was lucky enough to hit a pack of dogs that were fast gaining on us, but that did not deter the mob, they kept on chasing us.

We reached the river at a bend where it narrowed. Rupert was ahead of me, and he jumped in. The poor fellow didn't stand a chance. Alligators came from everywhere and tore him to pieces in a matter of seconds. On seeing that, I turned around, saying to myself that it is better to face the mob than be killed by the alligators, but remembering the stories of torture that Rupert had told me, I made an abrupt turn, and headed up stream. I ran full speed and jumped and skipped on what I thought were two floating logs that turned out to be the backs of two large alligators.

About two hundred feet from the river's edge, I stopped and stared at the mob standing on the other side. I was bewildered, being more than three hundred miles from base, with no vehicle, and no companion. My wrist-watch showed a quarter to two. I began to walk in a Southerly direction, and after an hour or so, thirst and exhaustion begun to set in. I felt glad that I had my bag with the trinkets, biscuits and confectioneries, and best of all; I had my revolver fully loaded, so I lay in an open field, and went to sleep.

One hour later, as I was on my back asleep, I felt the strap of my bag being removed from under my shoulder. I slowly opened my eyes and gazed at about ten male Aborigines standing over me with wooden spears, stone axes and two torches. I reached for my revolver, but immediately I noticed that they had no idea what that was. None of them had even moved a muscle. They made talking sounds at me, but I couldn't understand anything they said, so I began to make signs with my hands. They asked me where I came from, and I made signs and told them that I came from the river. They shook their heads and told me with signs that no man can cross the river. I asked them why, and they showed me the signs of the alligators. They were not convinced that I had come by way of the river, and beckoned one to another that I had fallen from the sky.

They formed a tight circle and whispered among themselves, and then one by one they touched my face, and looked into my mouth the way a horse trader would look at a horse, and surprisingly they uttered one word that I understood. "The word god".

As it turned out, those men were hunters from another tribe. They had a thing like a gurney, made with two six foot pieces of wood, about two and a half inch in diameter and held together by a large piece of animal skin. They put me on their contraption, and four of them carried the ends of the two staves on their shoulders. Their village was no less than five miles away, and they ran the entire distance.

On reaching the village, I was in for more surprises. The population was about fifty; men, women and children of different ages. They were as primitive as one could imagine. Each wore only loin cloth made from animal skins, and their tools were limited to what they made from stones, wood and animal bones. Their houses were small; only big enough for a hammock.

I was placed in a sitting position on a crude wooden table in an open area among the houses, and each person came and touched me at different parts of my exposed skin, and then they formed a circle and shouted "God"," God", while they danced. This went on for about two hours. I desperately tried to tell them that I was not God, only a son of God. However, they refused to think otherwise, so I decided to play along with them.

I took out my revolver and fired one shot into a goat they had tied up on a nearby tree, killing the animal on the impact of the bullet.

One by one they rushed to the goat in total disbelief, wondering what they had just experienced. They tried propping the goat in a standing position; however, the lifeless animal fell from their arms, as they gathered around with puzzled looks on their faces. Some of the men from the group, with their hand signs, asked me if they can eat the meat. I nodded my head to the affirmative. Within an hour I smelt the meat roasting on an open fire. I was salivating at the scent.

While the meat was being roasted, I took the opportunity to learn as much of their language in the shortest possible time. With the aid of my notebook and pencil, I drew common objects like tree, and the alligator, and so on, and asked them what they were. By the time the roast was ready my vocabulary of their language was probably fifty of the words I thought were most important to communicate with them.

They were as anxious to learn about me as I was about them. They thought that they were the only one of their kind in the entire world, and none of them knew how old they were. I asked about the children's age, and they counted their fingers and toes and pointed to each one. It puzzled me that they pointed only to the babies, and then I realized that each digit they counted represented a new moon, one month, and after they counted fingers and toes a few times, they stopped counting. Two hands with a narrow gap represent a young person, and arms stretched from side to side represent an old person. They all knew who the eldest one was. They pointed him out to me, maybe because he might have outlived all his companions, or his shriveled skin, or his missing teeth.

My next surprises came not long after. Every one of the fifty who could chew and swallow had a piece of the roasted meat. I was not given any, and I thought to myself that maybe they were of the opinion that god does not eat.

Night was falling fast, and I wondered if I was going to spend the night sitting on that crude wooden table. I could tell that so far, they trusted me to do them no harm, and I appreciated that. They were a loving set of people, but as far as what they expected of me going forward, was my puzzle. I had biscuits and nuts and honey in my bag, and I was hungry, but I wanted to be alone to eat, or as I imagined, it would all be gone the moment I took it out. They lit torches, and they sang and danced until I called one of the men and told him by hand sings that I wanted to sleep. He relayed the information to his people, and they dispersed to their tents.

Moments later the same man beckoned me to follow him, which I did. We stopped at a newly erected tent in the middle of their housing cluster. It was a simple construction of seven pieces of wood; each about eight feet long by three inch diameter. The shape was triangular, with three pieces of wood on each side and one piece at the apex; held together by vines. The long sides were covered with animal skins from top to bottom, and the short sides were open. Close to, and all around the base of the tent was a one foot wide and deep trench, filled with leafless tree branches.

The man pointed, and gingerly, I entered, and lit a match. In the dim light I saw a hammock hanging from the top of the tent. I felt glad that at least I would not have to sleep on the dirt floor. Just as I was about to climb into the hammock, I heard someone cleared their throat immediately behind me. I lit another match, and saw a naked woman smiling at me. I showed her out, and she reluctantly walked out, while trying her best to explain to me why she was there.

In the darkness of the night I watched her frame disappear between the cluster of tents, and again I attempted to climb into the hammock. I had only gotten one foot up when the woman was back, a man was with her. He explained to me with hand signs and whatever little of the language that I understood, that she was one of his mates, and that they both wanted me to have sex with her, so that they could have a god-child. I told him that I did not want to, but he insisted, and iterated that he was my friend. He pushed her inside my tent and left.

As I stood and wondered how to position my seven foot, two hundred and forty pound body to have sex with a woman in a hammock, she probably was reading my mind, because without hesitation, she loosened the hammock, and spread it on the floor. As soon as I obliged her, she hastily got up and walked away. Again I watched her frame disappear between the tents, and I stood in the opening with my revolver in hand, not knowing what to expect next. I did not have to wait long. Within minutes the man returned. He had both hands in the air, assuring me that he was unarmed. There was another woman with him. He hugged and kissed me, and beckoned for me to have sex with her also.

Considering, that by my count, there were about thirty-five women and young girls in the group; it would be an arduous task for me to impregnate them in a hurry, not to mention all the other implications, so I told him to call a meeting. I went and sat on the crude wooden table and, within minutes they and their torches were gathered around me. I explained to them that there were people just like them on the other side of the river who were savages and cannibals, but they have no god-babies, so if they have some god-babies, the savages would be afraid of them. They clapped and cheered. 'But', I said, 'for you to have god-babies, I will need to have sex with the same woman for three moons to make sure she has baby god in her. And one more thing, I will choose the woman'.

They were satisfied with my explanation, and they all retired to their tents, and then finally, I had a chance to enjoy a can of beans, some biscuits and some honey.

The next morning I was awakened by the crowing of roosters. I decided to go for a walk, only to find out that two of the men with their spears and stone axes had kept watch at my tent. I took my bag to make sure that no one could rummage through it while I was away, and with note book and pencil in hand to write my observations, I toured my new community. The two men followed closely behind.

The observations were many, first; their entire village was only the size of two adjoining soccer fields, and the clay earth was dry and cracked. It was fenced by a three feet wide by three feet deep trench filled with leafless tree branches that had prickles like porcupines. Between the trench and the living quarters was a bank of the clay soil, dug out of the trench, and on the other side of the trench were wooden spikes, the kind that flattened the tires on the Jeep. Secondly; the only vegetation in the village was cactuses, and mint bushes. All the vegetation was heavily mulched with pieces of cactuses. There was also a pen with chickens, and another with some female goats with young ones.

As the population rose from their slumber and moved about in the bright morning sunlight, I was able to see them on an individual basis, and noticed that all the men were about the same five foot five inch height, muscular, and about a hundred and fifty pounds. They all looked alike; dark complexion, broad nose, and straight black hair tied in one at the back of their heads. It was difficult, if not impossible to tell one from the other, except for their voices. Both, men and women wore the same type of animal skins as loin cloth. The women are discernible by their protruding uncovered breasts, and their hair style which was noticeably parted in two, and tied over their ears. All the children; boys and girls stayed naked.

The thing that amazed me the most was that there was no water supply. They had a container made from animal skins in which they stored some water, but it was only used for special occasions, such as childbirth, and for certain ceremonies. The only liquid in their diet was from the cactuses, and from the goats' milk. The gel of the cactus was used for bathing, for hair shampoo, as beverage, and for anything that water would normally be used for, except cooking. All their foods were consumed either raw, or roasted.

After a meal of roasted eggs, goats' milk and cactus gel, the hunters told me that they wished to have my company on their hunting trip. Again, they ate without offering any to me. We were heading in the direction which they found me the day before, and I suggested that we go the opposite way towards some hills that seemed to be in the clouds. They told me that the hills are evil, and that they only go there to leave their dead. I insisted that we go there and reminded them that I was god and would guard them. They told me that the wild animals in the hills ate their companions when they took their dead there. That was when I learned that the torches were their most formidable weapon against attacking animals.

We walked briskly through the dry shrubs. One man used a six foot stick to brush the path in front, and snakes slithered from us. It took just over two hours to travel the five mile distance, and we were facing the first hill. They pointed to me where they leave their dead, and we avoided that area. I had to cajole them to climb the hill, and promise each of them that their mates would be next in line to carry the god-baby.

All the animals we encountered on the hill scattered as we approached, except a tiger which I had to shoot in the head. They stopped long enough to remove most of the skin. At the top of the hill, the view ahead was the clouds lifting off the most beautiful meadowland that could be imagined, and as we descended towards it we found many edible fruits fallen from the trees grown there. I ate some of the fruits to show them that they could eat them too. That was the first time they saw me eat. They had no idea that such a place and those fruits exist. Prior to that day, all that they could see were the top of the hill and the clouds.

The men gathered as much of the fruits as they could in their hunting bags. They also found a variety of eggs and young chicks of the kiwi, of ducks and other birds, but the most valuable thing that I insisted we collect were seeds.

When it was time to leave, they all refused to return the way we came, saying that it was bad omen. All my inducements meant nothing. Finally I relented, and started walking in a direction that would take us around the hill. Within a half an hour, we came upon a narrow river. At first they were very afraid, thinking that we would have to go across it, and that it too might be infested with alligators, but on close examination they were satisfied that there was no gators, and much to their delight they saw fish. They referred to the fish as baby alligators. I showed them how to spear a few, and how to descale and clean them. They wanted to eat them raw, but I told them to wait and roast them at the village.

As we were about to leave the river, a shaft of rain came down. It was so hard and fast that in a matter of minutes I who was the only one fully clothed, was soaking wet. It was then that I knew that those Aborigines were afraid of the rain. They explained to me that some of their elders had been struck by lightning during rainstorms.

Their lack of water lifestyle was a result of them being afraid of the rainfall, which only occur for one or two days in a whole year, and when it does, it moistens the clay, which sticks to their feet, and that disgusted them. The lightning that usually accompanies the rains had more than once claimed lives. Collecting water from the alligator infested river invariably was in exchange for a life or two. Their main source of water was mainly a catchment of dew, stored in a leather pouch.

The heavy rain had put out their torches, and they were worried about being attacked by wild animals. The sun was out and was as bright as it was before the rain. I retrieved a small mirror that I had among the trinkets in my bag, and with a leaf from my notebook, reflected a sun beam unto the paper until it blazed. They lit the torches, and chanted 'god, god.

It was night when we got back to the village, and was grateful that the old men we left had the intelligence to light a torch and hoist it on a pole to guide us. That same night they roasted the fish, and for the first time and ever since, their diet includes fish and fruits. I looked at my wrist-watch and noticed that the time was exactly nine o'clock, the time that I was due back at the base. I took the watch off my wrist, and was about to throw it away, but changed my mind and gave it to one of the villagers instead. I was god where I was, and had no need for time.

Over the next fifteen years, other than fathering a child every three months, I taught the villagers how to protect themselves from each other and from the invading tribes, how to hunt and fish, even from the alligator river, how to make bricks from the clay soil, and thereby build proper houses, how to live and trade with other tribes, I even taught them drama, and had them performing stage shows for other villages. Now my children can read and write, they wear proper clothing, and maybe best of all they knew that the world is much bigger than where they live".

"*Wha mek yu lef*", asked one man. "What made you leave?"

"Well my first child, a girl was fourteen, and I was afraid of starting the cycle again. Besides I needed new clothes", Newman replied. The rain subsided and one by one his listeners left.

Missed Opportunities.

Linval Lewis was fifteen years old in nineteen fifty-nine when he seriously began to think about what he wanted to be, or could be as an adult a mere six years away. Prior to that he thought that at age twelve he would be sent off to the Kingston Technical High school like his cousin Donavan and some other boys from his elementary school. He was very disappointed when his father told him that there would be no money for him to attend High School.

Elementary School rules did not allow students past the age of fifteen to attend full time. However, they were allowed to attend part-time to study for the Jamaica Local Examinations.

Linval at fourteen had taken the 1st year J.L.E. and failed. His failure was due to a mix-up of papers at the Examination Center, and he happened to have been one of the unfortunates. The following year he transferred to a neighboring school that was served by a different center. There he studied for and passed the 2nd year Jamaica Local Examinations.

It was a very rough year for Linval. The new school was more than two miles from home, and although classes didn't start until four in the afternoon, he had a multitude of chores that he had to perform, such as taking care of the animals by providing water and feed for the day before he walked the two mile distance to the school. The chores were the same each day that he performed when he attended the first school, but then he had some done in the mornings before school and the rest he did after school in the afternoons. With the new school hours he didn't get home until after ten and then he had to stay up late to do his homework assignments.

He had some bright spots though. Maybe, he had too many bright spots. One; he was very handsome, and he knew it. All the ladies, young and old told him so. Secondly; he was very smart. He was number one in most of his classes.

He had an uncle in England who sent him expensive and fashionable clothes and shoes which he wore to school on Fridays that was the casual dress day, that made him appear as a teenager dressed for the GQ magazine. It was not his intention to be a show-off, but those were the only clothes he had.

All those attributes made the girls love him and the boys envied him. He only had one male friend in the whole school, a boy named Curtis. He and Curtis lived in the same neighborhood and were friends before he changed schools.

Because of the remoteness and the economics of the country-side, there were no telephones. The main form of communication, other than face to face talk was by letters through the Post Office, or hand delivered. There were weeks when Linval received dozens of love letters from not only the girls from his old school, but mostly girls from his new school. Some of the letters had money as gifts; some had fancy handkerchiefs with scents of girl's perfumes.

It was hard for Linval to reply to all the letters. At one time he was devoting four hours every Sunday to writing replies to love letters.

He was very good at composing love verses, and his hand writing was excellent, so very often the girls he wrote would archive his letters, and after many months his verses, sometimes slightly altered would return to him.

At seventeen he was employed on a temporary basis with the Public Works Department as a Ticket Writer over the summer holidays. That position took him to parts of his parish that he had only heard about, and through that position he was introduced to more girls in the expanded areas, and they all wanted to be his friend.

Because there wasn't enough time to keep up with all of them, he became selective, and only replied to the pretty ones from the different districts and to those that sent him money. Sometimes he used money sent to him to buy presents for some of his favorite girls.

One of his younger brothers was secretly profiting from his prose. Some of the girls could not wait on the Postal Service, so for a fee, little brother hand delivered their letters. At times he collected from the sender as well as the receiver.

Linval considered it as 'one of those things' when on a Sunday he was replying to a bunch of letters. Except for the name of the girl a letter was addressed to, they were all the same. The same love verses, the same promises of spending a lifetime together, and so on. One letter however; recounted a special event with a particular girl. The script was placed in the wrong envelope. He had no idea what he had done, until a younger sister of one girl told him. He lost both girls, but gained the younger sister.

When he turned eighteen, his father who was a maintenance supervisor at a nearby sugar factory, begged him to get a job where he worked. He flatly refused, saying that the factory work was too dirty. With that, and his staying out late at nights, he was put out of his parent's house. He went and stayed at his grandmother's with her. At first she was glad to have him there, because she lived alone, but when she could not take his staying out late at nights, she told him that he either had to be home by nine or leave.

A friend got him a job in Kingston, and he left. The job was to aid an elderly travelling salesman who traded in ladies cosmetics and lingerie. It took him all over the island, four days per week, every week. He met the most beautiful young girls in the whole wide world through his travelling. Many of them fell in love with him at first sight, and exchange letters with him every time he visited the stores where they worked.

Life was good in Kingston. He enjoyed going to night clubs, beaches, cinemas, and everywhere else that he could have a lot of fun and meet interesting girls. There were so many new girls that he stopped writing to those he once corresponded with in and around his home town.

On one of his trips out of Kingston, he met seventeen year old Pauline D of New Market in the parish of Westmoreland. She was a petite five foot five inch beauty with long black hair, copper colored skin that was smoother than that of an infant baby, and she had the prettiest green eyes ever. She was also a 3rd year Jamaica Local Exam (J.L.E.) student. They became pen-pals, and letters were exchanged on a weekly basis. They had many aspirations that could potentially keep them together. She would try to get her parents to send her to Teachers College in Kingston; he would get his driver's license and a new job that would allow them to see each other frequently, especially on the weekends when they both had more time to drive and explore the countryside.

Everything changed when one weekend he visited his parents in the country side. His mother was very distraught over the drinking and smoking habit that he picked up in Kingston, not to mention that she thought that he wasn't eating right. His once chunky frame was gaunt. She begged him to come home.

His father, who was still employed at Holland Sugar factory, showed him a paper from the factory bulletin board. It stated that positions for apprentices in the Chemist Laboratory and the Maintenance Machine Shop were available to immediate family members.

'Wa u doing now may mek yu feel good', said his father. *'But dat is only a jab. Yu caa lose e any time. Specially how yah hangle money. Yu need to av a trade ar a profession. Wen yu av dat ina yu head, yu caa lose e'*.

'What you are doing now may make you feel good, but that is only a job. You can lose it at anytime, especially the way you handle money loosely. You need to have a trade or a profession. When you have that in your head, you cannot lose it'.

'Tink bout wa u Pa seh bwauy', his mother said.

'Think about what your father says boy'.

Linval went back to Kingston, at the prodding of his mom and dad, he resigned his job.

When he reported for work at the factory a week later at eight o'clock the Monday morning everyone stopped working and steered at him. He thought to himself that the workers must be thinking that they were looking at a U.W.O. (Unidentified Walking Object).

His hair was cut low and was brushed back, displaying shiny black waves. He was clean shaven with a pencil-thin bat-wing mouth stash. His attire was a red Fred Perry shirt, a tight fit Wrangler jean, and Eaton suede shoes. When he spoke, a glittering gold capped upper front tooth was plainly visible. He naturally looked like a famous actor.

The Chemist Laboratory position that he was hoping to get was already taken, so he was placed in the Machine shop. His father gave him a pair of cover-all, and someone else loaned him a pair of old shoes.

At lunch time he sat with his father and shared the meal his mother had prepared for both of them. After he ate, he took an unopened pack of Chesterfield cigarettes from his pocket and opened it to smoke one. He looked around, and saw more hands reaching for cigarettes, than his pack of twenty could handle. He obliged them until the pack was empty. That was the last day that he smoked.

The shop foreman was a cousin of Linval, about seven or eight years his senior, but the two never got along from day one. He never called Linval by his name. Whenever he needed to get his attention, it was always 'Hey Faceman! Linval complained to his father who told him that his cousin who was single, was jealous of him, because he feared the competition for girls.

The apprenticeship pay was not much, compared with what he was earning in Kingston, and the pay in the Lab. was a little more, but since he was not put there, he decided to make the best of where he was.

Although he had moved back to his parents household, his cost of living expenses were high, because he had to help with the grocery bill, pay for his laundry, and transportation to and from work. He had stopped smoking and reduced his night life to Saturdays only.

The first letter he wrote was to Pauline. He wanted to tell her that the plans they had made needed to be altered because of this new job. He lied to her because he knew that the small amount of money he was earning could not allow him visit her and to help support her in college as he had promised. Moreover they would still be apart. The lie to her was that the new job would be sending him to Florida on a four-month study course, and his next letter would be coming to her from there.

The months went by, and Linval became extremely efficient in his trade, to the point where he got overtime pay to equal his base pay. He was able to save enough money to purchase a motor-cycle. He had developed a good rapport with a fellow apprentice by the name of Emerd who also rode a motor-cycle. They shared lots of their stories. Emerd had at one time lived in Kingston and was familiar with places and some of the people that he knew. They showed one another photos of girlfriends past and present.

One work-day morning Linval walked into the shop at the usual time. Emerd was already there, which was a surprise, because he was usually late. He had one hand behind him and as Linval approached him, he shoved the newspaper he was holding behind his back into Linval's face and grinned. It was the centerfold of the morning's paper, and on it was a half-page picture of Pauline D.

She had won the island-wide beauty contest for the parish, and would be competing with fourteen other girls for the Miss Jamaica Title. He was extremely happy to learn that she was competing for the title of Miss Jamaica. However, he thought to himself that this was a missed opportunity not to have a potential Miss Jamaica as his girlfriend.

Two weeks before that newspaper incident, Linval had passed by the bus stop across from the market and saw a girl he thought was about fifteen or sixteen standing there. She was alone. First he passed, and glanced at her, then, he had second thoughts and turned around. He stopped his bike at her feet, introduced himself and asked her if she wanted a ride. She did not respond, except she turned her back. She was a very pretty girl, medium built, five foot six-ish, black shoulder length hair and brown eyes.

He passed by the same bus stop the following Saturday at the same time, but she was not there.

Emerd was teasing one day about Pauline, when Linval wanting to change the subject, told him about the speechless girl at the bus stop. He described her to him, and he immediately recognized who she was.

"Oh," he said. "Her name is Mercedes, she is a friend of some friends of mine, but she is only fourteen. She is a student of the newly opened Saint Elizabeth Technical High School. STETHS."

"I like her," responded Linval.

"Good luck on that my friend," Emerd remarked. "She doesn't talk to any boy. I do know a few including myself who have tried without any success."

That was a challenge to Linval, so he decided to use a tactic that had worked for him many times before. He wrote his name and address on a three-by-five index card and folded it in two, so that the next time he saw her he would stealthily get beside her and stick it into her handbag, or her book, or anywhere he could.

He got his chance a full three weeks later. As it turned out Mercedes' grandmother sometimes go to the market to sell vegetables that she cultivated, and she goes there to meet with her, then travel by bus to Santa Cruz where attended boarding school.

Linval's plan was carried out. He visited the Post Office every other day with hopes that she would write. Four weeks had passed. He received lots of other letters, but none from her.

Finally it came. It was in the form of an invitation to a dance at her school. She stated that she would be chaperoned, and he could meet her at the school, but there was a stipulation that he first had to meet with her host.

The time of the meeting was noted and Linval promptly appeared to meet with the host. When he got there, he was met by Mercedes and five other girls of her age who also boarded there. The other girls were constantly giggling, and two of them purposely touched him with their fingers, maybe to prove that he was real. The host was not there, and Linval learned later that he was tricked into going there at that time, for the other girls to see that Mercedes had a date for the dance. That was her first date.

The fete was a great success, at least for her. Although she and the other girls had a mid-night curfew, she and Linval stuck together, and danced to every tune from the start of the music until her chaperone touched her on the shoulder for them to leave. That night, she had her first dance, her first real kiss and her first romantic hug.

Over the next three and a half years, Linval excelled at his job, and his earnings improved dramatically. With more money to spend, he lavished Mercedes and some of his other girlfriends with lots of expensive presents. He also moved from his parent's home, and rented a house that he shared with a friend. Together they furnished the house with exquisite furniture and appliances. The setting was so cozy and romantic that some of the girls that visited had to be tricked, or physically forced to leave. What made it worse was that the house was at a cul-de-sac that allowed for extra privacy.

Linval was only months from completing his apprenticeship program when a rumor started that the factory was being sold, and that the prospective owners would no longer produce sugar, but different crops that did not require a factory. This came as a shock to everyone, and left them all with a feeling of despair.

Without hesitation he resigned and moved back to Kingston where within days he was hired as a Machinist at a small Automobile parts repair shop. The pay was not fantastic, but he had made application at places that paid higher wages and was hopeful.

He made a lot of new friends, male and female. One such friend was rookie policeman by the name of Celburne Gayle. He became his handball team-mate. They practiced every afternoon after work between five and six, mostly for physical exercise.

Celbourne was very humorous and was always fun to be around. In his spare time he would devise ways to pick up girls. One of his favorite was to call to a young lady, saying;

' Hey young lady! Can I speak to you a minute'.

When the girl gave him her attention, he would say;

'There is a reward offered for your capture'.

Startled, the girl usually asked;

'What are you talking about?'

Then he would reply;

"Yes ma'am. Heaven is missing an angel, and you fit the description to the tee'.

Linval was back to having fun again. Just like his former days in Kingston. By his own standard, life was good; with lots of friends, a good job, and best of all, he had no curfew. He challenged himself to have a girl from every parish, just like his buddy Celbourne. He would keep Mercedes from Saint Elizabeth, and then there was Doreen from Saint Mary, Lovie from Manchester, Doreth from Saint Catherine, Avery from Clarendon and a few others from some other places which he wasn't sure of.

On his calendar he assigned a name to every other weekend and sent out letters to the girls inviting them to spend the particular weekend with him.

The first girl to visit was Lovie, but she returned the same day, saying that she wasn't allowed to stay out over-night. The second was Avery. Everything went fine with her. She came Friday night and returned Monday morning.

The third was Doreen. She came on a Saturday with a huge suitcase that she packed with everything, from clothes enough to last until the fashion change, to pots and pans. She had no intention of returning to her home. The following day, Sunday, Linval hired a taxi and rode with her all the way to Saint Mary. There he met with her mother whom she lived with. He told her that he really loved her daughter, but where he was living was not suitable for her to live, and that he was saving to buy a house and marry her. The mother seemed satisfied, but Doreen was sad.

Two weeks later was Mercedes' turn. He wasn't sure she would be able to make it. He had timed her visit to coincide with the last week of her final exams at school. However she did turn up Saturday afternoon, and said she had to run away, because her grandmother had seen his letters and dared her to leave. Linval was faced with a situation that was worse than it was with Doreen. One; he had known this girl for four years, and she was faithful to him. Two; there were no place else for her to go, even temporary. Three; he had on his schedule for other girls to visit.

Saturday night Celbourne stopped by with one of his girls, and the foursome went on the town. Sunday all four went to the beach. Linval told Celbourne of his predicament, and he advised him to take a wait-and-see attitude. Monday just before lunch time a clerk from Linval's workplace handed him a note. It was a telephone message that she received for him. It stated;

'Got on the bus at ten, will be there before three. Please do not play any handball today'.

He used his lunch time to rush home. There he saw Mercedes sleeping. She was exhausted with all the travelling on Saturday, the night club on Saturday night, and the all-day sun and swimming on Sunday, not to mention whatever else that had transpired, that she was glad that Linval went to his job, so that she could get some well needed rest. She awoke, sat up in bed, and with glary eyes, looked at him.

"Merce, honey," he said. "We have a problem."

"Yeh what?" she asked.

They had thoroughly discussed her situation, and had concluded that if in a month she did not get a job, then she would return to live with her grandmother, but she was confident that she would be employed, so she was not willing to hear anything else.

"Remember the girl from Saint Mary that I told you about?" said Linval, in a non-enthusiastic tone.

"She just sent a message that she is on the way here. Here is what I want you to do. Put those verandah chairs inside. That girl knows them very well. And then remove the window curtain and replace it with a bed sheet. When she gets here, tell her that I have moved and you are the new tenant. I have to get back to work. Love you."

He went back to work, and she went back to sleep.

At a quarter to four Linval was watching the clock. In another forty-five minutes he would be clocking out to go home to his Merce.

Celbourne drove up in the police Jeep.

"Buddy, what's up?" asked Linval. "You know I am not playing handball today, and you are in uniform."

"This is serious man," said Celbourne. "A domestic disturbance call came into the station from your address, and by coincidence I was dispatched to it. To my surprise it was your new girl and another one from Saint Mary fighting. I did not make an arrest, but I escorted the one from Saint Mary to the bus station and saw to it that she got on the bus."

That night Linval and Mercedes moved to a different address and have been together ever since.

Note; Where destiny leads, you must follow.

The following seven pages tell of some lesser known facts about Jamaica.

Black River

The Black River is the longest river in the island. It starts in the Cockpit mountains in the parish of Trelawney, and winds its' way through meadows, valleys and down many steeps for forty-four miles to the Caribbean Sea. That area where the river meets the sea was called The Black River Trading Post at first, then Black River, and later became a vibrant industrial town. It became the capital of the parish of Saint Elizabeth.

The river was so named, because at one stretch in history the water was actually black from the dye of the Logwood that loggers floated down the river to be picked up where the river and the sea meets. The logs were then loaded onto ships and taken to England. Today, although, the water is as clear as crystal, the river looks black, because way back then, the dye from the logs stained the bed, and the banks of the river, and the stained surfaces remained black.

The town of Black River was the first place in Jamaica to have electricity. The Leyden family had it installed in their residence in 1893. That building has had many owners and occupants since then; the address is 44 High Street. In the nineteen fifties to sixties, it was a high school, of which this author is a past student, and in the late sixties to seventies, it was occupied as a government run health clinic. Recently, it was extensively renovated and refurbished, and is being used as a guest house.

Falmouth

In 1799 a twenty foot water wheel and tower was built on the estates of Martha Brae. The Martha Brae estates had a river approximately 32 kilometers and was named after it's owner a British settler who owned most of the land that the river ran through. The strong water current of the river on the property turned the wheel and lifted about a hundred gallons of water per revolution to an elevated trough. Cast-iron piping carried the water gravity- fed to a large storage tank located in the town of Falmouth. That area where the tank was built was called 'Water Square', and the name remains up to present time.

Believe it, or not; in 1799 nowhere else in the Caribbean had running water.

Lucea

Lucea is a coastal town in Jamaica and the capital of the parish is Hanover, which is the smallest parish, founded in 1723. This town in the parish of Hanover has a functional clock tower built in 1817, and stands in the town center near the Old Lucea courthouse. The top of the clock tower is shaped in the fashion of a German military helmet. The construction of this tower was financed by a wealthy Jamaican of German descent.

Coffee

It is said that the best tasting coffee is the Blue Mountain coffee, from Jamaica. It takes its' name from the Blue Mountains, where it is grown. The area of the coffee plantation on the mountain has an almost constant day time average temperature of seventy-two degrees and the humidity of fifty percent. Even though, rainfall is scarce; at nights the dew falls heavily; added to that is the loam soil of rotted and compacted leaves, and the morning to midday sun makes the coffee growing conditions perfect.

Ironically, The Blue Mountain Coffee is not sold on the retail market in Jamaica, but is exported and sold for astronomical prices in Ritzy places in Morocco, Tokyo, London, Paris and others.

Marijuana (Ganja)

Many vacationers from North America and Europe go to Jamaica to enjoy the marijuana grown there. It is said to be the most potent in the world. The main reason for its potency is the soil it is grown in. There are caves in the northwest section of the island that contains thousands of tons of bat dung. This deposit has accumulated since before human history, and has now become the most fertile soil ever. Because of the labor intensity of retrieving it from deep in these caves; the cost of the crops it produces is astronomical, and is only economical for the growing of Ganja. This soil is often referred to, as black gold, and Ganja, as green gold. Pound for pound, most times, bat dung and Ganja are the same price. Ganja price however, does fluctuate, depending on supply and demand, whereas; bat dung price moves with the economy. The possession of Ganja is illegal, but the trading of rat-bat dung, as it is called is quite legal, and generates mucho money.

Jerk Chicken, Jerk Pork

Mention the word Jerk in Jamaica and its' not only synonymous with someone who is referred to as no-good, but most likely you would be referring to a special taste of cooked chicken or pork. There are plenty of stories of how this word came to be associated with food, but just like the dialect Patwa; one has to go back to the days of slavery for a very believable one.

It is no doubt that the J Wray and Nephew white rum, Reggae, coffee and a few other things had put Jamaica on the social map, but the Jerk recipe for preparing certain meats had been around for hundreds of years. Jerk chicken especially, is a featured dish in restaurants all over the world since the recent years.

Turtle meat and turtle eggs were the primary sources of protein for the slaves. Turtles were plentiful, particularly, in the eastern parishes. It was less time consuming to procure the meat and eggs than it was for other kinds of meat. The meat however; was hard to chew, regardless if it was boiled or roasted. The meat is said to have the taste and texture of beef, mutton and poultry all together, and for years the slaves were satisfied to make soup only with it, but as time went on; they experimented with different seasoning and methods to tenderize it.

There is a certain species of turtles known as the 'Alligator Snapping' type, commonly called the 'Snapper' turtle. The slaves used garlic, vinegar, lime-juice, salt, hot-pepper, ginger and every kind of seasoning that they could find to marinate the meat before they roast it on the open fire. They even used special types of wood and leaves in the fire to enhance the flavor. The meat has the characteristic of twitching (muscle contraction and relaxation) in response to the absorption or the dissipation of heat. This twitching was observed and referred to as jerking. The meat jerks, even when it is on the plate; ready to be eaten. Hence the Jerk, but whoever heard of jerk turtle? The turtle became an endangered species, and the chicken and pork took over. And now you too know a JERK story.

This author asked a man who sold jerk pork by the side of the road in the parish of Portland, 'What made his jerk so finger-licking good that people traveled many miles for his product?'

He said, "The first day I marinated it with the regular seasoning; salt, hot-pepper, vinegar, lime-juice, garlic, ginger and so on. The second day, I spice it up like a cake; a little rum, a little sugar, cinnamon, nut-meg and so on, and on the third day, I raised a pimento-wood fire under it. Try it----you'll like it, and may even say------I can't believe I ate the whole ting"

Credits

Many thanks, posthumously, for the help received in this work from; my parents, Mr. and Mrs. Vernon G Daley, also now deceased, my dear friend Harold Smith. To all the people I've met over the years in rum bars, restaurants, in fields and in homes; who were happy to relate this material to me. Special 'Thank you' to Editors; Linton Atkinson and Janet Simpson, and also to my dear wife who allowed me the time, late at nights and early mornings to work on this piece.

Other books by Laxleyval Sagasta:

News Flash--- Published by Outskirts Press

Gloria Gant (e-book only) Published by Book Baby

Colorado to Woodstock and Back-----Published by Outskirts Press

And coming soon: News Flash (Revised)

Warriors and Duds of the Bible.

Available from the publishers, at all book retailers and at:

Caribbean Sunshine Bakery and Restaurants, Orlando, Florida. USA

Caribbean Sunrise Bakery and Restaurant. Jacksonville, Florida. USA Fireside Restaurant. Lithonia, Georgia. USA

D'Flava Restaurants, London and Liverpool, England.

Aerostar Restaurant. Accra Airport. Ghana.

Printed in the USA
CPSIA information can be obtained
at www.ICGtesting.com
LVHW051636041123
762866LV00076B/2395

9 781954 304314